He felt the wetness on Cassie's cheeks and knew she was crying.

He couldn't bring himself to ask her why. He was too damned close to tears himself. And Jared Walker hadn't cried in twenty-four years.

When she slipped into sleep, her cheek still damp against his shoulder, he cradled her closer, guarding her rest against anything that could hurt her. Himself included.

Staring blindly at the ceiling, he wondered if he should sleep on the couch. Even as the thought crossed his mind, he knew that he couldn't make himself leave the woman who lay in his arms.

"You're feeling trapped because it won't be so easy to leave this time," she'd said. And he'd known it was the truth.

Walking away this time *would* probably be the hardest thing he'd ever done. But finding the courage to stay might prove to be the toughest challenge he'd ever faced.

Dear Reader,

Welcome to Silhouette **Special Edition** . . . welcome to romance. Each month, Silhouette **Special Edition** publishes six novels with you in mind—stories of love and life, tales that you can identify with—as well as dream about.

April has some wonderful stories for you. Nora Roberts presents her contribution to THAT SPECIAL WOMAN!—our new promotion that salutes women, and the wonderful men that win them. *Falling for Rachel,* the third installment of THOSE WILD UKRAINIANS, is the tale of lady lawyer Rachel Stanislaski's romance with Zackary Muldoon. Yes, he's a trial, but boy is he worth it!

This month also brings *Hardworking Man,* by Gina Ferris. This is the tender story of Jared Walker and Cassie Browning—and continues the series FAMILY FOUND. And not to be missed is Curtiss Ann Matlock's wonderful third book in THE BREEN MEN series. Remember Matt and Jesse? Well, we now have Rory's story in *True Blue Hearts.*

Rounding out this month are books from other favorite authors: Andrea Edwards, Ada Steward and Jennifer Mikels. It's a month full of Springtime joy!

I hope you enjoy this book, and all of the stories to come! Have a wonderful April!

Sincerely,

Tara Gavin
Senior Editor

GINA FERRIS

HARDWORKING MAN

SPECIAL EDITION®

Published by Silhouette Books New York

America's Publisher of Contemporary Romance

SILHOUETTE BOOKS
300 East 42nd St., New York, N.Y. 10017

HARDWORKING MAN

ISBN: 0-373-09806-5

First Silhouette Books printing April 1993

Books by Gina Ferris

Silhouette Special Edition

Healing Sympathy #496
Lady Beware #549
In from the Rain #677
Prodigal Father #711
Full of Grace #793
Hardworking Man #806

*Family Found

GINA FERRIS

declares that she is Southern by birth and by choice, and she has chosen to set many of her books in the South, where she finds a rich treasury of characters and settings. She particularly loves the Ozark mountain region of northern Arkansas and southern Missouri and the proudly unique people who reside there. She and her husband, John, live in Jacksonville, Arkansas, with their three children, Courtney, Kerry and David.

Monday's child is fair of face.
Tuesday's child is full of grace.
Wednesday's child is full of woe.
Thursday's child has far to go.
Friday's child is loving and giving.
Saturday's child has to work hard for its living.
But the child that is born on the Sabbath Day
is fair and wise and good and gay.

—Anon.

Prologue

"Tony? It's Cassie. I've found him."

"You've found Jared Walker? You're sure you've got the right man? My wife's brother?"

Huddling against the light September morning rain blowing under the eaves of the convenience store outside of which she stood, Cassie Browning tightened her fingers around the pay telephone receiver and turned her back to the impatient teenager waiting in line for the phone. "I'm sure it's the right man, I've got his driver's license photo—he hasn't changed that much from the childhood photograph we have of him."

Cassie's employer, private investigator Tony D'Alessandro, was obviously quite pleased with her report. "Cassie, this is great! I can't wait to tell Michelle. She and Layla have been so anxious to see their brother, especially since I told them how close you were to finding him."

"Um—Tony? You might want to hold up on telling Michelle and Layla that Jared's been located. There's something I haven't told you yet."

Her boss's voice grew sober, wary, as though the gravity of her tone had suddenly gotten through to him. "What is it, Cassie?"

She took a deep breath, then blurted, "Jared Walker's in jail, Tony. He was arrested last night. He's been charged with armed robbery."

reserved, very private, but reliable and very hardworking. Would a man like that suddenly turn to crime at thirty-five?

She *would* clear this up, Cassie thought with a surge of determination. She was twenty-six years old and had held more jobs than she could count on both hands, but this was the first one she'd utterly loved from the day she'd started. She'd finally found her niche in private investigation, and though she was only an apprentice now, she fully intended to be a partner someday. And what better way to start than to clear the name of her employer's brother-in-law—assuming, of course, the man was innocent. Cassie crossed her fingers.

And then Deputy William "Slim" Calhoun led in the prisoner—and Cassie's breath caught somewhere in her throat.

She hadn't been prepared for the emotional impact of actually seeing Jared Walker, a man she knew only from an old driver's license photo and a faded family portrait in which he'd been eleven years old. He'd looked innocuous enough in those photos, though he hadn't been smiling in either. But reality was a lean, dangerous-looking man in a regulation orange jumpsuit, his short brown hair disheveled, roughly carved features grim, dark blue eyes holding a wealth of anger, bitterness and a deep-seated pain.

And suddenly Cassie knew that nothing about this case was going to proceed as she'd hoped. This may just prove to be the challenge of her career—her entire life, perhaps.

The first thing Jared noticed about the woman was her shoulder-length mop of carrot red curls glittering like fire in the fluorescent lighting. Her eyes were wide, green, ingenuous, her pert nose scattered with faint freckles. She looked maybe twenty, twenty-one, though he supposed she could be a few years older. Not much.

He'd never seen her before. But, then, he hadn't expected to find anyone he knew waiting in this dingy interrogation room. Slim had told him he had a visitor representing his family. Since Jared Walker had only one family member that he could account for, he'd known from the first that the woman had lied.

He suspected from looking at her that she was an eager cub reporter, hoping for a juicy story for her tiny town newspaper. He didn't particularly care what her angle was as long as he could find some way to use her for his own advantage.

He was innocent of the crime with which these clods had charged him, but proving his innocence would be no easy task in a small town where he had no friends and no alibi. He couldn't even make bail, though he'd already placed a call to the one person who could possibly help him with that.

Jared had one particularly compelling reason to get out of this place as quickly as possible. Not that he intended to share that reason with anyone else—including the young woman watching him so anxiously as he was led in.

The woman gave Calhoun a look that had the paunchy forty-something officer preening in his wrinkled uniform. "Thank you so much, Deputy," she told him, her pleasant voice dripping with gratitude and admiration. "Would you mind if I talk to Jared in private?"

Calhoun frowned. "I don't know, Miz Browning. He could be dangerous. He was armed when he perpetrated the crime."

"*Allegedly* perpetrated the crime," Cassie reminded him gently. "And I assure you I'm in no danger. Am I, Jared?" she asked, looking at him in a manner that dared him to say he'd never laid eyes on her before.

"None at all," he replied, watching as her fair cheeks flushed at his response. Interesting.

"Please, Deputy," Cassie persisted. "This is family business. You could wait right outside the door so I could call if I need you."

Calhoun hesitated, then caved in to the entreaty in those wide, clear eyes. "Okay," he said, nudging Jared to a chair at the other side of the table where Cassie sat. "You behave yourself, Walker," he ordered sternly, scowling in an admirable imitation of Barney Fife at his most ferocious.

"Yeah. Right," Jared muttered, attention still focused on the woman as he took his seat.

"You call out if you need me, Miz Browning. I'll be standing right outside the door," Slim assured her, patting the grip of his .38 and glaring at Jared as he spoke.

"That's . . . very comforting to know," the woman murmured, only the slightest break in her voice betraying the amusement dancing in her eyes.

Jared felt his interest in her quickening. And then they were alone, the door to the room left open an inch or so despite her request for privacy. The woman clapped a hand over her mouth to stifle a giggle, seeming to need a moment before leaning across the table to speak softly. "Is everyone here like him?"

Jared nodded, his mouth quirking with his first smile since he'd been grabbed in the parking lot of his cheap motel. "Yeah, pretty much. They're all aquiver at having caught themselves a real, live criminal—even though they've got the wrong man."

Her expression sobered abruptly. "*Have* they got the wrong man?" she asked bluntly.

"Yeah." He met her eyes across the table without blinking. "They have."

Cassie searched those penetrating dark blue eyes for a long, taut moment, trying to read the truth in them. So much evidence against him—and yet she simply couldn't imagine this man robbing a fleabag motel office, no matter how hard she tried. She found herself wanting to believe in his innocence—for Michelle's sake, for her career's sake, but mostly because she suddenly had a hunch. . . .

Despite her friends' groaning distrust of her many impulsive hunches, Cassie had rarely been wrong in her instincts about people. Everything she'd learned about Jared Walker in her investigation, everything she saw in his clear blue eyes now, told her he was a man who lived quietly, honestly and carefully. Robbing the very motel where he was staying, leaving the alleged weapon in his room, returning openly and carelessly to the scene of the crime—none of those actions seemed to fit the man who sat across from her now, watching her so intently, so steadily.

"I guess we'll just have to do something about proving your innocence, won't we?" she said evenly, knowing she'd need his full cooperation if she were to find that proof.

His head cocked at her matter-of-fact tone. "Who the hell is 'we'?"

She cleared her throat. "Us. You and me. That's all I meant, of course." She cursed her lifelong inability to lie to anyone she really liked. When necessary in the course of her work, she could lie like a trouper to strangers and people she didn't care for, but she had a very hard time misleading anyone whose opinion mattered to her.

So why couldn't she consider Jared Walker just another stranger?

Don't screw this up, Browning, she warned herself sternly.

"I need some information about last night," she went on quickly. "Everything you were doing, everywhere you went during the time of the robbery. As I see it, our main problem is your lack of an alibi during the hours of eleven and midnight, when the robbery occurred. So what we need to do is—"

"Just wait a minute," Jared broke in shortly, leaning slightly forward so that his low voice was audible only to her. "First I think you'd better tell me who the hell you are, and why you're so all-fired intent on getting me out."

Okay, Browning, watch your step. If you're ever going to be a partner in D'Alessandro Investigations, your career is riding on the next few minutes.

Her fingers clenching in her lap with the pressure she was inflicting on herself, Cassie took a deep breath. "My name is Cassie Browning," she told him softly. "And I'm a private investigator."

He looked startled. "*You?* A P.I.?"

She wasn't flattered by his skepticism. She drew herself up stiffly and nodded. "I could show you my identification, but I don't think this is exactly a good time for that. Slim could walk back in, and he thinks we already know each other."

"Yeah, right. You told him you're representing my 'family.'"

She cleared her throat again. "It was all I could think of on short notice."

"So who are you working for, *Miz* Browning? Who hired you to clear me? Was it Bob Cutter? When I called, I was told he was at his hunting camp and couldn't be reached until Monday."

"I'm sorry," she murmured, making a mental note of the name Bob Cutter. "I can't answer that. I have instructions to keep my client's name confidential for now. I'm sure you understand."

"No, I sure as hell don't," Jared answered roughly. "I have something at stake here. I deserve to know exactly what's going on."

He had a point there. But Cassie had an employer to answer to—an employer who'd been known on occasion to lose his formidable Italian temper when an operative blew a case. "You'll know soon enough. Right now the important thing is to get you out of here, wouldn't you agree?"

Jared sighed, looking anything but satisfied. "Yeah," he grumbled after a moment. "I want out."

"Good. Then let's get started. Why were you staying in that motel last night? What are you doing in this two-bit town?"

She could have added that she knew he'd left instructions for his last employer to forward his final paycheck to general delivery at the post office in this "two-bit-town"—which was the way she'd located him in the first place—but she kept that to herself, wanting to hear the whole story from Jared.

Jared didn't look as though he appreciated being questioned about his activities. Knowing him to be a loner, she suspected he didn't often find it necessary to explain his actions. But this time it was important. This time his freedom depended on it.

"Jared?" she prodded.

He scowled, but nodded. "I was just on my way through," he explained. "I'm headed for Arizona, where I hope to find ranch work for the winter. I'd worked out my route on a map and told my last employer to forward a check to general delivery here, which I picked up yesterday. So I had some money on me," he added. "I didn't need to rip off the motel office."

Again, she studied the expression in his eyes, analyzed his tone. He sounded very much like an innocent man, she thought soberly. Was she being incredibly naive to find herself wanting to believe him? Despite her characteristic impulsiveness, her habitual snap judgments, the past ten minutes had hardly been long enough for her to get to know Jared—much less to form such sweeping judgments about his character. And yet . . .

"I'd like to believe that," she said slowly, holding his gaze with her own. "I'd like to help you prove it, if I can."

He crossed his arms on the table and locked his gaze with hers. "Why?"

Flustered by the unblinking intensity of his stare, Cassie squirmed. "Let's just say it's my job."

She quickly changed the subject, becoming all business again. "All right, here's the situation. You checked in to the motel at around 9:00 p.m. The motel owner, Gus Turley, noticed you particularly because there weren't but a few other guests and you didn't look like the usual trucker or weary tourist he generally gets. He also remembered that you paid cash in advance and didn't list a permanent address on your registration card. He said he tried to start a friendly conversation with you but you weren't very polite in response."

Jared grunted. "I was tired. Wasn't in the mood for small talk. So the guy fingered me as an armed robber because I hurt his feelings when I checked in?"

She frowned reprovingly at him. "There's a little more to it than that. The man who robbed him at gunpoint somewhere around 11:30 p.m. wore a ski mask, but he was approximately your size. He had on jeans, boots and a denim jacket, and Turley said he remembered you were wearing a similar outfit when you checked in."

"Me and most of the other guys in town," Jared muttered.

He had a point there. That had been her own instant response when she'd heard the description of the robber's clothing. Jeans and a denim jacket were the norm in this part of the country.

"Anyway," she continued, "the cops went to your room, knocked, didn't get an answer. They went in, found the bathroom window open, your duffel bag still in the room. They didn't find any money, but they found a gun."

"It's not illegal to own a gun," Jared pointed out. "And from what I hear, it wasn't even the same make of handgun Turley claimed the robber had used."

Point two. Cassie had pondered that rather significant error herself. "Yes, well, now he says he was so shaken up he could have been mistaken. It could have been your gun, he says."

"He's wrong."

Cassie nodded and went on with the facts as they'd been presented to her. "The cops staked out the room, caught you coming back at around 1:00 a.m. You resisted arrest."

"Hell, I didn't even know they were cops! They just came out of the shadows and grabbed me the minute I stepped out of my truck. I thought they were muggers. I hit a couple of them, but I think I had good cause."

It didn't surprise Cassie that Jared hadn't been taken easily. She sensed he was the type who'd hit first, ask questions later. Yet, despite her instincts that he was capable of violence, she felt no fear of him. His was a violence kept sternly leashed, she suspected, released only when necessary to protect himself—or someone he cared for. And where the hell had *that* observation come from? she wondered in exasperation.

Immediately distracting herself from that line of thought, she went on. "You said you'd been unable to sleep and had taken a drive. You claimed to have stopped at an all-night diner for a cup of coffee, but the waitress said she didn't remember seeing you.''

"She didn't want to get involved, most likely," Jared growled. "They never do."

"Can you describe her for me?"

He shrugged. "Fiftyish. Twenty pounds overweight. Hairstyle twenty years out of date—lots of tight little curls on top of her head. Bleached. Name tag on her pocket said 'Nellie.'"

Cassie lifted an eyebrow. "You told that to the cops?"

He snorted. "Yeah. They said I could have been in anytime yesterday afternoon and seen her."

"Damn."

"They want this conviction, Cassie. I get the impression I'm the most excitement they've had around here in months."

A shiver of awareness coursed through her when he said her name in that rough, deep voice. Why hadn't she noticed right off how sexy he was, despite his scowl?

Whoa, Browning. None of that. Rule number one: Never get involved with the clients.

Not that Jared was a client, exactly.

She avoided his too-knowing gaze as she hesitantly broached the next topic. "Turley thinks you were working with an accomplice, who now has the money you allegedly stole from him. He swears he saw you enter your motel room with someone, though you registered as a single."

"I travel alone."

Jared's expression was shuttered, his voice flat, brooking no argument. It took all her nerve for Cassie to ask, "Did you have any visitors in your room? A—er—woman you'd met in town, perhaps?"

"No."

Unaccountably relieved, she nodded. "So Turley was wrong about that, too. He was probably looking for a way to explain that the money wasn't found on you."

Jared remained silent. She frowned, studying him more closely. "Jared? Is there something you're not telling me? I have to know everything if I'm going to find the proof that you're innocent."

"That's the whole story," he replied flatly. "So what are you going to do now?"

"Talk to Turley, I suppose. And Nellie, of course."

"If you're so convinced of my innocence, how about bailing me out of here? I can help you come up with the proof I need."

Cassie bit her lip, knowing it must have been hard for him to ask her to bail him out. Jared Walker wasn't a man who'd ask for help easily. She could identify with that. Having always been the stubbornly independent type herself, she knew how hard it was to swallow pride and admit the need for assistance. Why was she beginning to think she and Jared Walker had quite a few things in common? Had the stress of this complicated morning affected her more than she'd thought?

"I'm sorry," she murmured, avoiding his eyes. "Your bail is so high, I don't have enough to cover it. Don't you have anyone to call? A friend? An attorney?"

Was he really so very much alone?

He shrugged. "I've called a friend in Oklahoma, the one I mentioned earlier. He's unavailable for the weekend. As soon as I get in touch with him, I'm sure he'll come through with bail and an attorney—I don't think I want to risk having one appointed for me here. God knows who I'd get, if Deputy Fife out there is anything to judge this town by."

"When do you think you'll be able to reach this friend?"

He shrugged again. "Two, three days."

Distressed, Cassie clenched her hands more tightly in front of her on the table. She hated the thought of Jared spending two or three more days behind bars.

She made a sudden decision to call Tony the moment she left the jailhouse, hoping to persuade him to wire her the money for Jared's bail. After all, Jared was Tony's brother-in-law. And Cassie was here to make sure he didn't jump bail. What could it hurt to get him out of this ridiculous excuse for a jail until he could be brought to a fair trial—or until Cassie found evidence to clear him, which she hoped would be soon.

"I'll do everything I can to get you out of here, Jared," she promised impulsively. "Please believe me."

They'd both leaned across the table to carry on their low-voiced conversation, their faces close together, their gazes locked. Now Cassie felt her stomach tightening at their proximity, at the look in Jared's eyes as he looked her over with almost insolent leisure. She couldn't remember any other man looking at her in quite that way before—and her reaction made her breath catch in her throat.

"I suppose I'll have to believe you, won't I?" he murmured finally. "I don't know who you are or what the hell you're doing here, but you're the only hope I've got. Do what you have to do, lady. Just get me out of here."

"I'll try." Her voice came out as little more than a whisper.

He seemed to come to a sudden decision. "Cassie—"

But whatever he might have said—and something told her it had been important—was cut off when the door swung open and Deputy Calhoun swaggered back into the room. "Sorry, Miz Browning, but your time's up. Got some officers out here that have some more questions for the prisoner."

Reluctantly, Cassie stood. "I hope they realize very quickly that you're holding the wrong man," she told the officer curtly, finding it very easy to play the part of offended family friend of the accused. "You're wasting your time questioning Jared while the real criminal is getting away."

"Now, Miz Browning, that's for the law to decide," he told her with an indulgent condescension that set her teeth on edge. "You just run along now and see about getting Mr. Walker an attorney, since he's refused to have one appointed for him."

Cassie paused by the door and looked back at the hard, dark man in the orange jumpsuit, and hated having to leave him like that. He looked so very much alone. "I'll talk to you soon, Jared. Very soon."

He only nodded.

With one last, distressed look back at him, Cassie made herself leave.

She would call Tony the moment she found a telephone that offered privacy. And, for once, she intended to convince her skeptical employer that he should listen to her intuition and wire her the money that would free Jared Walker. And she hoped with everything she had that she wasn't making a huge mistake in believing Jared Walker's declaration of his innocence.

Chapter Two

"But, Tony, we can't just leave him in jail! I'm almost certain he's innocent."

"You can't know that for sure, Cassie. Not without more proof. The cops had probable cause to take him in. Look at the evidence against him. He's the same build as the perp, was wearing almost identical clothing, even had a gun in his room. And all you have is his word that he's innocent. You wouldn't really expect him to tell you if he's not, would you?"

"I just can't believe he's guilty," Cassie repeated stubbornly, frustrated with the unsatisfactory communication offered by a pay phone in a grocery store parking lot. "I've met him, Tony. I've talked to him. I just can't believe he was dumb enough to rob that motel and then get himself caught like that. It doesn't make sense."

Her employer's sigh came quite clearly through the otherwise fuzzy connection. "You've got a hunch, right?"

She made a face she wouldn't have dared had he been able to see her. "Yeah. I've got a hunch."

Tony was silent for several long moments, building Cassie's hopes, but then he dashed them. "Sorry, Cassie. We can't risk it yet. If I wire you the money and he bolts, we've lost the cash and Michelle's brother. Damn, I wish I could get away to join you there this afternoon, but all hell's broken loose here."

Cassie knew Tony would have liked the chance to meet Jared and judge his character for himself, but her ego was still piqued that he didn't quite trust her to handle the case alone. "What's going on there?" she asked somewhat grudgingly.

"Chuck tried to serve a warrant on a father who's delinquent on child-support payments and got two teeth loosened in the process. He's out on sick leave for a couple of days. Michelle's uncle from California's still kicking up a fuss about her looking for her brothers and sisters—says he's going to court if he has to to protect the Trent money from outsiders. He hasn't got a leg to stand on, of course—Michelle's money is hers to do with as she wishes—but he's making her miserable. And Carter Powell has disappeared."

"Disappeared?" Cassie repeated in surprise. "Totally?"

"Yeah. Jumped bail," Tony informed her meaningfully. "It happens."

Cassie thought of the once-prominent attorney who'd been found to be skimming money from several of his clients—Michelle Trent, for one—something Tony had uncovered when he'd begun the search for Michelle's long-separated siblings. "Are you looking for him?"

"No. As long as he stays away from my wife, I don't care where he goes, and I haven't been hired to find him. That's a job for the cops. But I can't get away from here until Monday, at the earliest.''

"You're going to make Jared sit in that jail until Monday?'' Cassie asked indignantly.

"Unless you come up with more than a hunch to show me he shouldn't be there.'' Tony's voice softened. "Look, Cassie, I know you've worked hard on finding Jared, and I'm relieved that you think he's been arrested in error. But it won't hurt him to wait a day or two until we've got something more to go on.''

"I hate thinking of him there. It's a ridiculous, grubby little jail and he's a man with a lot of pride, Tony. I want to get him out.''

"So get busy and find your proof. You're still on the expense account. Since this guy is my brother-in-law, you can consider me your client.''

"And if he asks again who I'm working for?''

"We'll talk about that after we clear up this other mess.''

She sighed soundlessly. "You're the boss.''

"Nice of you to remember that occasionally. Now, do you know what you're going to do next? Need any advice?''

Her chin lifted. "I know the procedure.''

He chuckled. "All right. Keep in touch, Cassie. And good luck.''

"Thanks, Tony. Talk to you later.'' She hung up with a muttered curse, not at all satisfied with the outcome of the conversation. Jared was still in jail, and Tony still didn't completely trust Cassie to handle a case alone.

Her stomach growled, making her frown as she glanced at her functional oversize watch. Nearly noon, and she'd skipped breakfast, hoping to arrive in town early enough to verify Jared Walker's identity before he moved on. And then, of course, she'd learned he'd been arrested, and she'd lost her appetite. But now she was hungry again. She decided to have lunch before questioning Gus Turley.

The morning rain had ended hours earlier, leaving the air fresh and clean, the sky clear and deep blue. Cassie hated to think that Jared was spending such a lovely day in jail. The little town wasn't large enough even to merit the familiar golden arches, but she found a passably reputable-looking burger place. She noticed a few odd looks as she entered alone and slid into a booth, but they didn't particularly bother her. She doubted many single women strangers came into this place, which looked as though it were frequented by local regulars.

She ordered a cheeseburger, fries and a large soft drink, to be followed by a slice of cherry pie. The food wasn't bad, though it lost part of its flavor when she found herself wondering what Jared Walker was eating in his cell. That thought had her hurrying through dessert, already anxious to get back to work.

It occurred to her that, even though she'd always taken her work very seriously, she'd become more involved in this case than any of the ones she'd worked on before. She tried to believe that it wasn't because she'd found herself unexpectedly attracted to the man she was working so hard to clear. But she found it all too easy to remember every detail of his rough-hewn face, the sound of his deep, rough voice, the way his dark blue eyes had swept over her so slowly, so very thoroughly.

It was early afternoon when Cassie drove her small car into the parking lot of the motel where Jared had checked in the night before—the motel he'd supposedly robbed during the night. She winced at the name emblazoned on the garishly lettered sign. The Come-On-Inn. *Yuck.*

The place looked clean enough, if in need of paint and new shingles. She couldn't say much for the landscaping, which consisted of a few grubby, thirsty-looking shrubs and a badly rutted asphalt parking lot. Why would Jared have chosen to stay here? Because it was one of the few motels in the area? Because it looked cheap? Or because it was relatively secluded? But then, why would he have cared about that?

Knowing those questions could only be answered by Jared, she shrugged them off and walked into the motel office.

A short, balding man with a heavy paunch bulging over his tooled leather belt looked up at the jingle of the bell over the door. "Help you?"

"Are you Gus Turley?"

His expression turned suspicious. "Yeah. Why?"

She pasted on her brightest smile and leaned comfortably against the blue Formica counter, offering him her business card. "My name is Cassie Browning. I'm a private investigator."

Turley took the card and studied it carefully, then looked back up at her. "This got something to do with that robbery?"

"Yes, sir, it does. I'm trying to determine exactly what happened."

"Yeah? On whose behalf?"

"I'm sorry, my client wishes to remain confidential at this time. Would you mind if I ask you some questions, Mr. Turley?"

Turley glowered, and tapped one blunt, dirty-nailed finger on the paperwork in front of him. "I got things to do. And I already answered plenty of questions for the police. Ask to see their report."

"I've seen the report, Mr. Turley," she answered patiently, still smiling, "but there are just a few things I still need to know. Couldn't you give me just a moment of your time?''

He grumbled beneath his breath, but nodded curtly. ''All right. What is it?''

''The man who robbed you—you're sure he was the same size as Jared Walker? Wasn't there anything in particular you noticed about him? The color of his eyes, perhaps? An accent or other unusual speech pattern?''

''He talked a little different—not as deep, I think, but he could have been disguising his voice. Probably would have, since he knew I'd remember him checking in. And the robber was wearing a ski mask,'' Turley answered. ''I didn't see the color of his eyes. All I saw was the barrel of his gun.''

''A gun you identified as a 9 mm semiautomatic. Yet the only gun found in Mr. Walker's possession was a .45.''

Turley shrugged. ''They look a lot alike—especially when you're facing the wrong end of one.''

''But you were sure it was a 9 mm. You told the investigating officers it looked like a police issue to you.''

''So I might have been wrong,'' Turley blustered. ''Or maybe he gave that gun to the other guy, along with my money.''

''What other guy?''

''Whoever it was went into the room with him that evening. Saw them myself, though Walker swears he was alone.''

''You're sure it was a man?''

''Could've been a woman. Whoever it was was a lot smaller than Walker, wearing jeans and a jacket, like him. I was here in the office, looking through that window across the parking lot. Hard to tell much from that distance.''

Cassie checked the view from the window. As Turley had said, it was a considerable distance. Yet the door of Jared's room—number sixteen—was visible enough for him to have seen whether one person or two had entered. "You never saw the smaller person leave the room?"

"No. I got busy later, watched some TV. Next thing I knew I was being held up. Got nearly five hundred dollars, dammit. I hadn't had a chance to make my deposit yesterday."

"But neither the money nor the mysterious other person were found."

"I'll tell you what I think," Turley confided, leaning heavily on the counter. "The bathroom window was open when the cops went in. I think the little guy took the money—maybe the other gun—and skipped out when the cops knocked on the door."

"So why would Walker have come back so openly?" Cassie inquired, wondering at Turley's apparent conviction that there had, indeed, been someone else with Jared.

She remembered her hunch that Jared had been holding something back when she'd questioned him on that point. "I travel alone" was all he'd said. But *had* he been traveling alone? Was it possible that he was protecting someone by claiming to have been by himself?

Did Jared Walker know more about the robbery than he'd led her to believe?

Was she crazy to still think someone else had committed the robbery, despite all the evidence?

No. Picturing Jared's face, the frustration and pain in his dark blue eyes, she still found it too difficult to believe he had anything to do with this. Turley had to have been mistaken about the second person in Jared's room, just as he'd been mistaken about the gun.

Turley had taken his time answering her question, but finally he shrugged and spoke in an impatient snarl. "Why'd he come back so openly? Hell, I don't know. The guy's just stupid, I guess. It don't take brains to aim a gun and say, 'Give me your money.'"

Cassie would have questioned him more, hoping to shake him on some point of his story, but he brought the conversation to an end, telling her firmly that he had things to do. If she had any other questions, he said, ask the cops.

She sighed. "All right. Thank you for your time, Mr. Turley."

She had her hand on the outside door when he stopped her. "Hey, Miss Browning."

Cassie looked hopefully over her shoulder. "Yes?"

"Tell your buddy Walker that I don't appreciate having my hard-earned money taken from me at gunpoint. He'll find out we don't take kindly to sleazebag crooks around these parts."

Cassie lifted her chin, forcefully swallowing the impulse to tell him that he was all wrong about Jared Walker. But it wouldn't do to antagonize him at this point. He was still the prime witness against Jared. "Thank you again for your time, Mr. Turley. Good day."

She was almost to her car when she spotted movement out of the corner of her eye. She turned her head to find a grubby teenager running away from the motel.

Frowning, she looked back at the window of the motel office. What made her think the boy had been hiding beneath that window, listening to everything she and Turley had said? And why would he have done so?

Impatiently, she shook her coppery head and climbed into her car. Nothing much made sense about this case so far.

"This is *not* the way to get yourself a partnership, Browning," she muttered crossly, starting her engine.

Jared stared blindly at a gray concrete-block wall and tried to ignore a growing urge to slam his fist into its unyielding surface. All that would net him was a fistful of broken knuckles—and he didn't need any more pain at this moment.

A flick of his gaze took in the barred door locking him into the cell. Jail. He'd been down on his luck before, hit plenty of low points in his life, but this was the first time he'd landed quite this low. Sitting in a jail cell, accused of armed robbery, only two people that he knew of who believed he didn't belong here. A frightened, confused teenage boy, and a mysterious young woman with flame-colored hair and oddly trusting green eyes.

Cassie Browning. Who was she? Who had hired her? And why did he instinctively believe she would do her best to help him, when he'd learned at a very early age that it was foolish to ever rely on anyone but himself?

He closed his eyes and felt the walls of his cell closing in on him. His fist clenched on his thigh.

Whatever it is you're doing to clear me, lady, make it fast.

It wasn't hard for Cassie to spot the waitress Jared had described in the twenty-four-hour diner. There were only two waitresses working the evening shift, one a pretty young Latino, the other a slightly overweight women of perhaps fifty with heavily lacquered bleached hair and the name "Nellie" embroidered on her pocket.

For the first time since she'd left Gus Turley five hours earlier, Cassie felt her confidence swelling again. In the meantime she'd checked in at a hotel—one with a little more class than the Come-On-Inn—and made a few calls, biding her time until she thought Nellie's shift would begin.

Her fingers closed around the photograph in her lap as the woman approached her table. "What can I get you, hon?" Nellie asked, her polite smile not quite reaching her bored eyes.

Cassie thought of the cheeseburger and fries she'd eaten for lunch. "I'll have the chef's salad, please. And iced tea."

"What kind of dressing?"

Haunted by the memory of the cherry pie that had followed her cheeseburger, she ordered the diet dressing. Before she could show Nellie Jared's photograph, the waitress had already hurried away with Cassie's order, other tables claiming her attention.

Cassie glanced at the grainy driver's license photo she held, and her impatience grew as she thought of this proud-looking man still sitting in a tiny cell. She stared at Jared's roughly attractive face for several long moments before breaking her gaze away with a slight start.

Just a case, Browning. He's just another case. Another step toward that partnership.

Yeah. Right. She sighed imperceptibly and looked up as Nellie bore down on her again with an enormous salad and a quart-size plastic tumbler of iced tea. "Thank you. I..."

But the efficient, no-nonsense Nellie had already moved on, taking an order from a man and woman who'd just been seated in a nearby booth.

Muttering beneath her breath, Cassie picked up her fork and stabbed it into her salad. After all, she had no intention of leaving this diner until she'd asked her questions. Might as well try to enjoy her dinner in the meantime.

She'd finished all she could eat of the salad by the time Nellie returned. "How about some dessert?" the woman offered.

"No, thank you. But I would like to ask you a question if you don't mind."

"What question?" Nellie's face took on the same suspicious expression Turley had worn when Cassie had approached him the same way. It seemed that people in these parts didn't take well to questions from strangers.

Cassie smiled winningly and held up the photograph. "Have you ever seen this man before?"

Nellie exhaled gustily. "That's the guy the cops were asking about, ain't it? The guy who robbed Gus Turley."

"He's only been charged with the robbery, not convicted of the crime," Cassie reminded the woman, trying not to sound too defensive on Jared's part. "He says he was here last night when the robbery took place, having pie and coffee. He described you quite well."

"Look, lady, like I told the police. We get lots of guys in here off the freeway. I can't remember everyone who comes in. And I don't want to get involved. I got problems of my own."

"Please," Cassie said when the woman would have moved away. "Please just look at the photograph. Maybe you'll remember this one."

Nellie hesitated, studying Cassie's face, then nodded shortly and reached for the photo. She frowned at it. "Yeah. I remember him."

"You do?" Cassie's heart leaped into her throat. "You're sure?"

Nellie nodded and returned the print. "Quiet type, but polite enough. Spent a long time over his pie and coffee, like he was thinking about something."

"He was here last night, between the hours of eleven and midnight?"

Cassie was extremely disappointed when Nellie shook her head. "That I can't say. Could've been earlier, maybe later. I get off work at three. I don't keep one eye on the clock while I'm working."

Cassie sighed. "I understand. But you would be willing to tell the police you saw him here last night?"

"I guess," Nellie agreed reluctantly. "I ain't taking off work to do it, but I'll give 'em a call tomorrow. Not that it'll probably do you any good," she added.

"It couldn't hurt," Cassie replied. "Thank you, Nellie. I really appreciate this."

The waitress shrugged. "Can I get you anything else?"

"No, thank you."

"Then you can pay at the register on your way out." In response to a summons from the couple at the other booth, Nellie nodded to Cassie and went back to work.

Cassie left a generous tip. Nellie's identification of Jared's photo wasn't much to go on, she thought as she walked to her car, but at least it was a step in the right direction. One bit of evidence that Jared had been telling the truth.

She'd just put her key into the door lock when she saw the boy again. He was standing in the shadow of the diner, staring hard in her direction. She knew immediately that he was the same teenager she'd spotted at the motel office. She knew, as well, that it was more than just coincidence that he was watching her now.

Who was he? And why was he following her?

Deciding to find out, she started toward him. Only to stop in frustration when he turned and ran, his young legs taking him away too rapidly for her to even hope to catch him.

"Hey, kid!" she yelled after him. "Wait up."

But he didn't stop, of course. Nor had she really expected him to.

"What the *hell* is going on here?" she asked aloud, staring at the spot where the boy had been, ignoring the startled looks she was getting from the couple just exiting the diner.

Damned if she wasn't going to ask for a raise when this case was over.

On that thought, she climbed into her car and started the engine. She had one more stop to make before calling it a day. She wanted to see Jared Walker just one more time before he spent his first full night behind bars.

Cassie was rather surprised to find Deputy Calhoun at the tiny police station. "You're still here?" she asked him. "You're putting in a long day, aren't you?"

"Got two men off with the flu," he replied wearily. "Some of us are having to pull double shifts. What you doing here, Miz Browning? It's after eight o'clock. Visiting hours are over."

"Couldn't I see him just for a moment?" Cassie begged sweetly, using the same rather awed tone that had gotten her in to see Jared earlier. "I promise I won't stay long."

"I'm sorry, Miz Browning, but it's against the rules. The boss would have my head if I brought Walker out again this late."

"Then maybe I could speak to him in his cell? Please, Deputy Calhoun. I just want to tell him good-night."

The deputy's tired face softened at the entreaty. "Oh, hell, Miz Browning—pardon my language. You're gonna' get me in all kinds of hot water, but ..."

"You'll let me see him?" Cassie asked hopefully.

He grunted. "All right. But I'm staying with you this time. And you got five minutes—that's it."

"You're being more than generous," she assured him, trying to look properly grateful.

As she followed the officer down a hallway, Cassie found herself wondering why she was really there, why it had seemed so important to see Jared tonight. Maybe she'd just needed to test her faith again by looking straight into his eyes while he assured her one more time of his innocence. Maybe she needed to convince herself that she hadn't been crazy to believe him the first time, with so little reason to do so.

Yet even as the doubts crossed her mind, she knew she hadn't really changed that hastily formed opinion during the hours since she'd last seen him. Everything within her told her that Jared Walker was innocent. And it was up to her to prove it.

Jared was lying on his cot, still wearing the orange jumpsuit, one arm behind his head as he stared motionlessly at the ceiling. He glanced up when Calhoun said his name, then came to his feet in a hurry when he spotted Cassie.

She regretted having to quell the fleeting look of hope that crossed his hard face. "I haven't arranged bail yet," she said, her fingers closing around the cold, hard bars of the cell door. "I'm sorry."

His expression closed again, he nodded as he approached the door. "Why are you here?"

Cassie glanced at Calhoun, who turned partially away in a small effort at giving them privacy. "I talked to Turley today. And to the waitress, Nellie."

"And?"

"Turley's still convinced you did it, though his identification doesn't stand up very well under heavy questioning. He still insists that you had someone with you when you checked in yesterday. Says he saw you enter the room with someone—either a woman or a small man." She watched him carefully as she spoke, dwelling on this one issue that still bothered her about Jared's story. Turley had seemed so positive, at least about this.

Jared's expression didn't change. "He's wrong."

Making sure Calhoun couldn't hear her, Cassie whispered, "Jared, you're sure you're telling me the truth? You're not trying to protect anyone?"

"Who would I be trying to protect?" he growled, without really answering her question.

"A woman?" she asked reluctantly.

"I told you, there was no woman."

Even more reluctantly, she asked very carefully, "Then is there something else I should know?"

"Like what?"

"Like maybe—you had a guy with you? It's okay if you're—well, you know," she assured him hastily, and not quite truthfully. "I'd understand."

Jared's appalled expression would have been amusing if his situation hadn't been so very serious. "I am most definitely straight," he told her in a low growl. "I'd be happy to prove that to you if we were alone."

She flushed deeply at his meaningful tone, though she told herself the words were nothing more than a hasty reaction to her implication. Still, she couldn't help wondering what it would have been like to meet him under different circumstances. She was well aware that she was deeply, unreasonably drawn to this angry, complex man, though she wondered if Jared Walker would ever allow anyone to get close to him, even under the best of conditions.

She quickly changed the subject. "I showed Nellie your photograph. She's willing to testify that you were in the diner last night, though she can't be pinned down as to the time."

Jared looked grim. "That's not much."

"No. But it's a start," she reminded him, knowing how bleak his case must look to him at the moment. "They're not going to convict an innocent man, Jared. The system doesn't work that way."

"The 'system' doesn't work at all," Jared answered bitterly. "Believe me, I know. The cops would just as soon lock up an innocent man if they can call the case closed and make themselves look good.''

''I can't believe that.''

''Yeah, well, that's your problem. If you want to keep on believing in fairy tales, go right ahead. I just hope you don't find out the hard way that you've been wasting your efforts.''

The embittered cynicism in his voice hurt her. What must it have taken to make him so hard? Had it begun when he'd lost his mother and then been separated from his younger brothers and sisters when he was only eleven years old?

But, of course, she couldn't tell him she knew about that without revealing that she'd found him on behalf of his sister, and Tony had strictly forbidden her to do that.

''I won't give up trying to clear you,'' she could only insist softly.

His hard face softened, so fractionally that she wouldn't have noticed had she not been watching him so closely. ''I haven't even thanked you for what you've done today.''

Her throat tightened. She knew that expressing gratitude would be as difficult for Jared as asking for help. It touched her that he was making an effort for her. ''That isn't necessary.''

''Yeah,'' he said gruffly. ''It is. Thanks, Cassie.''

''You're welcome,'' she whispered.

Their gazes held for a long, taut moment, and then Jared moved closer, glancing warily at Calhoun before speaking in a low, private tone. ''Cassie, there's something I want you to do for me. I need you to—''

''Sorry, Miz Browning. Time's up,'' Calhoun broke in, stepping closer.

Jared abruptly stopped speaking, his eyes mirroring the frustration Cassie felt. What had he been going to say? She sensed that it had been very important to him. But, whatever it had been, he'd shut her out again with Calhoun's interruption. She glared at the deputy.

Calhoun cleared his throat forcefully at finding himself pinned between two hard stares. "Uh—sorry," he muttered. "But I really can't let you stay any longer."

Cassie tried to soothe her expression, reminding herself that she might need the deputy's assistance again before Jared was released. "I understand," she assured him. "And I appreciate what you've done."

She turned back for one last look at Jared. "Good night." She knew better than to suggest that he get a good night's sleep. She suspected he wouldn't sleep much at all. She wasn't expecting to get much rest herself, knowing that Jared was spending the night in this dreary cell, and racked with doubts about his innocence and her ability to prove it, one way or another. "I'll see you tomorrow."

He only nodded.

Cassie didn't dare look back as Calhoun escorted her out. She was afraid to risk releasing the tears she felt burning at the back of her eyes at the thought of Jared standing so still and alone, watching her walk away.

You owe me for this, Tony.

Chapter Three

Still wishing she knew what it was Jared wanted to ask her, Cassie crossed the parking lot of the police station toward her car. She was only a couple of feet from the vehicle when she realized that she was being watched again—and she thought she knew who was watching her. But this time, she had no intention of being outsmarted by a grubby kid.

With a noisy exclamation of disgust, she dropped her purse, spilling its contents on the pavement at her feet. "What a klutz!" she complained aloud, kneeling as though to gather her belongings.

In response to a movement out of the corner of her right eye, she launched herself in that direction, calling on all her training as a private investigator. A moment later, she had her hands full of squirming boy, and found herself using all the energy she had to hold him. Not for the first time, she regretted her lack of height. At only five feet four inches,

Cassie stood almost eye to eye with the boy, whose fear was lending him strength.

"Either be still or I'm calling for help," she warned him. "I'm sure Deputy Calhoun will come running if I start screaming. Is that what you want?"

The boy froze. "No! Don't call the cops! Please, lady."

"You'll stand still?"

He nodded unwillingly.

"Promise?" she insisted, not quite trusting him.

"You have my word," he answered, and his stiffly dignified tone was strangely familiar.

Frowning, she turned him toward her—only to find herself looking into Jared Walker's dark blue eyes in a weary, defiant, dirt-streaked young face. "Who are you?" she demanded, though she thought she already knew.

"My name is Shane Walker." He looked uneasily at the police station. "Could we get out of here? Please? I don't want them to see me."

"You're Jared's son," she breathed, her knees weakening with the realization. So Jared *had* been protecting someone. But why? Why wouldn't he tell someone that this boy was out on the streets alone while his father fretted in his cell?

Shane froze, his eyes widening in fear. "You're not going to turn me in, are you? Please, don't tell them about me. They'll send me away from him. And I won't go—I *won't!*"

"Hey, take it easy," she said when he struggled in her grasp again. "I'm not going to turn you in. I swear," she added, tightening her grip on his skinny arm. "My name is Cassie Browning. I'm a friend."

He looked at her suspiciously. She wasn't surprised that he didn't trust her yet. Like his father, Shane Walker seemed to be the cautious, reserved type. "If you're a friend of my dad's, how come I've never seen you before?"

She nodded at the logical question. "I only met him this morning," she explained. "I'm a private investigator, and I'm working to clear him of charges. I know he's innocent, and I'm not going to stop asking questions until I've got proof."

"He didn't rob that motel."

"I know." She cautiously loosened her grip. "I know, Shane."

He relaxed marginally. "You're really a P.I.?"

"I've got identification in my—well, it's here somewhere," she said ruefully, glancing at the scattered contents of her purse. "I'd be happy to show you."

He seemed to reach a decision. "All right. I believe you."

She made a face. "Thank you for that magnanimous concession."

"Huh?"

"Never mind. How about helping me pick this stuff up and then let's get out of here before someone sees us."

He hesitated only a moment, looking from her car to the door of the police station. And then he nodded. "All right."

She gave a silent sigh of relief. She still wasn't feeling quite steady. The discovery that Jared Walker had a teenage son had rocked her all the way to her toes, though she couldn't have said exactly why, even if she tried.

"You hungry, Shane?" Cassie asked when they were in her car, leaving the police station—and Jared—behind.

Shane drew his gaze from the rear window, his expression tearing at her heart. "Yeah," he said. "I haven't eaten since dinner yesterday."

She forced herself to speak cheerfully, wanting to ease the pain in his too-old eyes. "Heavens! You must be starving. I remember the way my brother ate when he was your age. Couldn't fill him up."

"You've got a brother?"

"Yes. Cliff's a pilot in Alaska. Delivers freight to the remote areas there."

"Wow. Cool job."

She managed not to laugh at the unintentional pun. "Yeah. He's a cool guy."

But Shane's attention didn't stray long from his father. "I saw you talking to those people today—the motel guy and the lady at the diner. You were asking about my dad?"

"Yes."

"Did it help?"

"Maybe," Cassie replied, not wanting to raise his hopes too greatly at this point. "The waitress remembered seeing him."

"They still think my dad did it, don't they?" Shane asked dispiritedly.

"He's only been charged, Shane. Now they have to prove it. Remember, he's innocent until they've proven guilt without a reasonable doubt. And since he didn't do anything wrong, they're going to have a tough time proving he did."

"My dad says the good guys don't always come out ahead," Shane informed her. "He says you can't always trust the system. That's why he hasn't told anyone about me since he was arrested. He knows they'd stick me in a foster home. My dad hates foster homes."

Knowing Jared had spent seven years in foster care, Cassie bit her lip. Obviously, Jared's experiences had been more difficult than those of the two sisters who'd already been reunited—Michelle, who'd been adopted by a wealthy, prominent family, and Layla, who'd lived with one foster family until her graduation from high school. Again, Cassie was frustrated by her orders not to reveal any information about Jared's family—Shane's family, as well.

"Surely your father doesn't think you should be on the streets alone," she fretted, not entirely comfortable with Jared's silence despite her understanding of his motives.

Shane cleared his throat. "Well, uh—"

She turned to look at him. "What is it?"

"Dad gave me some money a long time ago, when we started traveling together. Said I was supposed to use it to buy a bus ticket to a friend's house if anything ever happened to him or if we ever got separated—like now. He probably thinks I did what I was told and went to Mr. Cutter. But I couldn't leave him here all alone. I just couldn't."

"I understand." Now Cassie thought she knew what Jared had wanted her to do for him. She thought maybe he'd trusted her enough to tell her about Shane, and to ask her to check on the boy's welfare. She could be wrong—but somehow she knew she wasn't. And it warmed her to think he'd trust her with something this important to him.

"Think you'll be in trouble when your dad finds out you didn't follow orders?" she asked casually.

Shane grimaced. "He's going to be mad as a hornet. But he'll get over it. He always does."

Cassie pulled into the drive-through lane of a fast-food restaurant. "I'll get some food and take you to my hotel to eat it," she explained. "That way we won't risk being seen by anyone who might start asking questions."

Shane gave her suggestion a moment's consideration, then nodded. "That's a good idea," he said approvingly. And then he reached for his pocket. "I'm buying."

"Oh, no. I've got it."

Proudly lifting his chin, the boy pulled out a shabby wallet. "You're working to clear my dad, so that means we already owe you. I'll buy my own food."

Realizing that Shane Walker was every bit as proud—and as stubborn—as his father, Cassie shook her head. "Look,

I'm on an expense account, okay? Everything's taken care of."

Looking as though he wasn't quite sure what an expense account was, Shane eyed her suspiciously. "Yeah?"

"Yeah. Trust me." And darned if she wouldn't turn it in, she thought. Buying the kid's meal was the least Tony could do after refusing to make Jared's bail.

"I've got a bag stashed in a locker at the bus station," Shane told her after she'd purchased enough food to satisfy two starving adults. She'd figured that would be just about enough for one hungry teenager. "Would you mind if we pick it up on the way to your hotel?"

"Of course not. Just tell me how to get there."

"Turn right at the next light."

Cassie looked speculatively at him. "You seem to know your way around pretty well for a stranger in town."

Shane shrugged, sniffing appreciatively at the odors coming from the paper bag in his lap. "I've learned to get by on my own when I have to. I lived on the streets for almost three months once."

Appalled, Cassie stared at him, nearly running a red light before bringing her car to a stop. "When?"

"Two years ago. When I was twelve. My dad found me. I've been with him ever since."

She didn't understand; Shane seemed so devoted to his father. "You ran away from home two years ago?"

"From my stepfather's home. Me and him didn't get along, and my mom stayed too drunk to care. I knew Dad would find me as soon as he came back."

"Came back from where?" Cassie asked, thoroughly confused.

"He was in the navy, stationed on an aircraft carrier. Soon as he could, he got out and came after me. Now he has full custody—my mom and stepfather were really relieved to hand me over to him, I think.''

Cassie swallowed hard against words of sympathy she doubted the boy would appreciate. She still wasn't sure exactly what had transpired in Shane's short life, but it was a wonder he'd turned out as levelheaded and well-behaved as he seemed to be. Three months on his own at age twelve! How had he survived?

Shane slipped in and out of the deserted bus station with a stealthy ease that reminded Cassie forcibly of the few homeless youths she'd encountered back home in Dallas. He tossed his bag into the back seat. "We'd better hurry," he said, squirming into his seat belt. "I think my food's getting cold."

Cassie smiled shakily and headed toward her motel. Once there, she settled Shane in her room with his food and a soft drink purchased from the machine outside her door. And then she walked into the office and booked the room adjoining hers, which had fortunately been vacated earlier that day.

Worried about possible inconvenient questions, she'd thought of having Shane stay in her room overnight. But then she'd decided that was an even more potentially awkward situation. She was relieved that the hotel clerk didn't even seem curious as to why she wanted the second room, accepting Cassie's money without hesitation.

Shane had inhaled every bite of the food by the time Cassie returned. She tossed him the key. "You've got the room next door," she said, motioning toward the connecting doorway. "You must be tired."

Shane nodded, his young shoulders slumping a bit. "Yeah. I didn't get much sleep last night."

"Can you tell me what happened last night, Shane?"

His expression grew grim, and he looked so much like his father that Cassie couldn't help staring. "Me and Dad had been on the road all day—he had a lead on a job in Arizona, just north of Flagstaff," he added, confirming what Jared had told Cassie. "I was tired, so I turned in early. Dad couldn't sleep, so he went out for a while. He does that sometimes to keep from disturbing me when he's feeling restless.

"Anyway, about midnight someone started pounding on the door, yelling that they were the cops and for me to open up. I thought something had happened to Dad and they were there to take me to a foster home," he explained unhappily, once again displaying his fear of the child welfare system his father had taught him to avoid. "I grabbed my stuff and went out the bathroom window. Then I waited in the bushes for Dad. I watched them arrest him."

His tone was so bleak, his eyes so haunted, that Cassie blinked back tears. "Did you hear the reason why?"

"Yeah. Everyone was yelling—and that Turley guy was shouting something about Dad robbing him. I knew they were crazy, of course, but I didn't know how to help him."

"You couldn't have helped him," Cassie assured him gently, her voice husky. "Not then."

"I know. Dad gave me the sign to clear out, so I did. I even went to the bus station—but I couldn't leave him here in jail. I just couldn't, no matter what he'd told me."

"Your dad gave you a sign?" Cassie repeated in surprise. "He saw you?"

Shane nodded. "Yeah. No one else did, but Dad spotted me. That's when he quit fighting them. He jerked his chin and I knew he was telling me to get going. And then they put the cuffs on him and pushed him into the cruiser."

He stopped to clear his throat before continuing. "I hung around the jail for most of the night. I was snooping around the motel, hoping maybe to find some proof that Dad was innocent, when I heard you questioning Turley. Then later I went over to the diner Dad had said he was going to, thinking maybe I'd have something to eat and ask some questions, but you were already there. I couldn't figure out who you were, but I thought maybe you were trying to help."

Cassie smiled at him, her heart already firmly captivated by the resourceful young man. "You thought right."

Shane returned the smile, making her realize it was the first time he'd smiled at her all evening. The smile made him look suddenly younger, like the boy he was rather than the man he was trying so hard to be.

Again, Cassie felt tears pricking at the back of her eyes. "You'd better get some rest," she said. "I'll wake you in the morning for breakfast. We'll decide then what our next move will be."

But she already knew what her first move would be the next morning. With or without her employer's permission, she was bailing Jared Walker out of jail, even if she had to empty her savings account. Shane Walker needed his father. And Cassie couldn't bear to think of Jared spending even one more day behind bars.

Shane glanced from the connecting door to the key in his hand. "You paid for the other room already?"

"Yes. Don't worry about it."

He grinned crookedly. "Expense account, right?"

"Right." She could seriously like this kid.

He paused on his way out, shuffling his feet in awkward embarrassment. "Uh, Miss Browning—thanks, okay?"

"It's Cassie," she murmured. "And you're welcome. Good night, Shane."

"'Night." He gave her another of those endearingly sweet smiles before closing the door behind him.

Cassie sighed and ran her hands through her tangled curls. "God, Browning. What have you gotten yourself into now?" she asked before reaching wearily for her night-gown.

Shane wasn't the only one in desperate need of rest.

Jared lay wide awake on the hard, lumpy cot, his thoughts torn between worrying about his son and wondering about the woman who was supposedly working to clear him.

He had to believe that Shane had followed orders and headed straight for Bob Cutter's place in Oklahoma when Jared had given him the sign to take off. They'd been through the drill enough for the boy to know what was expected of him, and he was perfectly capable of buying a bus ticket and making the trip alone, though Jared wasn't entirely comfortable with the prospect. Still, it beat being alone on the streets again. And even though Jared knew Cutter was away from home for the weekend, there was an excellent housekeeper who'd take Shane in without a question. The boy would be safe there, though Jared knew Shane would be worrying himself half-sick.

His distrust of the legal system was deeply ingrained, but Jared would have trusted Cassie Browning to check on Shane for him if he'd had a chance to talk to her in certain privacy. He'd been surprised by his own impulse to tell her about the boy. Trust wasn't something he gave easily, and almost never to strangers. But then, few strangers had gone to so much trouble so willingly on his behalf.

Who the hell was she? How did she know of him? Who was she working for? And was she really as honest and trustworthy as she seemed, or was he only being set up yet again?

He *had* to get out of here, he thought, grinding his teeth in frustration. Dammit, he had to. For his son, for himself.

And because he was growing increasingly more impatient to find out for himself exactly why Ms. Cassie Browning had suddenly appeared in his life.

Cassie didn't sleep well. Her disturbing dreams were filled with images of dark blue eyes. Jared's—angry, tortured, wary. And Shane's—frightened, unhappy, heartbreakingly hopeful. Both of them counting on Cassie to help them. And she felt so helpless in response.

When her restless tossing and turning woke her at 1:00 a.m.—twenty-four hours after Jared's arrest, she couldn't help noting—she padded into the tiny bathroom to wash her face and drink some water from a plastic cup.

As she returned to bed, hoping to be more successful with this attempt at sleep, she wondered how she'd managed to become so involved with the two Walker men in such a short time. She'd already lost her heart to Shane—and something told her it wouldn't be too difficult to do the same with his father. And wouldn't *that* be one of the most foolhardy mistakes she'd ever made?

Don't get involved with the cases, Tony had told her over and over again. And yet, Tony had fallen head over heels in love with Jared's sister Michelle the day she'd walked into his office only a few months ago and hired him to find her missing brothers and sisters. Maybe there was something about the Walker siblings that neither Tony nor Cassie had been able to resist.

Deciding she was being silly, trying to blame her emotional fancies on exhaustion, she buried her head in the pillow and ordered herself to sleep. If only she could order herself not to dream....

It was just past 6:00 a.m. when Cassie was abruptly awakened by a heavy pounding on the outer door to her room. She sat up with a gasp, taking a moment to remember where she was and why before reaching for her robe.

"Coming," she called out, assuming it was Shane at her door. He could have knocked on the adjoining door, of course, but who else could it be? Maybe he'd awakened disoriented, too.

It was, indeed, one of the Walkers at her door—but it wasn't Shane.

"*Jared!* How—? When—?"

"The real crook struck again last night. They caught him with Turley's bank bag still under the seat of his pickup and a 9 mm semiautomatic stuck in the waistband of his jeans. I was released with a grudging apology and a warning to 'be more careful in the future.'" Jared's mouth twisted for a moment. "I checked every motel in the area to find you. Why have you registered in two rooms here?"

Cassie was delighted, of course, that Jared had been released. She told herself it was mean and petty of her to be just a bit disappointed that she hadn't been the one to clear him.

"Come in," she urged him, tightening the belt on her robe and smoothing futilely at her wildly tousled curls. "I'll explain as much as I can."

"Yeah, I want you to do that," he assured her, stepping past her into the room. She couldn't help noticing how much more virile and confident he looked in his flannel shirt, skintight jeans and battered boots, rather than the regulation jail jumpsuit she'd seen him in before.

"But first," he said, glancing at the nightstand, "would you mind if I use the phone? I've got to call a friend to check on someone."

"You're checking on Shane? If so, I—"

Jared stiffened, his dark gaze stabbing into hers. Cassie felt a chill slither down her spine. "How do you know about Shane?"

"I—"

The connecting door opened without warning. "Cassie?" Shane asked, stepping into the room, wearing only a pair of jeans. "I thought I heard my—*Dad!*"

Jared's look of surprise changed quickly to relief. He held out his arms and Shane pelted unselfconsciously into them. Almost unbearably touched by the scene, Cassie had to look away from the expressions on their faces. She was pleased to realize that Jared Walker loved his son as deeply as Shane adored his father.

The embrace didn't last long. Jared held his son away, hands gripped firmly on Shane's thin shoulders. "You're supposed to be in Oklahoma," he said, obviously trying to sound stern. "Why aren't you?"

"I couldn't leave you," Shane answered simply. "I just couldn't, Dad."

Jared sighed. "After all the times we talked about what you should do..." He stopped and shook his head. "You're lucky the welfare services didn't get you."

Shane lifted his head proudly. "They wouldn't have kept me for long."

Jared winced and glanced at Cassie. "They wouldn't have, either."

"No," she agreed with a shaky smile. "I think Shane is very much like his father. The independent type."

Both Shane and Jared looked rather pleased with the comparison, though she hadn't exactly meant it as a compliment.

"Grab a shower and get your things together, son, while Ms. Browning has a chance to get dressed," Jared said, giving Cassie a lingering, all-encompassing glance that had her pulling the lapels of her robe more tightly closed. "I'll be there in a minute," he added, giving Shane a slight shove in the direction of his room without taking his gaze from Cassie.

Glancing speculatively from Cassie to his father, Shane quickly followed instructions, closing the connecting door behind him. Cassie's room seemed suddenly to grow smaller when she found herself alone in it with Jared.

"I don't know how you hooked up with my son," he said, taking a step toward her. "But thanks for watching out for him. And for everything else. It was good to know there was at least one person besides Shane who didn't think I'd robbed that motel. I consider myself in your debt."

She wrapped the tie of her robe around both hands, all too aware of her sleep-tousled appearance and lack of makeup. "You're welcome," she whispered, nervously moistening her lips. "But you really don't owe me anything for what little I did."

"I don't agree," he murmured, his hands settling on her shoulders. "And I don't think what you did was so little. Thank you, Cassie Browning."

While her hands were still tangled in the fabric belt of her robe, he lowered his face to hers, taking her mouth in a long, thorough, heart-stopping kiss. Cassie was trembling by the time it ended, dazed by the intensity of the sensations he'd aroused in her with nothing more than that one kiss.

"I'll be back in fifteen minutes," he told her, stepping away from her just a bit too quickly. "I've got a few questions for you."

Shaking off her lingering bemusement—had she *ever* been kissed like that before?—Cassie dove for the telephone the moment the door to the other room closed behind Jared. Doubting Tony would be at his office so early on a Friday morning, she dialed his home number. The housekeeper answered.

"Hi, Betty, it's Cassie. Is Tony around?"

"Sorry, Miss Cassie. He had a breakfast meeting with a client this morning. Michelle's here, if you'd like to speak to her."

Cassie hesitated, then declined. "I'll try to reach Tony later. Thanks, Betty."

She hung up, wondering if she should have asked Michelle for permission to disclose her client to Jared. But she couldn't, not when she wasn't sure Tony had let Michelle know Jared had been located.

Stripping out of her robe and nightgown, Cassie dressed rapidly in slacks and a sweater, then hurried into the bathroom to brush her teeth and do what she could with her hair and makeup in the short time Jared had allotted her. Trying to tame her unruly curls with a gold clip at the back of her head, she ran through a list of vague answers to the questions she knew Jared would ask. Questions like who she was working for, why she'd been looking for him, how she'd found him.

She couldn't think about the kiss—had it only been his way of expressing gratitude?—or she'd never be able to function coherently. And she knew she was going to need all her wits about her when he returned.

Dammit, Tony, why'd you tie my hands like this? You don't know how hard it's going to be to tell Jared Walker that I can't answer his questions yet!

Finally satisfied that she'd done the best she could with her appearance, Cassie stepped out of the bathroom, only to find Jared Walker calmly and openly going through the contents of her purse.

"What the—get out of that!" she snapped, making a grab for the leather bag.

He allowed her to take it, seemingly content with her wallet, which he held open. Easily avoiding her snatch at the wallet, he studied her driver's license, then her business card. "D'Alessandro Investigations, Dallas, Texas," he murmured. "That's who you work for?"

"Yes," she answered crossly. "And haven't you ever heard of invasion of privacy?"

"As a matter of fact, I have. I'm trying to figure out if my privacy has been invaded." He looked up at her, and he was no longer the man who'd kissed her until her toes had curled, but a faintly menacing stranger. "Who's your client, Cassie?"

She lifted her chin in a gesture of defiance. "I told you, that's confidential until I have permission to discuss it with you. If you'd wait just a couple of hours until I can contact my boss..."

"I thought maybe my old navy friend Bob Cutter hired you, that he must have sent you as soon as he heard I was in trouble. Though I can't figure why he'd hire someone from Dallas when he lives in Tulsa. Did he?"

"Not as far as I know," Cassie admitted.

"So who are you working for?"

She looked pleadingly at him. "I'm sorry, Jared. I'm under orders. And I don't want to lose my job."

"You've got a copy of my last driver's license photo," he commented, nodding toward the purse she held. "Which means you were looking for me even before I was arrested. Why?"

She remained mute, her fingers clenched around the soft leather.

Sighing his impatience, he tossed her the wallet, which she caught by reflex. "Call your boss. Now. I want some answers. With or without his clearance."

"I just tried to call him," she said, annoyed at the curtness of his command. "He wasn't in."

"Try again."

"Now see here—"

"Fine. I'll call him myself." He displayed the business card he'd kept when he'd returned her other things.

Cassie muttered a curse and snatched up the telephone. "I'll call him," she grumbled, punching in Tony's office number. "But we're wasting our time. He's not . . . Tony?"

"Yeah," her boss replied, apparently unperturbed by her surprise at having him answer. "I had an early meeting that didn't last long. Thought I'd come on in and work on some overdue paperwork. What have you got, Cassie?"

"Just a minute." She put a hand over the mouthpiece and looked from Jared to the connecting door. "Maybe you could give me a few minutes to talk to my employer in private?"

"Forget it."

"Dammit, Jared—"

"This concerns me," he replied implacably, crossing his arms over his chest. "I'm staying."

She glared at him, but took her hand away. "Tony?"

"Yeah. What's going on, Cassie?"

"Jared Walker's here, in my room. He's been cleared of all charges—and he wants to know who my client is."

"Immediately," Jared confirmed quite clearly.

Tony obviously heard. "I see. Then I guess you'd better tell him."

Cassie turned her back to Jared in a futile effort to shut him out. "Um—you'll tell Michelle?"

"I've already told her," Tony admitted. "Never could keep anything from her for long. She and Layla will be greatly relieved to hear their brother's been cleared."

"So it's okay now to tell him everything?"

Tony hesitated only a moment. "You trust him, Cass?"

She knew what he was asking. He wanted to know if Jared Walker proved any threat to his wife. "Yes, Tony. I do."

"Then tell him. And ask if he'd like to come to Texas to meet his sisters. If not, I'm sure they'd be delighted to meet him wherever he chooses."

"I'll let you know."

"Do that. Good work, Cassie."

Warmed by his praise, she managed a smile. "Thanks, Tony. I'll talk to you later."

She hung up the telephone and turned to face Jared. She wasn't prepared for his first question.

"Who's this Tony guy?" he demanded. "And what is he to you?"

"He's my boss," she replied in surprise. "And my friend. He also happens to be your brother-in-law," she added, taking small revenge for his arrogance with the blunt statement. "He's married to your sister Michelle. My client."

Chapter Four

Jared shook his head in response to Cassie's disclosure. "Try again. I don't have a sister named Michelle."

"How about Shelley? Shelley Marie? She would have been two years old the last time you saw her."

His eyes widened, then narrowed again. "Shelley?"

Unable to hold on to her irritation with him, Cassie nodded, speaking more professionally. "Next to the youngest of your three sisters—her name was changed to Michelle Culverton Trent when she was adopted soon after you were separated. She and Tony, my boss, were married this summer. She met him when she hired him to find her biological family."

Jared seemed to struggle to understand what she was telling him. "My little sister Shelley has hired you to find the rest of us? After all these years?"

"Yes. She's already found the oldest sister, Layla, the one who's a year younger than you. Layla lives in Ft. Worth, and she and Michelle have become quite close during the past few months.''

Jared inhaled sharply. "Layla," he murmured, his eyes focused somewhere in the past. He ran a hand through his crisp brown hair. "Damn."

Cassie tried very hard to read his expression. "You remember them?"

"I was eleven years old when we were separated," he answered. "I remember them."

"I hope you understand why Tony was reluctant for me to tell you at first," she said, nervously clenching her fingers in front of her. "I mean, you were in jail, and even though I believed from the beginning you hadn't done anything wrong, Tony wanted to be careful. I tried to talk him into making your bail, but he—well, he's a really nice guy, but when it comes to Michelle, he's very protective. He wanted to be sure."

Jared inclined his head. "Yeah."

She waited for him to say something else. When he didn't, she offered, "Tony's still coordinating the search for your youngest sister and your two brothers. He hasn't located any of them yet, but—"

"*Two* brothers?" Jared repeated. "There should be three."

"Oh." Cassie bit her lip before explaining. "One of them died in a car accident several years ago."

"Which?" he asked sharply.

"Miles. As far as we know, the twins are still living."

Jared's only reaction was the twitch of a muscle in his jaw. He shoved his hands in his pockets, looking away from her.

Cassie suspected that he was more shaken by the news than he would have her believe. "I'm sorry, Jared. I guess I didn't handle that very well. I'm not very good at breaking bad news.''

He flicked her a glance. It wasn't unkind, just…detached, Cassie decided, wondering if she'd made a mess of everything with her usual lack of tact.

"Jared?"

"I haven't seen them in twenty-four years," he told her. "I didn't know whether any of them were still alive. I'm not so sure this search is such a hot idea."

"How can you say that?" Cassie demanded, perplexed by his attitude. "They're your family. Don't you want to see them again?"

"As far as I'm concerned, Shane is the only family I've got," Jared returned brusquely. "We've gotten along fine, just the two of us. These other people are strangers."

Cassie was stunned by his callousness. Perhaps she'd taken her own loosely knit family for granted at times, but she'd always known they were there for her, should she need them. She couldn't imagine walking away from them for good. "Jared—"

He exhaled through his nose, shaking his head in apparent incredulity at her dismay. "Still living in that fairy-tale world, Cassie?" he murmured. "Believing that every story leads to a happy ending?"

She strongly resented his condescending tone. "You weren't convicted for a crime you didn't commit, were you? Didn't I tell you the system works most of the time?"

"Right. But if the jerk who robbed the motel hadn't been such an idiot and gotten himself caught, I'd still be sitting in that cell and the cops would be quite certain they had their man. It was dumb luck, not the wheels of justice."

She decided it wasn't worth arguing about. "Believe whatever you want."

His mouth twitched in a smile that held little humor. "Thanks. I will."

Cassie thought she'd take almost as much satisfaction from hitting this infuriating man as she had in kissing him. Almost. She clenched her fists behind her back to keep them away from temptation. "Your sisters really want to see you again, Jared. They've gone to a lot of trouble to track you down."

His faint smile deepened just fractionally. "I can see they put the best investigator on the case."

She scowled. "There's no need to make fun of me," she told him with all the dignity at her command.

"I wasn't," he replied, his tone unexpectedly gentle.

Eyeing him uncertainly, she asked, "Will you come back to Dallas with me to see your sisters?"

He hesitated only a moment. "No. Sorry, but I'd best head on toward Arizona. I need a job for the winter. Got to get Shane back in school. He's already missed a week."

"There are jobs in Texas," Cassie said wistfully, reluctant to let either Jared or Shane leave her life now that she'd found them. "And schools."

He shook his head. Again, his expression wasn't hard or unkind, but he didn't look as though he'd change his mind. "I don't belong there, Cassie. I've been on my own too long now, wouldn't know what to do with a lot of family. Tell my—tell your clients that I appreciate their concern and I send my best regards, but I think I'll pass on a family reunion for now."

"You wouldn't have to go to Dallas," Cassie said, taking one last shot, which she already knew would be futile. "They'd come to Arizona. Or anywhere you like. They only want to see you."

"Maybe some day," Jared replied firmly. "Not now."

He glanced at his watch, a clear indication the conversation was over. "I'd better get moving. Oddly enough, I can't wait to get the hell out of this town."

"A real loner, aren't you?" she grumbled, thoroughly dissatisfied with the outcome of the case on which she'd worked so hard. The case with which she'd become all too deeply involved. "You're walking away without a regret."

"Oh, I don't know," Jared murmured, stepping close and touching the fingertips of his right hand to her cheek. "Maybe one regret."

Cassie looked longingly up at him. Whatever unguarded expression he saw in her eyes made him groan. And then he kissed her again, and Cassie found herself clinging to his shirt as though that tenuous grip would keep him with her.

He took his time, his mouth moving hungrily on hers until neither of them could wait any longer for the kiss to deepen. Cassie parted her lips, and Jared thrust inside with a rough, heated skill that made the blood pound in her veins, bringing every inch of her to tingling awareness. And this time, she didn't even wonder if the kiss was motivated by gratitude. She might not be widely experienced when it came to men, but she knew enough to tell the difference between gratitude and desire.

"Uh—Dad?"

Cassie would have torn herself out of Jared's arms had he not held her where she was. Without the least evidence of embarrassment, he slowly lifted his head and glanced toward the doorway. "Be right with you, Shane."

His dark head cocked to one side, Shane looked from Jared to Cassie with what seemed to her to be amused approval. "Guess there's no need for you to hurry. It's just..."

"You're hungry, right?" Jared spoke with the confidence of parental experience.

Shane grinned. "Yeah."

Jared gave Cassie a rueful glance and released her. "We'll stop for breakfast at the next town," he told his son. "I've had enough of this place."

"I know the feeling," Shane agreed heartily. He turned his attention to Cassie. "Are you going with us?"

Jared answered instead. "Cassie's going back to Dallas. That's the opposite direction from where we're going."

Shane looked disappointed. "Oh."

Jared tossed Cassie's business card on her unmade bed. "I'll put your things back in the truck, Shane. You can take a minute to thank her for all she did for us and tell her goodbye."

"Take my card with you," Cassie said, retrieving it and holding it out to Jared. "My work and home numbers are on it. You could call me—you know, if you change your mind."

He glanced at the card, but didn't take it. "I won't be changing my mind. And I know how to find you. Goodbye, Cassie. Thanks again for all you did for us. Tell your boss you deserve a bonus for this case."

She winced at his mention of her job. Jared and Shane had become much more than just another case to her, though damned if she knew what she was going to do about it.

She turned to find Shane looking indignantly after his father. "He's not always that rude," he seemed to feel obligated to say. "He's just had a bad couple of days."

"I know," she murmured, moved again by Shane's consideration. He really was such a sweet young man.

She pressed the rejected card into his hand. "Keep this, okay, Shane? If you ever need me, you can call anytime."

He studied the card curiously. "Maybe I'll write you sometime?" he suggested rather tentatively. "You know, let you know how we're doing, how things are going in Arizona."

Her smile felt shaky around the edges. "I'd really like that."

"Yeah? Maybe I will, then." He stored her card carefully in his battered wallet, treating it with touching care. And then he slid the wallet into the back pocket of his jeans and looked back up at her. "I'm going to miss you, Cassie. You've been a good friend."

"I'll miss you, too," Cassie whispered. "And we're still friends, okay?"

"You bet." Impulsively, he reached out to hug her, the embrace awkward, but obviously sincere. Cassie blinked back tears as she fervently returned the hug.

A horn honked briefly outside the room. "That's my dad," Shane said, drawing back with his young face rather flushed. "He wants to make it as far as Winslow by tonight. I'd better go."

"Take care of yourself. And your dad."

"I will. 'Bye, Cassie."

"'Bye, Shane."

And then Cassie was left alone, staring wistfully at a closed door.

"Damn," she said aloud, unable, for the moment, to think of anything else to say.

Jared was aware of his son's unblinking regard for a full ten minutes after they'd left the town behind them. He ignored it at first, fiddling with the radio until he found a station that played the contemporary country music Shane preferred. When Shane continued to look at him without saying anything, Jared sighed gustily and slanted the boy a questioning glance.

"All right. Get it said. What's eating you?"

"I liked her, Dad. She worked real hard yesterday to try to clear you, even though she'd just met you. And she didn't talk to me like I was some helpless kid, or call the welfare service or anything. Why'd you have to treat her so bad?"

"I did *not* treat her badly," Jared returned, unaccountably defensive. "I thought I was nice enough. I thanked her for helping us."

"You kissed her off. Literally."

Jared scowled at his son's phrasing, as well as the uncomfortable sensations that coursed through him at the mention of that kiss. He hadn't really wanted to walk away from Cassie Browning—not just yet, anyway—but all her talk of sisters and family ties had made him extremely nervous.

Okay, he'd admit it. He'd sort of panicked. But, hell, he'd been on his own for a long time, responsible for and dependent on no one but himself and his son for the past two years. Maybe it wasn't an ideal life that he and Shane were leading, but they were getting by. Jared didn't see the need to make any radical changes at this point.

He hadn't told Shane about the family who'd initiated Cassie's search. Wasn't sure he wanted to tell him just yet. Not until he decided exactly how he felt about being found by them.

But, damn, the taste of Cassie Browning's pouty mouth had turned him on. Like no other woman had in a very long time.

Spotting a small restaurant ahead, he pointed it out to Shane, knowing only food could distract the boy from thoughts of his new friend at the moment. Now, if only a stack of hotcakes and a cup of coffee could do the same for himself...

But he knew, even as the thought crossed his mind, that he wouldn't be forgetting Cassie Browning anytime soon.

* * *

"Look, it's not your fault, Cassie. You did the best you could. You did a hell of a job on this case, actually."

A few days earlier, praise like that from her boss would have had Cassie doing ecstatic time steps across the motel room. Now she could only slump more dejectedly on the side of the bed. "I really tried to talk him into seeing Michelle and Layla. But he's been alone a long time, Tony. I think the idea of family unnerved him."

"I suppose that's understandable. We know he lost both his parents in less than a year, then was separated from his brothers and sisters and thrown into a series of unsuccessful foster homes. He's probably learned not to get close to people, that it's easier not to have personal ties."

"You're right," Cassie admitted regretfully. "Other than Shane, there seems to be no one special in his life except an old navy buddy who apparently lives in Oklahoma."

It had really been foolish of her to fall so hard for a man who'd almost made a career out of being a loner. And yet, she couldn't help remembering the way he'd looked at his son when they'd been reunited. If Jared could love Shane that intensely, couldn't he learn to love someone else? Someone very persistent, very stubborn and very motivated to teach him? Someone just like her?

"Cassie? You still there?"

"Mmm? Oh, sorry, Tony. I was just thinking."

"Uh-oh. I know that tone. What are you planning?"

"Shane mentioned where they'll be staying tonight. I thought maybe I'd follow—try to talk to Jared one more time. Maybe he'll change his mind."

"Cassie. Give it up. You've done all you can do. It's up to Jared to contact us if he wants to be reunited with his family. Neither Michelle nor Layla expect us to force their brother to see them."

Cassie stuck out her lower lip in an expression that her parents could have identified as one of sheer determination. "You know, I'm kind of tired after tracking Jared down for the past few weeks. All the stress and everything. I think I'll take a couple of days off, if you don't mind."

"I *do* mind, as a matter of fact," Tony returned immediately. "Chuck's still out, the guy I hired to replace Bob is still learning the ropes, Michelle's uncle's still raising a fuss. I need you here, Cassie. Come home."

Cassie coughed delicately, not bothering to cover the mouthpiece. "You know, Tony, I'm not feeling very well. I think maybe I'm coming down with something. Probably picked it up in that tacky little jail yesterday."

"Cassie..."

"Just a couple of days, Tony. I swear. And you can take me off the expense account as of now. I'm on my own time."

The word he said was probably illegal over the telephone wires. Since he spoke in idiomatic Italian, Cassie couldn't have said for certain. She winced, waiting with held breath for his decision.

"All right, Browning. You've got a couple more days. But this time, if he says no, you're going to give up. Got that?"

"Thanks, Tony. You won't be sorry. And you know how pleased Michelle will be if I talk her brother into coming there to meet her."

"That's the only reason I'm going along with this," Tony admitted. "Michelle would love to see her older brother—and her nephew. So, you're still on the expense account. But, dammit, Cassie, stay in touch. And don't be gone long."

"I won't. 'Bye, Tony."

She hung up quickly, before her boss could change his mind, and reached for her bag.

Jared Walker was about to find out that Cassie Browning could be as stubborn as he was. That he couldn't look at her the way he had, kiss her silly—twice—then walk out on her without a backward glance.

And she wouldn't turn in her new expenses, she decided, forcefully zipping her bag.

From this moment on, the case was strictly personal.

Though he'd quit smoking two years ago, figuring it was better for his health and a better example for Shane, Jared bought a pack of cigarettes from a vending machine in the corridor of another inexpensive motel, this one in Winslow, Arizona. He carried the pack only as far as a corner of the second-story landing outside the room where Shane slept, then leaned against the wrought-iron balcony and lit up. Jared was having another restless night, but this time he had no intention of wandering very far from his son.

He drew deeply on the cigarette, making a face at the dry, bitter taste. Had he really enjoyed it once? Shrugging, he brought it back to his lips. Might as well finish it now that he'd started.

It wasn't as though he had anything else to do.

Except think. He'd been doing entirely too much thinking today. Too much remembering. Things he hadn't allowed himself to remember in nearly twenty-four years.

The distant sounds of childish voices drifted through his mind. He sighed and gave up on trying to hold them back. His brothers and sisters. God, he'd missed them when they'd been taken away.

As the eldest, Jared had been the one in charge when his alcoholic father was gone and his poor, fragile mother working or resting. Jared had always felt responsible for them all, his mother included, particularly after his father had been killed in an industrial accident, which the insurance hadn't covered because Hank had been drinking that day.

Jared had never quite gotten over the crushing guilt he'd felt when his mother had died less than a year after giving birth to the child she'd been carrying when her husband died. He'd tried so hard to help her, as had Layla, his junior by a year. But their efforts hadn't stopped their delicate, overworked mother from catching pneumonia. Nor had they been able to prevent the siblings from being separated when the social workers decided that no family would be willing to take in seven children, ranging in age from eleven years to eight months.

It would be "best," they'd said, to split the kids up. *Best for whom?* Jared had demanded to know, but he'd never gotten a satisfactory answer.

He'd secretly grieved for his family for years afterward, until he'd finally learned to put them out of his mind so that he could get on with his own life. And he'd learned not to get so attached again. Not until he'd had Shane, whom he'd allowed himself to love more deeply than anyone or anything else in his entire life.

So little Shelley was married now. He held the smoldering cigarette between his fingers and stared blindly at the deserted parking lot below him. Hard to believe. He remembered her as a curly headed toddler, a bright, happy baby who'd loved jelly sandwiches and "horsey-back" rides from her oldest brother, whom she'd called Jerry. She'd been devoted to him, and to Layla, whom she'd clung to, crying when the social workers had come to take her away.

It was nice to know Layla and Shelley had been reunited, that they were growing close again. He was pleased for them, despite his own cautious reluctance to get involved.

Jared had been especially close to Layla, maybe because they'd been so close in age. Together they had made sure the younger ones were fed, bathed, clothed, tucked into bed. A pretty, loving girl, Layla had always been willing to listen, always ready to lend a hand with homework or to take over his chores for a few hours so he could join the neighborhood boys for a game of empty-lot baseball in their hometown of Texarkana, Texas.

And Miles. Eight years old when they'd been separated. Jared could still picture the boy's round, freckled face. Miles could always be counted on to make the others laugh, since he'd usually been laughing himself. A real little clown, with dreams of becoming a stand-up comic or an impersonator like his hero, Rich Little. He'd been pretty good, too, for a kid. Did a great imitation of President Johnson. And now he was dead. Had he ever made it to a stage, basked in the sound of an audience's laughter?

And what had happened to the five-year-old twins, Joey and Bobby? They'd been a handful, always into some sort of mischief. He and Layla had run themselves ragged trying to keep up with them. Jared remembered very clearly telling Bobby that it would be a wonder if he lived to see junior high—it had been a threat, actually. *Had* Bobby seen junior high? Where was he now?

Which left only the baby, Lindsay. She hadn't really had a chance to develop a personality when they'd taken her away, of course. Just a little thing, but she'd been a good baby. Jared still remembered how it had felt to rock her sweetly scented little body in the middle of the night so their mother could catch a few hours' sleep before going in to one of the two jobs she'd worked to feed her kids. Jared and Layla had taken turns looking after the baby, and he'd never really minded doing his part, no matter how much he may have grumbled at the time.

He'd missed them. But he didn't know them now. Why take the chance of an awkward, painful reunion when he had enough to do just taking care of himself and his son?

Shane. Jared scowled. Being arrested for a crime he didn't commit had made Jared all too aware of how very much alone he and Shane really were.

What would become of the boy if anything happened to Jared? He certainly wouldn't go back to his mother and stepfather, neither of whom would want him, anyway. Which left the streets—or foster care, both of which held approximately the same appeal, as far as Jared was concerned.

Should he give Shane the chance to meet these long-lost family members, hoping they would be there for the boy if he ever needed them? Or would he be imposing more stress on Shane by introducing him to these strangers who might have emotional expectations neither Jared nor Shane could satisfy?

"Damn," he muttered, annoyed with his uncharacteristic ambiguity.

It was usually so easy to make decisions, avoid messy entanglements, move on without regrets. Why did he suspect that Cassie Browning had all too much to do with his indecisiveness now?

"Hello, Jared."

Jared looked around sharply to find Cassie standing only a few feet away, watching him with a wary guardedness that showed how uncertain she was of her reception. Had he been the sort of man to believe in the paranormal, he might have wondered if his thoughts had conjured her.

He didn't have to ask why she was here. One of the first impressions he'd gotten of her was that she was the persistent type. Young, eager, reckless, stubborn, idealistic, impetuous. Desirable.

With his abysmal track record with women, he'd thought it best to walk away from this one, feeling he had much too little to offer her. But somehow, even as he'd driven away from her that morning, he'd suspected she wouldn't leave his life so easily. And, no matter how he might try to deny it, he was glad she hadn't.

He ground the cigarette beneath the heel of his boot, deliberately taking his time about it. And then he looped his thumbs in his belt and faced her. "Anyone ever tell you you're a pain in the butt, Cassie Browning?"

Chapter Five

Oddly enough, Cassie relaxed in response to Jared's question—more specifically, to the tone in which he'd asked it. He didn't sound angry that she'd followed him, just resigned. As though he'd really been expecting her all along.

She'd been watching him in tense silence for the past five minutes, working up her nerve to speak. He'd seemed so tough and unapproachable, leaning against the balcony and smoking in the shadows, lost in his own deep thoughts. And he'd looked so virilely sexy that she'd become aroused all over again, just from standing close to him.

She pushed her hands into the pockets of her slacks. "It's been mentioned a time or two," she quipped in response to his only half-joking question.

"Not surprising." He propped both elbows on the railing behind him, one boot resting on the bottom rail as he studied her in the dim artificial lighting. "It's getting late. Took you a while to find me, did it?"

She took offense at the subtle criticism. "I think I did pretty well," she retorted. "Considering that I've had to check the guest registers of twelve different hotels in the past two hours."

"Guess I don't have to ask why you're here."

"I'm sure you know," she replied, hoping his casual tone indicated that he was more receptive now to the idea of meeting his sisters.

"You want my body, right? Want to go to bed with me."

Cassie choked. *"What?"*

"Not so loud. There are people trying to sleep around here, you know. And damned if I intend to be accused of disturbing the peace and spend another night in jail."

She lowered her voice to a sibilant whisper. "You are the most obnoxious, arrogant, conceited—"

"Hey, it's okay. I understand. Those *were* dynamite kisses, weren't they? Can't blame you for wanting to follow up on them. Matter of fact, the same thought crossed my mind a time or two. I'm willing."

Cassie suddenly realized that she'd just been expertly played for a fool. Jared had been baiting her—and she'd swallowed it hook, line and sinker.

"You jerk," she said, more calmly this time.

"You mean you *don't* want to go to bed with me? Well, hell."

She couldn't help giggling, though she suppressed her amusement almost immediately. "You know why I'm really here, Jared," she said, crossing her arms in front of her.

He sighed faintly, abandoning the teasing. "Yeah, I know. Would you mind answering one question?"

"What is it?"

"What's in it for you if I agree to see my sisters? Why are you so determined to talk me into this?"

"Well..." She hesitated, then suggested, "It would look really good to my boss if I pull this off. He still considers me an apprentice, and I'm hoping to make partner someday."

"So I'm just a career opportunity to you, is that it?" Jared asked gruffly.

She dropped her arms to her sides, wishing just this once she could get away with dissimulation to someone she cared about. Knowing Jared would see right through anything but the truth. "That's not the only reason I followed you," she admitted.

"No?"

She gave him a quick, resentful look, annoyed that he was making this so difficult. "No."

He didn't move, though she sensed a change in him, a tension she felt echoed in herself. "Then why?" he asked, his voice a husky murmur.

Dragging both hands through her hair, Cassie attempted a quiet laugh, which came out much too shaky and tentative. "Maybe I just want your body."

When Jared started to move, she hastily held up a hand, palm outward, afraid he'd taken her sadly flat-sounding joke the wrong way.

"No wait. What I really mean is, I'd like to get to know you better. I'm—well, I'm attracted to you, of course, and I think Shane is terrific and—and I think it would be good for both of you to meet your family. Not just because it would be good for my career, but because I think you're both a little lonely and..."

"But, anyway," she hurried on when he took another step toward her, "I'd understand if you don't—uh—reciprocate my feelings, but I still think you should see your sisters, for your own—"

Jared put an end to her nervous babbling by smothering the words beneath his mouth.

Cassie didn't even try to resist him. She melted into his embrace like warm chocolate, her arms going around his neck to bring them even closer together. His arms locked around her waist, and for the first time she felt the full length of him against her.

They fit so well. He wasn't overly tall, maybe five-nine, just right for her height. But he was so strong, so lean and hard that she felt utterly, deliciously feminine in contrast. Intensely aware of the exciting differences between them.

The kiss lasted a very long time. As did the one that followed it, and the one after that. Cassie thought she'd be content to stay right here forever, locked in his arms, his mouth moving on hers.

And then he slipped a hand between them to cup her swelling right breast and she knew that it wouldn't be long before she'd need more. Much, much more. And, judging from the hardness she felt pressing against her abdomen, Jared wouldn't be content with kisses for much longer, either.

"You two at it again?" a young, sleepy voice asked cheerfully from behind them.

Dropping his hand, Jared groaned and rested his forehead against Cassie's, giving them both a moment to control their breathing. And then he lifted his head and glared at the grinning teenager standing in the doorway of the motel room. "You're pushing your luck, boy," he said, his voice still rough around the edges.

"Hi, Cassie," Shane said, ignoring his father's warning.

She returned his smile and pulled out of Jared's arms, wondering why she didn't really feel embarrassed this time at being caught kissing his father. "Hi, Shane."

"Good to see you again."

"You, too."

"You're looking well."

She really adored this kid. She nodded in grave acknowl-edgment of his teasing. "Thanks. So are you."

"Did you have a nice drive?"

"Yes, quite pleasant. And you?"

Jared gave a short laugh, putting an end to the gravely silly conversation. "All right, you two, knock it off. You got a place to stay tonight, Cassie?"

"No, not yet."

"Go back to bed, Shane. I'll be in as soon as I'm sure Cassie's got a room."

"Hey, no problem. Take your time, Dad."

"Shane?"

"Yes, Dad?"

"You want to live to see fifteen?"

Shane's grin deepened. "Yeah. I was kinda hoping to live long enough to get a driver's license."

"Then get back in bed. Now. I'll be in shortly."

"Yes, Dad. 'Night, Cassie. See you in the morning?"

"You bet. Good night, Shane." Cassie bit back a laugh as she looked up at Jared when the door had closed behind his son. "Did I mention that I like your kid, Jared?"

"I'm not surprised. The two of you have a lot in com-mon."

Cassie couldn't help wondering about Shane's mother as Jared escorted her to the motel office. Had Jared ever loved the woman? And how could any mother let go of a won-derful young man like Shane?

She remembered Shane's casual mention of his mother's drinking and, again, she marveled that he'd turned out so well. She thought maybe Jared had a lot to do with that.

Jared waited outside the office while Cassie registered. Fortunately, there were vacancies on this Friday night, since it wasn't exactly the peak of tourist season. She was pleased to be given a room close to the one Jared and Shane shared. She held up the key as she stepped back outside. "All set."

"Good. Where are your bags?"

"In my car." She nodded to the car parked close by the office. "I'll get it."

"I'll help you."

Jared was very quiet as they retrieved her bag from the back seat of the car and headed toward her room. Cassie wished she knew him well enough to guess at his thoughts.

He unlocked her door for her, carried the bag inside and dropped it at the foot of the bed. With what Cassie considered rather touching courtesy, he checked to make sure the utilitarian room was adequate, clean towels available, television functional, an extra blanket in the closet should she need it. "You'll be okay?"

"I'll be fine," she assured him. "I live by myself in Dallas. I'm used to sleeping alone."

His gaze locked with hers. "If it weren't for Shane, you wouldn't be sleeping alone tonight."

Her mouth went dry. She moistened her lips with the tip of her tongue, noting that Jared watched intently as she did so. "I know."

He hesitated, then seemed to force himself to turn toward the door. "Good night, Cassie. Sleep well."

"Thanks. You, too."

He snorted skeptically. "Yeah. Right."

Which meant, of course, that he didn't expect to sleep any better than she did. Sexual frustration wasn't exactly conducive to a good night's rest.

Jared paused with one hand on the doorknob, his back turned to her. She watched him curiously, sensing that he was struggling for words. "What is it, Jared?"

"I'm unemployed," he said, still without looking around at her. "My track record with women is lousy. I've got a teenage boy to worry about and a bank account that's a long way from being enough to buy the small ranch I hope to own someday. I'm not exactly a good risk for a relationship. I think you should know that before we—well, before we take this any further."

"Thank you for telling me."

He did glance back then, in response to her wry tone. "You don't look like you're taking me very seriously."

She managed a tremulous smile. "No."

"That reckless streak is going to get you in trouble someday, Cassie."

"So everyone tells me. It hasn't happened yet."

He exhaled wearily. "Just don't say I didn't warn you."

He was gone before she could respond, had she been able to think of anything to say.

Okay, Browning, you've been warned. The man's not looking for a long-term relationship. So, are you going to take his advice and keep your distance?

Her mouth still felt swollen and tingly from his kisses, the deepest feminine parts of her still moist and throbbing with desire for him.

Oh, no, Jared Walker. You're not getting off that easily. Cassie Browning doesn't give up so quickly on something this important.

It wasn't until she was tucked into bed, tossing restlessly on the pillow and trying to think of anything but her physical discomfort, that it occurred to her that Jared had never given her an answer about meeting his sisters.

Cassie was awakened the next morning by the telephone on her nightstand. Expecting to hear Jared's voice, she answered with a sleepy smile.

"Cassie? It's Shane. Good morning."

She wasn't really disappointed. "Good morning, Shane. What time is it?"

"Nearly eight. Dad wants to know if you want to join us for breakfast. I'm—"

"—starving," Cassie finished with him, her smile deepening.

He laughed self-consciously. "Yeah."

"I'd love to join you for breakfast. Think you can wait another twenty minutes without fainting from hunger?"

"I might last that long—but it'll be close," he returned cheerfully.

"Then I promise to hurry."

"I'd appreciate it," Shane drawled, sounding so much like his father that Cassie's throat tightened.

She jumped out of bed, took a record-breaking quick shower and subdued her wet curls into a French braid. She hadn't brought many clothes with her when she'd left Dallas four days earlier. She pulled a clean pair of jeans and a floral fleece pullover from her bag, trusting that Jared didn't have anyplace fancy in mind for breakfast, judging by the low-budget motels and inexpensive diners he'd frequented thus far.

She had just finished tying her tennis shoes when someone knocked on her door. She pulled it open eagerly, finding Jared and Shane waiting on the other side.

"Good morning." The greeting was meant for both of them, though Cassie looked at Jared as she spoke.

Jared's smile was as intimate as a kiss would have been. His gaze locked with Cassie's. "Good morning."

Shane cleared his throat noisily when several long, silent moments had passed. "So, is anybody hungry? For food?" he added daringly.

Jared cuffed his son's shoulder. "Mind your manners."

Shane grinned. "Yes, sir."

Cassie grabbed her purse and suitcase, knowing there would be no reason for them to return to the motel. Jared took the bag from her, their fingers brushing. Cassie could almost feel the electricity spark between them at the contact.

"Thanks," she said, rather breathlessly.

He looked down at her for another long moment. "Oh, hell," he muttered, then glanced at his son. "Turn around."

Shane laughed, but obliged.

Jared bent to Cassie, giving her a very thorough, quite satisfactory good-morning kiss. Her toes curled inside her tennies at the heat and hunger behind the embrace.

"*Now* we can have breakfast," he said, lifting his head with a rakish smile that made her shiver in response.

"It's about time," Shane proclaimed fervently.

Cassie just hoped she'd remember how to walk to the door. *Wow, could that man kiss!*

With Cassie following in her little car, Jared drove his truck to a small restaurant just down the road from the motel. Shane teased him about his obvious attraction to Cassie until Jared put a stop to it with a firm, "That's enough, Shane."

"Yes, Dad," Shane said, subsiding with a meek tone and a suspicious twinkle in his blue eyes. "But you *do* like her, don't you?"

"I like her," Jared answered, knowing even as he spoke that he wasn't being exactly truthful. He wasn't sure what, exactly, he felt for Cassie Browning, but *like* was far too tepid a word to describe it.

"Table for three?" a plain young hostess inquired when they entered the restaurant. "Smoking or nonsmoking?"

"Nonsmoking," Jared answered for them. He'd given it up again. He hadn't found much pleasure in the one cigarette he'd smoked the night before. He figured he could live without them.

Shane and Cassie kept up a rapid repartee as they ordered their breakfasts and waited to be served, making Jared feel, at times, like a chaperone with a couple of kids. The bond that was forming between Cassie and the boy was almost a visible one. Jared had never seen Shane take to anyone as quickly.

He guessed he could understand that. He felt much the same way.

"You got a boyfriend, Cassie?" Shane asked just a shade too casually, avoiding his father's eyes as he spoke.

"No," Cassie answered in the same tone, and she didn't look at Jared, either. "I guess I've been too busy with my job to have much time for a social life lately."

"Too bad," Shane commented, his expression saying just the opposite. "Did you know Cassie has a brother who's a bush pilot in Alaska, Dad?"

"No, I didn't," Jared replied, realizing with a slight start that he actually knew very little about Cassie's personal life. Odd that he should feel as though he knew her so well in some ways.

"Cliff," Cassie said. "He's a couple of years older than I am. He's a redhead, too, though no one else has been for generations back."

"Your family lives in Dallas?" Jared asked, suddenly wanting to know as much as he could about her.

She shook her head, causing the overhead lights to glisten in the still-damp, dark red braid. "My parents live in Tyler, Texas and Cliff's my only brother. I moved to Dallas because the job market looked better there."

"And you became a P.I." Jared commented. "You and your brother both seem to be the adventurous types."

Cassie smiled. "Yeah, I guess we are. My parents, who are very sweet, but just a little staid, seem to think we're changelings, that their real babies were mysteriously replaced by these two redheaded daredevils. They love us, but they don't quite understand our need to constantly challenge ourselves."

Shane laughed, but then defended his new friend. "I think what you do is cool. Your parents ought to be proud of you."

Jared gave Cassie a wry look. "It seems you've won yourself a champion."

Cassie only smiled and turned her attention to the breakfast their waitress had just set in front of her.

Jared waited until Shane had taken the edge off his hunger before bringing up the topic he knew Cassie was waiting anxiously for him to broach. Maybe it would have been better to talk to the boy in private, he thought, but for some reason he wanted Cassie there. He'd already come to value her matter-of-fact comments and her easy way of talking with Shane. And this talk wasn't going to be easy for Jared.

"Son, you remember asking me once if I had any family?"

Jared felt Cassie stiffen, but he kept his gaze on Shane, who looked up curiously from the remains of his huge breakfast. "Yeah, I remember. You said your folks died when you were a kid."

"Right. And I told you that I'd had some brothers and sisters who were separated and sent to different homes. That I assumed most of them had been adopted soon afterward."

Shane nodded, then his eyes widened. He looked across the table at Cassie. "Is that who you're working for? One of Dad's brothers or sisters?"

Damn, the kid was sharp, Jared couldn't help thinking with a touch of pride. Didn't miss a trick.

Cassie glanced at Jared before answering Shane. He nodded.

"Yes, Shane," she said, turning back to the boy. "Your father's sister Michelle is my client. Actually, she's married to my boss."

"Michelle?" Shane looked intrigued. "You remember her, Dad?"

"Yeah. She was just a little thing when we were split up. We called her Shelley."

"She was adopted by a family named Trent from Dallas," Cassie supplied. "She grew up thinking she was an only child, since she was too young to remember her brothers and sisters. She initiated the search for the others when her adoptive mother died earlier this year, leaving a letter telling Michelle about her biological family. Michelle hired my boss for the job, then ended up married to him a few months later."

"And you were assigned to find my dad."

Cassie nodded. "That's right."

"Guess they gave you the best, huh, Dad?"

Jared smiled at Cassie, remembering that he'd said much the same thing only the day before. She'd thought he was mocking her. He hadn't been, any more than Shane was now. "Yeah. Guess they did."

He was relieved that Shane was taking the news so well.

"So I've got an Aunt Michelle," Shane mused.

"And an Aunt Layla," Cassie told him. "And three cousins that we know of so far. Layla has three kids."

"My age?" Shane asked with interest.

"Younger," Cassie replied. "I think the oldest is maybe nine, ten years old."

"Boys or girls?"

"One boy, two girls. I'm sorry, I don't remember their names."

Jared shook his head in wonder at the thought of young Layla with a brood of her own now. Not that it was so hard to picture, really. She'd been a natural at mothering the little ones.

"What about the rest of Dad's brothers and sisters?" Shane asked, still addressing his questions to Cassie. "There were a bunch of them, weren't there?"

Cassie looked again at Jared, who motioned her to answer. He wasn't yet ready to join the discussion he'd initiated.

"Counting your dad, there were seven children. One died in a car accident several years ago, leaving twin boys and a girl still unaccounted for."

"I bet you'll find 'em, won't you, Cassie? You can find anyone."

Cassie flushed at the confidence in Shane's young voice. Jared found the blush sweetly endearing.

She avoided his eyes as she answered, "Tony—my boss— has several operatives on the case, actually, as well as his own efforts. I've spent most of my time just tracking down your dad through military and employment records."

"Operatives," Shane repeated in a murmur, obviously impressed by the term. "Cool."

"So here's the deal, son," Jared said, leaning forward and taking control of the conversation. "My sisters have invited us to Dallas to visit them and get to know the families. They're also willing to visit us here in Arizona, whenever we get settled. They're leaving it up to us to choose."

"Dallas," Shane repeated, looking speculatively at Cassie. "That's where you live, isn't it?"

"Yes."

Shane turned to his father. "I'd like to go to Dallas, Dad."

Jared frowned at the too-quick answer. "We need to discuss it a little more. I don't know if that's the best choice right now. After all, you've already missed a week of school, and I've got to get back to work before our money runs out. Might be better if we head on to Flagstaff and arrange a meeting later."

It never occurred to Jared to make the decision without asking for Shane's opinion. After all, this affected them both, and they'd become a team during the past couple of years.

"Aw, come on, Dad. Another week out of school won't make any difference. I can catch up, you know I can. Didn't I have all A's in Oklahoma?"

"Social studies," Jared reminded him, though he was already weakening at the entreaty in his son's eyes.

"Okay, one B," Shane conceded. "But I'll study real hard when I get back to it, I promise. As for the job, well, you didn't have anything firmed up, anyway. You can always talk to the guy next week rather than this one."

"You really want to go to Dallas? Why, Shane?"

"Well, gosh, Dad. You've got family there. Don't you want to get to know them?"

Jared was staggered by Shane's apparent eagerness to meet this newly discovered family. Had the boy really been so lonely? Had Jared been deluding himself that neither of them needed anyone else in his life? "The question is, do *you* want to get to know them?" he asked, watching his son closely.

"Well, yeah. I think it would be cool to have aunts and cousins and everything," Shane admitted. "Of course, it's been great just the two of us the past couple of years," he assured Jared hastily, as if concerned that he'd hurt his father's feelings.

Jared knew exactly how lonely Shane had been in the years before he had gotten full custody of the boy. Living in a home with an alcoholic mother and a distant, resentful stepfather, Shane had grown up isolated and withdrawn, eager for visits from his seafaring father. For the first time, Jared realized that Shane must have fantasized during those years about having a large family.

Jared's fist clenched beneath the table at the thought of the abuse his son had suffered at the hands of his mother, and the years Jared and Shane had missed together because the courts had denied Jared's repeated attempts to gain custody. The so-called experts had decided the boy would be better off in a home with two parents than with his single, military father, even though those "parents" had proven sadly inadequate for the responsibility they'd been given.

Was that why Shane had taken so quickly to Cassie, why he seemed so pleased that his father was obviously attracted to the friendly young woman? Was the boy starting to fantasize now about a new family, complete with father and mother, aunts, uncles and cousins?

Jared ran a finger beneath the open collar of his flannel shirt, as though it had suddenly grown tight.

Damn. He really didn't need this kind of pressure right now.

"We can't stay long," he warned. "Our money's not going to hold out forever. I've got to get back to work."

Shane shrugged with youthful unconcern. "You could always find something in Texas. Maybe Cassie knows of something," he added.

Jared felt a muscle twitch in his jaw. "I can find my own jobs."

He noted that Cassie was being very quiet, her hands folded in her lap, though she was concentrating intensely on the discussion between Jared and Shane. Just looking at her made his pulse quicken, his loins harden.

He couldn't remember wanting any woman as much as he wanted this one. But damned if he'd find himself married to her just to please his son. He was a long way from ready for a commitment like that.

"You remember what I said last night?" he asked her abruptly, not wanting to clarify his question in front of the boy.

"I remember," she answered evenly, her expression telling him that she remembered every word of warning.

"You willing to risk that it won't work out?"

Her eyes held his without wavering. "I'm willing."

Feeling just a bit cornered, Jared turned to Shane, who watched him hopefully. "You understand that if this doesn't pan out, we'll have to move on? Soon?"

Shane shrugged. "It's what we've always done before," he agreed, sounding suddenly older than his fourteen years.

Jared pushed a hand through his hair. "Okay. We'll give it a shot."

"We're going to Dallas?" Shane asked, eagerly seeking confirmation.

Jared nodded, his gaze still focused on Cassie. "We're going to Dallas."

And he knew, as he suspected the others did, that the decision had little to do with Jared's sisters and a great deal to do with whatever had developed between Cassie and Jared during that first visit in a New Mexico jail only some forty-eight hours earlier.

Chapter Six

"Too bad we can't all ride together to Dallas," Shane lamented as they left the restaurant, headed for their separate vehicles. "That would be lots more fun."

"We'll follow Cassie," Jared replied. "We'll stop and eat lunch together and stay in a motel somewhere tonight. This is a two-day trip."

"Two long days," Cassie agreed, not particularly looking forward to the drive. But at least she'd have their meals together to anticipate along the way. She almost suggested that Shane ride with her for a while, then decided not to deprive Jared of the boy's company.

"If you need to stop for anything, flash your taillights," Jared instructed, seeing Cassie to her car. "I'll flash you if we need to stop."

"I'll be watching," Cassie promised.

"You do that. But watch the cars ahead of you, as well."

"Yes, Jared," she said, making a face at his tone.

"Buckle your seat belt."

"Yes, Jared." She did so, thinking that he certainly was the bossy type. Rather sweetly protective, but bossy.

With a smile in his eyes, he leaned into the open doorway. "Kiss me."

She returned the smile. "Yes, Jared." She lifted her face eagerly to his.

The kiss was brief, a mere promise of better things to come. Cassie thought it just as well. If his earlier kiss had made her forget how to walk, another one like it would probably make her dangerous behind a wheel. But then, there were some people who said she was that, anyway, she thought with a chuckle, and started her engine.

They'd been on the highway for less than an hour when Jared flashed his lights. Cassie obediently pulled over into a roadside rest stop, assuming that was probably the reason, the guys had wanted a break. She rolled down her window as Jared approached her car.

"Lady, you drive like a maniac," he said, scowling as he leaned into the opening. Behind him, she could see Shane slumped in the seat of the pickup, his face buried in his hands.

"What's wrong with the way I drive?" Cassie demanded. She'd been on her best behavior, too!

"For one thing, you've been speeding."

"Only a little."

"And driving too close to the cars in front of you."

"They were going too slowly."

"And changing lanes without even checking the traffic."

"I did not! I always check the traffic before I change lanes."

"And turn down your radio. You're paying more attention to the music than to your driving."

Her jaw dropped. "Now how could you possibly know how loudly I was playing my radio? And don't tell me you could hear it—I know it wasn't *that* loud."

"I watched you bobbing up and down in time to the music," he returned crossly. "You're supposed to be driving, not bebopping."

"*Bebopping?* Hey, who do you think you are, my mother?"

"I'd just hate to watch you get hurt or killed in a car accident because you weren't paying attention," he said, sounding so virtuous and sermonizing that she could easily have hit him.

His bossiness—and his overprotectiveness—were becoming less endearing by the moment.

"I'll tell you what, Jared," she said sweetly, giving him a smile that showed all her teeth. "You concentrate on getting yourself and Shane safely to Dallas, and I'll do the same for me. Okay?"

He eyed her with sudden wariness. "You're annoyed with me."

"You could say that, yes."

"For caring about your welfare?"

"For not crediting me with enough sense to take care of myself."

He sighed. "Look, I wasn't trying to make you mad. It's just that I—well—"

"You what?" she probed, wanting him to finish what he'd started to say.

"I'm not used to caring."

The stark simplicity of the statement drained all the anger from her, replacing it with a warm, sappy feeling she didn't quite know how to handle. "Oh," was all she could think of to say.

He reached through the window to touch her cheek,. "Sorry, Cassie. I shouldn't have chewed you out like that. I won't again."

Her smile was both tremulous and skeptical. "You won't? Ever?"

He returned the smile with a rueful, rather sheepish one of his own. "Well, not until lunch, anyway."

She laughed, wondering how she could have gone so quickly from temper to humor. But then, Jared had been stirring up rapidly changing emotions in her since she'd first laid eyes on him. Something told her she'd always react strongly to this particular male.

"Let's move on," Jared said abruptly, shoving himself upright.

She craned her neck to look up at him. "Don't you and Shane want to—uh—you know?" She motioned toward the public rest rooms at the center of the paved area.

He gave her an incredulous look. "Here? Not hardly. Don't you know the type of weirdos who hang out at these places?"

Her Jared was definitely the prudent type, Cassie thought with a grin as he loped back to the driver's seat of the pickup.

And then her smile faded as she realized how she'd referred to him in her thoughts. *Her* Jared? In her dreams. They were a long way from establishing that sort of relationship.

Still, it was a nice feeling to think of him as hers. For now, at least.

By the time they stopped for lunch, Cassie was a nervous wreck from trying to drive in an exemplary manner, and Shane was a bundle of energy from sitting still for so long. It was a beautiful mid-September Saturday, so they decided in a roadside consultation to get take-out food and eat at a public park Shane had spotted as they entered the mid-size town.

The moment they arrived at the park, Shane was off, running as hard as he could down a trail marked for walkers and joggers.

Jared chuckled as he and Cassie followed more sedately, choosing one of the few empty concrete picnic tables left on such an ideal day for picnics. "He's about tired of traveling. We've been on the road for most of the week."

"I know," Cassie replied with a smile. "I've been right behind you since the day after you left your last job in Oklahoma."

Jared frowned and draped a leg over the bench, reaching for a canned soft drink as he sat down.

Studying his expression, Cassie realized that she was learning to read him. "You don't like the idea of someone tracking you down through your records?"

"Not particularly," he admitted.

"You're a very private person, aren't you?"

He shrugged. "Yeah. I guess."

She sat opposite him, her chin propped in her hands as her elbows rested on the cool concrete table. "If it makes you feel any better, I didn't learn that much about you in my investigation. Only some of the jobs you've held since leaving the navy two years ago. I didn't even know you had a son. I never found a record of your marriage."

"It was a long time ago," Jared replied, his eyes on Shane, who'd been invited to join a game of Frisbee with a couple of boys his age. "I was nineteen and just out of basic training, she was eighteen and ready to get away from a bad home life. Marriage seemed like a good idea at the time, though neither of us tried to pretend we were passionately in love."

"What's her name?" Cassie asked, though she wasn't entirely sure she wanted to hear about Jared's relationship with another woman, even if he hadn't been deeply in love with her. Still, the other woman was Shane's mother—and Shane was a very important part of Jared's life, as the boy would be to Cassie's, should this budding relationship go much further.

"Kay."

"Is she pretty?"

He gave her a rather odd look, but answered, "She was, sixteen years ago when we got married. She hasn't taken very good care of herself since, I'm afraid."

Cassie wondered how to bring up the next question, wondered if she even dared. But she had to know. "Shane said his mother has a drinking problem."

Jared's eyes hardened. "Yeah. That started right after he was born. I tried to tell Kay when we got married that I'd be away a lot—six months at a time on sea duty—but I guess she didn't really understand that she'd be the one left with the responsibilities of the household.

"I was on leave when Shane was born, but had to ship out again when he was only two weeks old. Maybe the next few months were just too tough for her. Anyway, by the time I came back, she'd already started drinking too regularly, though she did a pretty good job of hiding it. I really wasn't aware of the extent of her problem until she'd been at it for a couple of years. We fought a lot about it, but that only made it worse. We were divorced when Shane was five."

Cassie checked to make sure Shane was still involved in the game. "Who took care of him when he was little?"

"I did, on the rare occasions when I was home. I assumed Kay was taking care of him when I was away. I knew she was a lousy wife, but she had me convinced she was a fairly decent mother."

"And was she?" Cassie whispered.

"In her way. He was fed and clothed. And then generally ignored the rest of the time."

Cassie fought down the indignant comment that sprang to her lips. She wanted to know more, wanted to ask why Jared had thought a heavy drinker was a fit mother for his son, was burning with curiosity about Shane's mention of living on the streets for three months until his father had found him. Still...

"This is really none of my business, of course," she said apologetically. "I didn't mean to pry."

Again, Jared shrugged, his expression so distant and shuttered that she wished she'd never brought the subject up. They'd been having such a nice day so far—other than that rest-stop confrontation, of course.

"You may as well know," he said coolly. "I told you I was lousy with relationships. I'm not proud that I didn't even know my own wife was becoming a lush and that my son was being emotionally neglected."

Cassie felt compelled to defend him. "You were young."

"And gone more than I was home. But that's not really an excuse, is it? The real problem was that I had gotten so used to taking care of no one but myself that I just assumed Kay was doing the same for herself and our son. I loved Shane, of course, more than I ever thought it possible to love anyone—but I didn't know how to be a real father to him. My own father was certainly no example. God knows I never saw him much when I was a kid, and he was usually drunk when I did. As far as I knew, the only thing he and my mother ever did together was make babies they couldn't take care of."

Cassie couldn't bear the traces of pain in his voice, a pain he probably thought he concealed from everyone else. And maybe no one else *would* hear it. Maybe Cassie was beginning to understand him better than other people did, or could. She reached across the table to cover his hard, callused hand with her own smaller, softer one. "I'm sorry, Jared. We don't have to talk about this now."

He looked at their joined hands, then slowly back up to her face. Whatever he might have said was cut off when Shane loped up to the table. "You two sure look serious. Something wrong?"

Cassie pulled her hand back to her lap and forced a smile. "Of course not. Are you ready to eat? Our chicken's getting cold."

"It's okay," Shane answered, swinging a leg over the bench in a move very much like his father's. "I like cold chicken."

"Is there any food you *don't* like?" Cassie asked teasingly, distributing paper plates and napkins.

"Yeah. Chinese. Too many little squiggly things I can't recognize."

Cassie laughed, but said, "I happen to love Chinese food. You might just like it, too, if you'd give it a chance."

Shane shuddered dramatically and reached for a drumstick. "No, thanks. I'll stick to the basics. Chicken, cheeseburgers and pizza."

"A fine, healthy diet," Jared agreed gravely, pushing a container of coleslaw toward his son. "Here. Eat your vegetables."

Shane grinned and served himself a heaping portion.

Watching them both, Cassie wondered how any woman could have willingly let these two get away. How could Kay not have known how very lucky she was to have them?

She still wished she knew what, exactly, had happened in their lives two years ago. Whatever it was, it had to have been traumatic. Jared was still eating himself up with guilt. That was something else Cassie was beginning to understand about this multilayered, complex man. How many more layers would she have to uncover to ever know him completely?

And would he ever let her—or anyone—get close enough to really know him?

Sprawled in the shade of an enormous oak tree just starting to don its fall colors, Jared rested back on his elbows and watched indulgently as Cassie and Shane carried on a laughing, dodging, uninhibited game of tag. He found it hard to believe at times that Cassie was twenty-six years old, as her driver's license had said she was. There were moments when she seemed closer to Shane's age than his own.

She was beautiful with her face flushed from exertion, her green eyes lit with laughter, several springy red curls escaping her French braid. Her jeans fit her like a second skin, and she'd pushed the sleeves of her flowered sweatshirt up to expose her lower arms. He wanted her so badly his teeth hurt.

Was he making a mistake to go with her to Dallas, despite Shane's desire to do so? Being an utter fool to think he could ever have the chance at finding with her what he'd been unable to find with anyone else? Didn't she deserve a hell of a lot more than a burned-out, unemployed drifter with more emotional baggage than material possessions?

A hand touched his shoulder, making him realize he'd drifted into his own thoughts and had lost track of time. He blinked and looked up to find Cassie standing only a couple of feet away, breathing rapidly and poised on the balls of her feet as though prepared to run. Shane stood a few yards behind her, grinning broadly.

"You're it," Cassie said, eyeing Jared in open challenge.

He shook his head. "I'm not playing, remember?"

"Tough. I tagged you. You're it."

"Dad's it!" Shane added, his brown hair lifting in the afternoon breeze. Jared realized it was time for a trim—for both of them, actually.

"You two go ahead and play. I'll just watch."

"Being 'it' is too much for you, hmm?" Cassie taunted. "Can't handle it?" She took a step closer, daring him in body language to make a move toward her.

Seeing that she was still ready to run, and sensing that she was quite confident in her ability to evade him, Jared continued to sprawl with apparent laziness, though he felt the muscles in his arms tightening. "If I chose to chase you, you wouldn't get two feet."

Her laughter was ripe with disbelief. "Yeah. Right."

"*If* I were playing, of course," he added, watching from beneath his lashes as she took a tiny step forward.

"You're still it," she reminded him, beginning to relax when he made no move to respond.

He sighed.

Cassie turned her head to look at Shane. "What a wimp," she said. "He won't even—"

Jared was on his feet before she could finish the sentence. He had her pinned to the ground beneath him before she could even think about running. "Want to take back that wimp remark?" he asked, totally unruffled.

Winded and dazed, she blinked up at him, her bangs tangled in her eyes. She reached up to push them out of her face. "We're playing tag, not tackle," she protested indignantly.

He grinned at her disgruntled expression, trying to ignore how very good she felt beneath him. There was nothing he could do to prevent his body from responding to her. Her eyes widened, and he knew she was feeling it, too.

"Take it back," he prodded.

"I—uh—forgot to warn you, Cassie," Shane apologized from nearby, his voice quavering with laughter. "Dad's quick. Sneaky, too."

"So I've discovered," she said, without taking her eyes from Jared's.

"You still haven't taken it back."

"I take it back," she conceded in a rush. "You're not a wimp. You don't play fairly, but you're not a wimp."

"I can live with that." He brushed her mouth with his, very lightly, resisting the imprudent temptation to deepen the kiss. And then he released her and sat beside her, one knee raised to disguise the condition of his jeans.

Cassie lay where she was, wiping her brow with one hand. "I'm dying."

Shane dropped down beside her, twisted into that boneless position unique to young people. "I'm sure Dad would just love giving you CPR."

Cassie growled. "The boy needs a trip behind the woodshed, Jared. Do your paternal duty."

"I've got better ways of punishing him."

"Yeah? Like what?"

"Hey, Shane. How'd you like me to tell her about you and Penny Bennett?"

"*Dad!*" Shane flushed crimson, as Jared had known he would. "You wouldn't!"

"Then don't push your luck, boy," Jared answered mildly.

Cassie giggled. "You're right. That's much better than a woodshed any day."

Jared noticed that her top had ridden up to expose an inch of smooth, pale skin above the waistband of her jeans. He cleared his throat and climbed abruptly to his feet. "We'd better get back on the road. Lunch break's over."

"Bossy," Cassie sighed, though she obediently pushed herself upright. "So bossy."

Jared ignored her. Or tried to.

"Want me to ride with you for a while, Cassie?" Shane offered.

Jared noted that she looked to him before giving the boy an answer. She seemed to be taking a great deal of care not to step on his parental toes. "It's okay with me," he assured her.

"Then I'd like that," Cassie said with a smile for Shane.

"Great! I'll get my tapes." Shane loped toward the truck.

Jared grinned at the look on Cassie's face. "Hope you like Garth Brooks and Vince Gill."

"Are they anything like U2 or Guns N' Roses?"

He chuckled and turned toward his truck. "Have fun."

Cassie did have fun with Shane, as a matter of fact. He introduced her to contemporary country music, and she insisted that he listen to one of her classic rock tapes in return.

"Eric Clapton," she breathed at the opening refrains of "Layla." "No one else handles a guitar like that."

"That's what my dad says. But then I'll bet you've never heard Steve Wariner when he really gets wound up."

"Steve who?"

"Oh, man!"

Cassie laughed, thoroughly enjoying herself, though she couldn't help glancing wistfully in the rearview mirror at the lone man in the pickup truck behind her.

They were somewhere in central New Mexico that evening when Jared suggested they stop for the night. "We'll have to make better time tomorrow," he said, looking at his watch, "or this is going to become a three-day trip."

Cassie thought briefly of checking in with Tony, then decided to wait until they arrived in Dallas to call him. As far as she was concerned, she'd been on her own time since taking herself off the expense account the day before. This weekend with Jared and Shane was hers.

They had an early dinner at a cafeteria near their hotel, then took in a seven o'clock showing of a recent comedy film that Shane wanted to see. Cassie sat between the two guys during the movie. Listening to their chuckles—Jared's deep and sexy, Shane's less restrained—she decided she'd never been more content in her life. Especially when, halfway through the film, Jared reached over and took her hand in his.

The three of them were beginning to feel very much like a family. Maybe too much so. But she refused to allow herself to worry about it just yet. Perhaps she would end up brokenhearted, but she had no intention of missing out on this quiet happiness for fear of what might come later.

Jared had driven to the theater, so Cassie climbed into the cab of the truck to sit in the middle again after the movie. Jared slid behind the wheel and started the engine. "It's still early," he said. "I thought maybe you'd like to have a drink with me somewhere."

"Hey, sounds good to me," Shane said cheekily.

Jared gave him a look over Cassie's head. "I was talking to Cassie. *You* can raid the motel vending machines for your usual bedtime snack, watch some TV and then get some rest. We've got a long ride ahead of us tomorrow."

"Can't blame a guy for trying," Shane muttered to Cassie, apparently resigned to a quiet evening.

"Cassie?"

"Yes, Jared. I'd love to have a drink with you," she accepted without hesitation.

He nodded, saying little more during the ride back to the motel. Shane more than made up for his father's silence with his chatter about the movie. And as much as she enjoyed Shane, Cassie looked forward with a mixture of eagerness and a strangely shy nervousness to being alone with Jared.

Though Jared said it wasn't necessary, Cassie insisted on changing out of her jeans before going out again. She slipped on clean slacks and a brightly patterned sweater, pulling the top of her hair back with a gold clip and allowing the rest to tumble to her shoulders in a mass of tight curls. She added small gold earrings and a touch of makeup, the entire process taking less than twenty minutes.

She was running out of clean clothes, she noted, closing her suitcase again. She had one pair of clean jeans and one top left for the trip home tomorrow. If they were delayed any longer on the road, she was going to have to find either a department store or a Laundromat.

Jared was waiting outside her door when she stepped out. He, too, had changed, she noted, into dark twill slacks and a white dress shirt. She tried for a moment to picture him in an Italian suit and a silk tie. The image was mind-boggling. Jared was born to wear jeans and boots.

It was much easier to imagine him in a Western hat and sheepskin-lined jacket, riding the pastures of the small ranch he'd said he hoped to own someday. Carrying the fantasy a bit further, she could imagine Shane riding behind him— and maybe a little girl with long, red braids.

Whoa, Browning. Better not start looking that far ahead. You haven't even got him to Dallas yet.

Jared had spotted a bar close to the hotel. It didn't look too bad from the outside, but they soon realized that the patrons were made up mostly of rednecks spending this Saturday getting drunk and making noise.

Jared cursed beneath his breath when a heavyset bottle-blonde in two-sizes-too-small jeans and a T-shirt that barely stretched over her massive bosom stumbled into the table he had found in a relatively quiet corner. Jared's beer sloshed over the rim of his mug, splattering his slacks.

"Oh, sorry, honey," the blonde said, leaning so close to him that her unbound breasts almost brushed his face. "Guess I've had a few too many, you know?"

Her hands wrapped around the stem of her wineglass, Cassie watched sympathetically as Jared almost reeled from the fumes of the woman's breath. "No problem," he muttered, drawing as far back in his chair as physically possible.

"Hey, you're kinda cute." Ignoring Cassie altogether, the woman threaded her scarlet-taloned fingers through Jared's hair. "Want to dance."

"No." He added belatedly, "Thanks."

She sighed deeply, causing Jared to choke again. "Oh, well. It was worth a shot." And then she staggered away, her attention already focusing on a would-be cowboy at the bar across the room.

Scowling, Jared reached up to smooth his hair by briskly running his own fingers through. "Sorry about this," he said. "Not a very classy place I've brought you to, is it?"

"You couldn't have known," Cassie replied, excusing him with a smile. "And, anyway, that woman was right about one thing."

He eyed her suspiciously. "What?"

"You are kinda cute."

She laughed when he growled something unintelligible and took a long drink of his beer. She would have sworn she saw a tinge of red touch his lean cheeks, though the lighting in the bar was hardly bright. The thought of Jared blushing was so endearing that her throat tightened.

She was really getting in deep this time. And making very little effort to stop herself from falling any farther.

Jared set down his mug and glanced at the crowded, undersize dance floor. "I'm a lousy dancer," he said, sounding as though he were apologizing.

Cassie took a sip of her white wine, wondering what he expected her to say in return. She liked to dance, but she was perfectly happy just to sit in a shadowy corner with Jared, their knees brushing beneath the tiny table.

He cleared his throat. "If you don't mind risking your toes, we could give it a try."

Surprised, she set down her glass. "You're asking me to dance?"

"Yeah. What do you say?"

She smiled and stood. "I say yes."

Jared gave her a rueful look and pushed himself to his feet. "Just don't say I didn't warn you."

The new song was a slow one—fortunately, since it was impossible to do much more than sway in place on the packed dance floor. Cassie had no complaints. Her arms around Jared's neck, his hands at her hips, she felt as though she'd died and gone someplace wonderful, even if that place smelled strongly of beer and tobacco and sweat.

Jared pulled her closer, his head bent to hers. She felt him nuzzling her temple, and her knees went weak, causing her to cling more tightly to him. Their thighs brushed seductively, and she found herself resenting the fabric that separated them. She ached to be pressed this closely against him with absolutely nothing between them. His hands moved at her hips, settling her more snugly, and it was obvious that Jared was as deeply affected by their dancing as Cassie.

His lips brushed her cheek. "Want to get out of here?"

She forced her heavy eyelids open. "Whatever you want."

Jared groaned. "I like the way that sounds."

"Is that right?" Cassie couldn't resist pressing a quick kiss to his firm, stubborn jaw.

"Mmm." He kissed her, his mouth pressing firmly, if all too briefly, to hers. And then he turned with her toward the exit, his arm wrapped securely around Cassie's waist as he guided her through the press of people.

Lost in tingly anticipation of the outcome of the evening, Cassie didn't at first understand why Jared suddenly went tense as they approached his pickup. She looked up to find three disreputable-looking young men in battered cowboy hats and pointed-toe boots leaning against the front fender and passing around a bottle as they laughed uproariously at the off-color jokes they were telling loudly enough for everyone within a block to hear. They quite effectively blocked Jared and Cassie's access to the truck.

Jared stepped slightly in front of Cassie. "Excuse me. That's my truck, and we're ready to leave. Mind moving out of the way?"

All three looked at Jared and then Cassie, obviously weighing his mild tone against the opportunity to flex their macho in front of a woman.

"What if we do mind?" one of them—the biggest, Cassie noted apprehensively—demanded.

"Then I'll have to ask you to move, anyway." Jared's voice was still quiet, but had taken on a steely note that couldn't be mistaken even by cocky young drunks. All three immediately straightened, bracing themselves in response to the subtle challenge.

Cassie looked anxiously from Jared to his potential opponents. They were younger, two of them taller and heavier, made reckless by alcohol. On the other hand, Jared was—well, Jared. She figured that made them almost even, but she wanted to avoid a fight if at all possible.

Another confrontation with the police was the last thing they needed on this trip.

"Please," she said, stepping forward even though Jared moved to hold her back. "We'd really like to leave now, if you'd be so kind as to let us get by."

One of the young toughs whistled. The second leered in what he probably thought was a sexy manner, but really made him look somewhat slow-witted. The third—the big one, again—looked Cassie up and down with insolent leisure. "Hey, red. How about dumping this old loser and having a party?"

Cassie put her hand on Jared's arm when he made a restless move. "Thank you, but no," she said firmly. "Now, if you'll please just..."

"Oh, we can please you, sugar," the big one drawled, eliciting a raucous laugh from his buddies. "We can please you real good. How about if we—"

"How about if you shut up and get out of our way before we call the cops?" Jared growled, stepping forward to face down the young man who'd become the leader of the confrontation. Cassie noted that the other two men fell back a little at the cold, deadly menace suddenly radiating from Jared's narrowed eyes.

Their friend cleared his throat, his hands lifting in what appeared to be capitulation. "Hey, don't get all bent out of shape. If you want past us, all you have to do is start walking."

"Stay close, Cassie," Jared ordered in an undertone, moving cautiously forward.

The big guy attacked without warning, his meaty fist connecting solidly with Jared's chin. Jared staggered back, though he didn't go down.

Cassie saw red. Without hesitation she started forward, fully prepared to do some damage herself. Jared caught her arm and pulled sharply.

"Get back," he ordered, just before the other two, emboldened by their leader's aggression, leaped forward. And then Jared was too busy defending himself to concentrate on keeping Cassie out of his way.

She had no intention of standing back and wringing her hands like some sort of helpless woman in a male-dominated action movie. She hadn't spent five years in self-defense classes for nothing.

She landed a solid kick square in the kidneys of the nearest opponent, making him howl and stagger away from Jared, hands pressed to his back. Without giving him a chance to recover from his surprise, Cassie quite effectively took his mind off that pain with a follow-up kick to the groin. He promptly curled into a whimpering ball on the pavement and lost most of the booze that had given him his foolhardy courage.

Judging him to no longer be a threat, Cassie whirled to help Jared, only to find him watching her in amazement, his hands on his hips, feet spread. The big guy who'd initiated the fight lay on the pavement behind him, moaning and holding a hand to his freely bleeding nose. The third man was nowhere to be seen. Cassie assumed he'd suddenly come to his senses and abandoned his buddies to their fate.

Already other patrons of the bar were approaching, trying to find out what was going on. Jared took Cassie's arm. "Let's get out of here."

She didn't hesitate to climb into the truck with him. Moments later, they'd left the bar and its customers behind them.

Jared didn't say anything for the first few minutes, driving with his right hand as he fingered the darkening bruise on his jaw with his left. When he spoke, it was without looking at her. "How tall are you? Five-three? Five-four?"

"Five-four. And a quarter," she added.

"You weigh—what? A hundred pounds?"

Watching him curiously, she answered, "A hundred ten."

He slanted her a sexy grin that all but melted her into the seat. "You can guard my back any time, tiger."

She looked at that smile, at the bruise on his chin and the lock of dark hair that had tumbled onto his forehead, and she felt herself sliding the rest of the way into love.

Not smart, Browning. Not smart at all.

But it was far too late for her to heed the warnings of her common sense.

Chapter Seven

The motel was quiet, no light showing through the crack in the curtain of the room Jared and Shane shared. "Shane must be asleep," Jared commented, leading Cassie past that door to her own, which was next to it.

"Don't you want to go in and check on him?" she asked, looking back at the other room.

"He's okay." Jared reached over and took her key out of her hand. He slid it into the lock and opened the door, though he made no move to go inside.

Cassie went past him, then looked over her shoulder when he didn't follow. "Aren't you coming in?"

"Is that an invitation?" he asked in return, his voice deeper than usual.

She swallowed hard, knowing exactly what he was asking. "Yes," she whispered through suddenly dry lips. "That's an invitation."

He took a step forward, though he left the door standing open. His gaze held hers captive. "I can't make any promises, Cassie. There are a lot of uncertainties in my life right now. I can't even guarantee what state I'll be living in by this time next week."

"I know." She was pleased at the steadiness of her voice. "I'm not asking for promises. I want this, Jared."

He closed the door very quietly behind him.

She moistened her lips with the tip of her tongue. She'd been completely honest with him. She wanted to make love with him more than she'd ever wanted anything in her entire life. But she was suddenly nervous, unable to pretend this was something she did casually or easily.

Rubbing her open palms against the legs of her slacks, she glanced around the sterile room, which seemed to be filled mostly with bed at the moment. Had she been at home, she'd have offered him a drink or a snack or something. Unfortunately, she had no such diversion available at the moment.

"Cassie." His hands fell lightly on her shoulders. "Relax. We'll take all the time you need. And there's no need to worry about protection. I'll take care of it."

She looked up at him gratefully. "You're a very nice man, Jared Walker."

"Don't start idealizing me," he warned her, his expression suddenly grim. "I'm nobody's hero—not by a long shot."

"I'm not looking for a hero," Cassie answered mistily, touching her fingertips to his battered jaw. "But I think I've been looking for you all my life."

His eyes turned wary at her unguarded words, but she didn't give him a chance to issue any further warnings. All remnants of nervousness vanishing, she went up on tiptoes to press her mouth firmly, hungrily to his.

Jared resisted only a moment. And then he gave a low groan and his arms went around her, crushing her against him.

Cassie couldn't get close enough, couldn't hold him tightly enough, though she tried desperately to do both. In response to her fervor, Jared abandoned all efforts to go slowly or cautiously, his mouth devouring hers, his hands racing over her straining body.

She wanted to touch him, wanted to stroke his chest, taste his skin. She slipped her hands between them and fumbled with the top button of his shirt. His mouth still moving over hers, Jared drew back an inch to give her better access, then grew impatient with her unsteady hands and attacked the buttons himself. Cassie shoved the fabric off his shoulders and down his muscular arms, sighing her pleasure when her hands were free to spread across his broad, hair-roughened chest.

His skin was hot, as if heated from inside, his muscles hard and well-defined. Her thumbs found the pointed nipples buried in the crisp dark curls. She rotated her thumbs and Jared inhaled sharply.

Delighted with his reaction to her, she stroked her hand slowly down his flat stomach to the waistband of his slacks, where she paused. Jared covered her hand with his and moved it lower, so that she found her palm filled with his rigid length, and even through the fabric of his slacks she could feel his pulsing excitement. She moaned in response.

It was a heady, stimulating feeling to be wanted so badly.

Jared twisted, bearing her down to the bed, his hand covering her breast as they fell. Cassie arched into him. He moved his fingers, and she gasped at the waves of sensation that coursed through her.

He parted her legs with one knee, pressing upward until he was wedged firmly in the notch of her thighs. Cassie shuddered. *"Jared."*

"I want to touch you." He tugged impatiently at her clothing, dispensing of buttons and zippers with ruthless haste.

"Yes." She squirmed to assist him.

Her clothes, as well as his slacks, socks and briefs, fell into a tangled heap on the floor beside the bed. Cassie released a long, unsteady breath when she finally felt him pressed full-length against her, nothing between them except their growing desire.

He was warm and vibrant and so very male, making her feel soft and pliant and feminine beneath his hands. She surrendered to the feelings. There were times when the traditional roles suited her quite nicely.

Aware of the need for quiet, Cassie swallowed her cries of delight as Jared took her higher and higher, pushing her precariously close to the edge of ecstasy. She wanted him inside her when she took that leap, but he was relentless. All too soon, she shuddered in waves of pleasure, racked with sensations more glorious, more vividly intense than anything she'd ever known.

He didn't give her time to recover, nor to regret that he hadn't been with her. Instead, he drew her inexorably back to that edge again, and this time when she tumbled over, it was exactly the way she'd fantasized—with Jared buried so deeply inside her that he had become a part of her.

She held him as they both slowly recovered their breath and their senses. She stroked his damp hair, loving the soft, thick feel of it. Loving him.

So long accustomed to blurting her feelings, she found it difficult to hold back the words brimming inside her now. She knew Jared wasn't ready to hear them—at least, not yet.

He'd think she'd lost her mind, of course. After all, they'd known each other only two days. He'd never believe she'd fallen in love with him the moment their eyes had met in that awful jail.

He wanted her, but he didn't love her—at least, not yet, she added with a secret, determinedly optimistic smile.

"What?" Jared said, raising his head to look at her curiously.

She blinked at him. "I beg your pardon?"

"I'm not sure I like that smile," he murmured, brushing a curl away from her eyes. "It looked just a little devious to me."

She chuckled. "Devious? You're imagining things."

"Mmm." He didn't sound entirely convinced.

Cassie stirred against the pillows. "I wonder what Shane found to eat in the vending machines. I'm starving."

He smiled indulgently. "Does great sex always make you hungry?"

She didn't at all like him trivializing the experience they'd just shared to nothing more momentous than great sex. She told herself that maybe he was trying to convince her, as well as himself, that that was all it had been. She believed it had been more. Much more.

For the first time in her impulsive life, she would have to learn to be patient so she didn't drive this frustratingly commitment-shy man away.

Ignoring his question, she reached for the robe she'd left lying on the chair nearby, slipping into it as she climbed from the bed, suddenly restless. "I think I've got some Gummi Bears in my bag. Want some?"

"I'll pass. Cassie?" He raised himself on one elbow to watch her rummage through the bag.

She found the bag of candies and ripped it open to avoid looking at him sprawled nude on her bed. "Yes?"

"What's wrong?"

"Nothing. Why?"

"You're acting funny. Was it something I said?"

"Of course not." She popped a soft red bear into her mouth.

"Something I didn't say?"

Her throat tightened, making it difficult to swallow. "No."

"You want me to leave? You've suddenly decided I'm a jerk? You regret going to bed with me? All of the above?"

"I really don't know what you're talking about, Jared." She wished she had a diet soft drink to wash down the candy. She wondered if anyone would see her if she made a dash for the vending machines in her robe.

It was so much easier to think about a late-night snack than to wonder if Jared Walker was going to break her heart.

Or would it be more realistic to wonder when, rather than if?

"Cassie. Come here." He patted the bed beside him.

She stalled. "Think I'll go get a Coke. You want one?"

"No, and neither do you. Now come here."

"You're being bossy again."

He only looked at her. Waiting.

Cassie sighed and sat stiffly on the edge of the bed. "All right, I'm here. What do you—?"

He grabbed her arm and pulled her down beside him, cutting her question off in a whoosh of surprised breath.

"Now," he said, tucking her into the crook of his arm. "Let's talk."

She couldn't quite resist snuggling her cheek more comfortably into the hollow of his shoulder. It felt so good to be held by him. So safe. "What do you want to talk about?"

"Whatever you like. You're not sleepy, are you?"

"No." Far from it. She was so wired with tension and worry and leftover sexual awareness that she wasn't sure she'd sleep at all that night.

"Neither am I. So let's talk. We haven't had much chance to get to know each other, have we?"

Beginning to relax when she realized that he wasn't going to push her to explain her sudden attack of nerves, she rested a hand on his bare chest and giggled. "Oh, I think we've gotten to know each other fairly well."

"I wasn't talking about biblical knowledge," he replied dryly. "Tell me about your life in Dallas. Do you live in a house, an apartment, a condo?"

"An apartment."

"Any pets?"

She shifted to fit herself more comfortably against him. Jared tightened his arm, willingly accommodating her. "No pets. I like animals, but didn't want to be bothered with finding a sitter or kennel every time Tony sends me out of town."

"Does he do that often?"

"Not really. Most P.I. work these days is done on computer or by telephone. And we specialize in security consultation for local businesses—analyzing their existing security measures, studying loss reports, researching the market for affordable, state-of-the-art security equipment, making recommendations for employee testing, monitoring and incentive programs."

"Incentive programs? What does that have to do with security?"

"A contented, well-treated employee is a much more loyal one," she answered with a smile. "Much less likely to steal."

"How's the search coming for my other sister and brothers?" Jared asked, his voice almost studiously casual. "Any leads?"

"Not on the twins," Cassie replied, trying to match his tone so he wouldn't know that she'd read him again. The question had been much more than casual to him, though it was obvious he wasn't looking for sympathy.

"They went into a series of foster homes after you were separated, were even considered for adoption by one family. But they kept getting into trouble—nothing serious, just mischievous and annoying—and kept being relocated. When they were nine, a social worker recommended they be split up. She said that would curb their mischievous tendencies."

Jared tensed. "That's the dumbest thing I've ever heard. Didn't she know what that would do to them? They're identical twins, for God's sake!"

"She was a fool," Cassie agreed flatly. "And it wasn't long before her suggestions were vetoed by the child welfare authorities. But the twins had gotten wind of the suggestion. That was the first time they ran away."

"They ran away at nine?"

"Yes. It took over a week for them to be located. From then on, whenever there was the least suggestion they were going to be split, they took off. Their habit of running away kept them in trouble from then until they were sixteen."

"What happened then?"

"They ran off again—and haven't been seen since. At least, not that we've been able to determine so far."

Jared lay quietly for a moment, then asked, "What are the odds that they're still alive?"

"Good," she answered firmly. "They were sixteen. Young, but not helpless. And they had each other to depend on. They're out there somewhere, and we'll find them eventually. Identical twins should be easier to locate than just one person—and we found you, didn't we?"

He shrugged, though he seemed to have taken some encouragement from her confidence. "I never made any effort not to be found."

"That did make it easier," she admitted.

"What about the baby?"

"Lindsay? She's hardly a baby now. She'll soon be twenty-five."

"Damn. I'd forgotten. Any leads on her?"

"Some. We know she was adopted very soon after you were separated. The adoption records were sealed, but Tony has interviewed several social workers who were assigned to your family. Though he hasn't been able to officially verify anything, he thinks he may have the name of the adoptive family, possibly a lead on how to track them down. It will take time, but he's hopeful that we're getting closer."

"And if she's found? Then what?"

"Then, like you, she'll be contacted to find out if she's interested in meeting her biological sisters and brothers."

Jared shook his head. "I can't imagine why she would. We'd all be strangers to her. I remember all of them, of course, but Layla and maybe the twins are the only ones who would've been old enough to share any of my memories. Even Shelley—Michelle—was just a toddler when we split up."

"Yes, but she still wants to see you. You're her brother, Jared. You had the same parents, the same genes—you even look a little alike. That means something to her."

"We look alike?" Jared sounded startled.

"You both have brown hair and blue eyes. And, yes, there's a family resemblance," Cassie acknowledged, lifting her head to study his face. "You'll like her, Jared. She's very nice."

"I think you should know—the main reason I agreed to see her is because of you."

"Because of me?" Cassie repeated, surprised. "Why?"

His hand settled on her robe-covered thigh, kneading gently. "Because you asked me to. If bringing me back with you helps you out with your job, I guess it's the least I can do after you worked so hard to clear me of that robbery charge."

Cassie shook her head, uncomfortable. "Oh, Jared, I didn't want you coming with me out of gratitude. I wanted you to do this for yourself and your sisters, not for me."

"Does it matter why I came?"

She chewed her lip, considering the question. On the one hand, it flattered her that Jared was making the trip on her behalf. On the other, she truly believed he needed this much more than she did.

Jared was more in need of family ties than anyone she'd ever met—if only he'd give his sisters a chance to form them with him.

He'd built such impenetrable walls around his emotions during the lonely years of his youth, walls that only Shane could get past now. Would Michelle and Layla ever be allowed inside? And, more importantly to her, would she? For as close as she and Jared had been only moments before, Cassie knew that there was a part of himself he still held back. A part of himself she longed to know.

"Cassie? You haven't answered me. Does it really matter why I'm going with you to Dallas?"

"No," she answered finally. "It doesn't really matter."

Not as long as you'll give me—give all of us—a chance to really know you while you're there. And maybe a reason to hope that you'll stay.

Jared lay quietly for a few minutes, toying with her hair. He seemed fascinated by the tight copper curls, twisting them around his fingers, watching them spring free when he released them. Cassie could feel her pulse picking up again, increasingly aware that he held her so closely to his nude body that only her thin, loosely tied robe separated them. She buried her fingers in the crisp hair on his chest, her palm pressed just above his heart. She felt it beating rapidly, and was delighted that she wasn't the only one affected by their nearness.

"Cassie?"

She turned her face into his chest, enjoying the spicy, male scent of him. "Mmm?"

"Have you always wanted to be a P.I.?"

She hadn't really expected that question—at least, not now. She tried to forget about sex for the moment and concentrate on the conversation. Not an easy task, especially when Jared slipped a hand beneath the hem of her robe to stroke her thigh.

"Um, no," she managed, her voice coming out rather hoarse. "I changed my major three times in college—from journalism to pre-law to computer sciences. That's what I finally got my degree in. I've had a dozen jobs since leaving college. I took a part-time job with Tony after leaving the last job, just because it sounded interesting and I had bills to pay. I've been hooked ever since. Working part-time gave me a chance to get my training while gaining job experience."

"Are you still part time?"

"No. He put me on full time this summer, after he fired Bob O'Brien."

Jared slipped his hand a bit higher, cupping the curve of her hip. "Why'd he fire the other guy?"

Her eyelids growing heavy, Cassie had to make an effort to remember. "He—uh—he was giving information on Michelle's case to the attorney who had been skimming money from some trust funds he'd helped her father set up for her."

Jared's hand stilled. "Michelle's attorney was stealing from her?"

"Yeah. Tony found the proof. He was really furious with Bob for cooperating with the lawyer, and hurt. He's always expected loyalty from his employees, and he'd always gotten it before."

"I hope they're prosecuting the bastard."

The attorney? Or Bob? Cassie was having a difficult time following the subject. Jared's fingers were unbearably close to a part of her that was beginning to throb heavily in anticipation of his touch. "They had the attorney, Carter Powell, arrested. But Tony told me the guy's disappeared. Jumped bail."

"Is Michelle in any danger?"

"Oh, I'm sure she's not. It turned out she wasn't the only client he was cheating. He's just making a run for it. He'll probably be caught soon. Bail jumpers usually are."

Jared relaxed. He nuzzled the hair at her temple. "Cassie?"

She caught her breath when he slid his thumb into the crease between her leg and her groin, tracing the soft fold with exquisite care. "Y-yes?"

"I think we've talked enough for now. Don't you?"

She twisted to wrap her arms around his neck. "Oh, yes."

His mouth covered hers, his fingers finally moving inward to drive the remaining breath from her body with his skillful pleasuring. Cassie arched helplessly against his hand, relieved that his questions had finally come to an end. At the moment, she couldn't even remember her name.

It was close to 3:00 a.m. by the time Jared forced himself from Cassie's bed. Though he'd never found it hard to leave a woman before, generally preferring to sleep on his own, he found it incredibly difficult to slip out of Cassie's arms.

He stood by the bed for several long, silent moments, just watching her. The faint light coming through the crack in the curtain robbed her of her vibrant coloring, leaving her porcelain pale against the white sheets. Her glorious hair was a dark mass of curls around her face, which looked so sweet and vulnerable in her sleep. It took all his fortitude not to crawl back into the bed with her.

His feelings for her were too strong, his reactions to her too intense. Their lovemaking hadn't been like anything he'd ever experienced before. Something told him he'd never get enough of it, that he'd never find quite the same satisfaction with any other woman.

He wasn't sure what, exactly, he felt for Cassie Browning, but an uncomfortable suspicion niggled at the back of his mind. And damned if he knew what he was going to do about it.

Chapter Eight

Jared had gotten maybe three hours' sleep by the time he finally gave up trying and climbed out of bed Sunday morning. Might as well get an early start, he decided. They still had a long drive ahead of them to Dallas.

He took a quick shower, then stood by the sink and lathered his face before waking his son. "Shane. Time to get up."

Shane stirred, yawned and blinked open his eyes. "What time is it?"

"Little after seven." Jared stroked a razor over his face, wishing he'd shaved before going out to the bar last night. Had his evening beard marked Cassie's delicate skin? There was certainly no part of her he hadn't rubbed it against at one time or another.

"What time did you get in last night? I was up till eleven."

Jared pushed the memories to the back of his mind, before his body embarrassed him in a way it hadn't done since adolescence. "Late. Now get on up and take your shower."

Shane swung his legs over the side of the bed, stretching. He was clad only in a pair of white briefs. Watching in the mirror, Jared was startled to realize that his son was growing rapidly, his arms and chest starting to fill out. At fourteen, his boy was becoming a man—and Jared had missed so much of his childhood. He turned, wiping the remaining lather from his face with a hand towel.

Shane lifted an eyebrow at his father's expression. "You sure look serious this morning. Is— Hey, what happened to your face?"

Jared had forgotten the bruise on his jaw. He glanced back at the mirror, noting ruefully that it had turned a deep purple during the night. That big drunk hadn't had much stamina, but he'd packed a mean right hook. "Nothing serious. A little altercation at the bar last night."

Shane grinned. "I bet Cassie gave it to you. You start bossing her around again?"

Jared couldn't help chuckling, remembering the way Cassie had thrown herself into the fight—and handled herself with impressive skill. "No. And after seeing her in action, I may not try it again."

"This sounds like a story I gotta hear."

"Later. Now take your shower or you might find yourself being left behind."

"Yeah, right." Shane didn't look particularly concerned. He rubbed his stomach as he headed for the shower. "Man, I'm hungry. Hope Cassie'll be ready to go eat soon."

"I'll give her a wake-up call." He could think of a lot of better ways to wake her, of course. He tried not to dwell on any of those possibilities as he lifted the phone and punched in her room number.

Her voice was still husky with sleep when she answered. "H'lo?"

His body reacted immediately and forcefully to the sound of her, and the accompanying image of her still in bed, nude, soft, her hair still tousled from his hands. He was relieved that his son was in the other room. What the hell had happened to his long-cultivated self-control?

Self-annoyance made his tone more curt than he'd intended. "Shane's in the shower. We'll be ready to leave soon."

"Good morning to you, too." The words were spoken just a bit too sweetly. Jared winced.

"Give me twenty minutes," she added. "I'll be ready."

She hung up before he could answer.

"Way to go, Walker," Jared muttered, replacing his own receiver with less force than she'd used. "You haven't even seen her yet today and you've already hacked her off. Real smooth."

What the hell had he gotten himself into by agreeing to this trip?

Seven hours after being rather rudely awakened by her decidedly complex lover, Cassie was still seething with irritation at him. She hadn't really expected him to jump her bones right in front of Shane, she told herself as she drove relentlessly toward Dallas, Jared's truck close on her rear bumper. But did he have to treat her like a passing acquaintance who just happened to be traveling in the same direction he was?

He'd been nothing more than distantly polite when they'd shared breakfast and, later, lunch, which they'd eaten only a half hour ago. Even Shane, who'd ridden with Cassie after breakfast, had looked at his father strangely during lunch, as though sensing for the first time that Jared wasn't being particularly friendly.

She certainly hadn't picked an easy man to fall in love with. How could he take her to paradise so many times during the night, only to treat her like a near stranger the next day? He hadn't even kissed her good morning.

She tried to console herself with the possibility that Jared had been as deeply affected by their lovemaking as she had. And that he was running in sheer panic from the intensity of the experience they'd shared. She liked the idea that his feelings for her weren't casual ones, but what if he succeeded in stifling them before they ever had a chance to fully develop?

Would they ever have another night like that together?

Tense, anxious, annoyed, restless, she twisted the dial on the radio, trying to tune in a decent station. She found a country station and left it on for a while, deciding to give Shane's favorite a try. Three brokenhearted ballads later, she turned it again. She wasn't really in the mood to listen to mournful songs about love gone wrong.

Maybe she could find something mindless and fluffy to take her mind off her troubles. Where were the Bee Gees when she needed them?

Jared cursed beneath his breath when Cassie's little car swerved dangerously close to the center line on the two-lane freeway. She was obviously playing with her radio and not paying enough attention to her driving. Fortunately, there were no cars traveling in the other lane at the moment, but what if there had been?

"She can't drive worth a damn," he muttered, relaxing a little when she straightened in her seat and brought the car back into line.

"Dad, did you and Cassie have a fight last night?"

Jared glanced at his son, who was watching him gravely. "No, we didn't have a fight. Why?"

"Well, you're both acting kind of...I don't know, funny today. Like you're mad or something."

"I'm not mad," Jared denied with a shrug. He was confused, bemused and scared half out of his boots, but he wasn't mad. Not that he expected Shane to understand, even if he should try to explain. Hell, Jared himself didn't understand.

"So you had a good time last night—other than being attacked by those three drunks?" Shane asked, having gotten the story out of Cassie at breakfast.

"Yeah. We had a good time." And that was something else he didn't intend to discuss in detail with his son.

"So what's the problem?"

Jared exhaled gustily at his son's persistence. "Nothing's the problem. We've just got a long trip ahead of us and we're trying not to waste a lot of time today. Okay?"

Shane didn't look particularly satisfied, though he was quiet for a few minutes before asking his next question. "Are you worried about seeing your sisters?"

Jared kept his eyes on Cassie's rear bumper. "Why would I be worried?"

"Well, it has been a long time since you've seen them. I guess I could understand if you were sort of nervous about being around them again."

"Yeah," Jared conceded. "I'm sort of nervous. I'm not sure what I'm going to say to them."

"Did you love 'em—when you were a kid, I mean?"

Jared's jaw twitched convulsively. "Yeah," he said after a moment. "I loved them."

"Do you still?"

Jared had been blessed with a son who was wise beyond his years, bright and funny and amazingly well adjusted, considering his background. He also had a knack for asking questions that could make his father squirm. But Jared had made a real effort during the past two years to be honest with the boy whenever possible and he didn't want to change now, though he wasn't quite ready to discuss his feelings for Cassie—whatever they were.

So, he tried to answer Shane's question candidly. "I don't know, Shane. Right now, I guess I'm just...feeling my way."

About a lot of things. Cassie, for example.

Shane thought about his father's words for a moment, then nodded. "Yeah. I guess I understand that, too. I love you, Dad."

"Love you, too, Shane." They didn't say the words often. But when they did, it meant something special to both of them.

Jared slanted his son a faint smile, warmed, as always, by the affection in the boy's eyes. "Why don't you find another radio station? You know I can take anyone but Willie Nelson."

Shane grinned and reached for the radio knob. "I'll see if I can find any of that prehistoric rock you like."

Jared chuckled. "Smartass."

But already his attention was drifting back to the car ahead of him, his gaze lingering on the back of Cassie's head as she reached up and wearily rubbed her nape.

She was getting tired. They really should stop for a break soon. And maybe this time he'd make an effort to be a little nicer to her. It wasn't her fault that Jared was in such an emotional tangle.

Not entirely, anyway.

They stopped at midafternoon at an ice-cream parlor and arcade Shane had eagerly pointed out to his father. Cassie was rather surprised when Jared slid in next to her in the booth they'd chosen, leaving Shane to sit opposite them.

She tried hard to concentrate on her hot fudge sundae, not an easy task with Jared's thigh pressed to hers. By accident? Or was he deliberately trying to generate enough heat to melt her ice cream? If that was his intention, he was doing a damned good job of it.

Shane wolfed down his supersize banana split with enough speed to give a normal person a major ice-cream headache, then excused himself and headed for the video machines. Jared looked at his son's empty bowl, then at his and Cassie's only half-finished smaller treats and shook his head. "I don't know where he puts it."

"He's a growing boy," Cassie answered with a smile. "He uses up a lot of energy."

"No kidding."

"All this car travel must be difficult for him. He must be getting restless."

"Yeah." Cassie noted that Jared looked a bit guilty with the admission. "He'll be glad when we get settled somewhere."

"Why did you leave Oklahoma?" she asked curiously.

He lifted one shoulder in a shrug. "Job played out. I heard about a job in Arizona, so it seemed like a good place to head."

Cassie bit her lip to keep from pointing out that a life on the road wasn't the most secure upbringing for a boy of fourteen. She didn't say anything, of course. It wasn't really any of her business. And, for that matter, Shane seemed happier than many boys she'd met of his age. He was loved, he was cared for and he was treated with respect. On the whole, Jared probably knew a lot more about raising his son than Cassie could even imagine at this point.

Jared pushed his ice cream away, leaving nearly half uneaten. "Cassie, about this morning..."

She promptly choked on a maraschino cherry. Reaching desperately for her soft drink, she took a bracing sip before trying to speak. "What about this morning?" she asked, realizing Jared was watching her quizzically.

"I just wanted to say I'm sorry. Shane accused me of treating you badly. I didn't mean to."

"You have been rather cool," Cassie admitted, toying with her spoon. "I couldn't help wondering why."

Jared was bending a plastic drinking straw around his fingers, winding it in one direction and then another, as though he, too, was uncomfortable with the direction their conversation had taken.

"I just...didn't know what to say," he said. He glanced quickly toward Shane, who was fighting an enthusiastic battle to save the universe from alien invaders. "Last night was—well, last night was pretty special. But I'm still not making any promises. I can't. Not yet. Maybe not ever."

"I'm still not asking for any promises," Cassie replied evenly, oddly encouraged by his stumbling explanation. He'd admitted last night was special. He seemed even more determined to disclaim any interest in commitment. Was he trying to convince her—or dare she hope that he was trying just as anxiously to convince himself?

She looked at him with a smile, her gaze moving slowly from his so-serious blue eyes beneath a disheveled lock of brown hair to the firmly carved mouth above his poor, bruised chin. "Last night was special for me, too, Jared. Very special. I'll never forget it."

His gaze catching hers, he slid a hand to the back of her neck, pulling her toward him. "Good," he murmured, his mouth hovering above hers. "I don't want you to forget."

And then he kissed her, oblivious of the public setting, the possible audience. Cassie was no more concerned about propriety when she tilted her head to kiss him back, feeling as though it had been days since they'd held each other.

By the time the kiss ended, Shane's galactic battle had ended. He stood beside their booth, grinning in obvious approval. "So, you guys going to sit here and make out or are you ready to get back on the road?"

"Someday, Shane..." But Jared was smiling now, the first real smile Cassie had seen on him all day. She was in a much better mood, herself.

"Hey, Dad. How about if I drive the truck and you ride with Cassie for a while?" Shane suggested, tongue-in-cheek, when they walked back out into the parking lot.

Jared reached out to cuff Shane's shoulder. "Yeah, right. As soon as you produce a valid driver's license."

"How about the fake one I use when I go out with the guys for drinks?" Shane asked, trying without much success to keep a straight face.

Jared shook his head. "Don't even joke about it. Get in the truck, son. I need to have a conference with Cassie."

"A conference? That's what they're calling it these days, huh?" Still grinning, Shane climbed into the pickup.

"Somebody's going to strangle that boy someday," Jared muttered, taking Cassie by the arm as he escorted her to her car.

She smiled at the fond exasperation in his voice. "It won't be you," she teased. "And he knows it."

"He suspects it," Jared corrected her with a quick grin. "He hasn't quite had the nerve to test me yet. He knows just when to back off."

Cassie loved his smile. She only wished she could see it more often. "Why *are* we having a conference?"

"I figure we're about five hours out of Dallas," Jared replied, glancing at his watch. "If we add an hour for dinner somewhere along the way, we should be getting into Dallas at around ten o'clock tonight."

"That sounds about right," Cassie agreed.

"Have you called yet to tell them we're coming?"

"No," she admitted. "I thought I'd call once we were in town."

He nodded. "Good idea. It'll be too late to call tonight. You can talk to them tomorrow and set something up for tomorrow evening, if it's convenient with my sisters."

"I'm sure it will be," Cassie said, knowing both Michelle and Layla would give up just about any plans they could have made to see Jared. She took a deep breath. "You'll stay at my place tonight, of course."

She eyed him as she spoke, wondering if he'd feel it necessary to protest. "I've got a spare bedroom," she added before he could speak. "You and Shane could share it."

"Or Shane could take it and I could share your bed," Jared answered quietly, a hint of a question in the suggestion.

She glanced at the pickup where Shane waited, then back to Jared. "I'd like that," she admitted. "But how would Shane feel about it?"

"In case you haven't noticed, my son is all but pushing us into each other's arms," he replied dryly. "He's been around more than most boys his age. I don't think we're going to shock him if we spend the night together. Unless it bothers you, of course."

"It doesn't bother me." Cassie didn't care if the whole world knew that she and Jared were lovers. She loved him, and she wasn't ashamed of that love. Though she couldn't help wondering what Tony would say when he realized just how deeply, personally involved she'd gotten with this particular case.

She was breaking all of the rules, of course. But Tony didn't have much room to criticize, since he'd done the same with Michelle.

Jared leaned down to brush her mouth with his. "Good," he said, straightening before the kiss could get out of hand—much to Cassie's disappointment. "We'll stop about seven for dinner. In the meantime, drive carefully. And leave your radio alone. You can't watch the road if you're playing with your dial."

Cassie gave him a sweet smile. "Someday someone's going to strangle you, Jared Walker," she said, paraphrasing his comment about his son.

He grinned and flicked her nose with the top of one finger. "But it won't be you," he answered, mocking her reply. And then he turned and headed for the truck, his sexy swagger all but making her mouth water.

Cassie sighed wistfully and climbed into her car, comforting herself with the knowledge that they were only some six hours away from being at her home, at which time she'd finally have him to herself once again.

The only worry dimming her anticipation was the fear that once she had Jared and Shane Walker in her home, she'd never want to let them leave. But would she be able to keep them there?

"Well, you're certainly in a better mood. I take it you and Cassie had a little talk while I was playing video games?"

Startled by Shane's question—as well as the realization that he'd actually been whistling along with the toe-tapping country song playing on the radio—Jared grinned somewhat sheepishly. "Yeah, We talked."

"And . . . ?"

"And—it's none of your business what we said," Jared answered.

Shane wasn't offended. "I'm just glad you settled whatever it was. I like it better when you guys are friends."

Jared concentrated hard on the road ahead, his fingers tightening around the steering wheel. "Cassie's invited us to spend the night at her place tonight. She has an extra bedroom."

"Yeah? Cool. I'm really getting tired of motels."

Jared's fingers flexed. "I—uh—won't be sharing the bedroom with you, Shane."

"I didn't think you would be," Shane answered dryly. "And I don't think you spent most of last night at a bar."

Jared winced. "Son, we've talked about this plenty of times. I don't go in for casual affairs, you know that. What I feel for Cassie—well, it's not casual. But that doesn't mean it's going to lead to anything permanent. I think you're mature enough to understand that by now."

"I understand, Dad. But I still hope it does," Shane added. "I really like her."

Jared couldn't help being pleased, despite his concerns that Shane would be disappointed if he and Cassie couldn't make it work out. "Yeah. So do I."

He hesitated a moment, then said, "She's a nice woman, Shane. This isn't casual for her, either. You know that, don't you?"

"Well, of course!" Shane said, sounding indignant on Cassie's behalf. "Jeez, Dad, I know Cassie's not the easy type. Anybody could tell by looking at her that she's crazy about you."

Which, of course, didn't make Jared feel any better at all. *Was* Cassie getting too deeply involved with him? Was she starting to expect more than he was capable of giving her, despite her assurances to the contrary?

Damn. A week ago he'd just had himself and Shane to worry about. Now there was Cassie, as well as two sisters who'd be expecting some sort of response from him. And he couldn't for the life of him have said whether he was more pleased or dismayed with the twist his path had taken.

"Tell me about the ranch you want to own, Jared," Cassie requested as the three of them lingered over dinner that evening. "How did a navy seaman ever get interested in ranch work?"

"Dad used to ride in the rodeo!" Shane informed her before Jared had a chance to answer.

Cassie lifted a questioning eyebrow. "When was that?"

"My last foster home, from the time I was sixteen until I graduated from high school, was on a ranch not far from Texarkana," Jared replied. "I showed an aptitude for the life then, rode in amateur rodeo competitions whenever I got a chance. My foster father encouraged me to stay on and work for him when I graduated from high school.

"I was tempted—I'd been happier there than at the other places. But I decided it would be best if I struck out on my own for a while. The military looked like a good choice—steady work, free job training, a chance to see some of the world."

Had he left because he'd found himself developing ties again for the first time since he'd been separated from his real family? Cassie couldn't help wondering. "Do you stay in contact with him? Have you seen your foster family since you joined the navy?"

Jared shook his head. "He died of a heart attack six months after I joined up. I never was as close to his wife, so we just lost touch after that."

"I'm sorry." So many people lost to him, she thought sadly. Everyone he'd ever cared about, it seemed—except

Shane, of course. And even Shane had been taken from him for several years. No wonder Jared had learned not to get too close.

Jared shrugged, his characteristic response when the conversation turned too personal, too intimate. "Anyway," he went on, his voice expressionless, "when I left the navy, I found work on a ranch in west Texas. Shane and I both enjoy the work, so we've been saving up for our own place for the past two years. Couple more years, and we'll have enough for a down payment on a small ranch. It'll take a while to make a go of it, but we plan on working together at it."

"We're going to call it the Walker Ranch," Shane agreed eagerly. "I kinda like the Double W, but Dad says it's too hard to say in a hurry. We're going to raise champion quarter horses. All we need's one good stud and a couple of fine mares. I want some cattle, too. Polled Herefords, the big red ones. Dad says maybe."

Cassie loved watching the two of them make their plans together. How she wished to see them have their dream come true, to be a part of that future with them!

"My uncle was a rancher in Wyoming," she said. "My parents used to take Cliff and me there to visit for a couple of weeks every summer. Once Cliff and I got to stay six whole weeks, while my parents went to Europe for their first overseas vacation. I loved the ranch."

"Does your uncle still have the place?" Shane asked, his eyes lighting up.

Cassie shook her head. "He passed away, and neither of his sons were interested in carrying on the business. One's a doctor, the other a musician. They sold the ranch right after Uncle Pete died."

"That's a shame."

"I miss him—and the ranch," Cassie agreed. "I understand why you enjoy the life. It's hard work, but it's a challenge."

"The woman likes ranch life and she's good in a fight," Shane said with an exaggeratedly blissful sigh. "Dad, if you don't grab her, damned if I won't. You wouldn't mind waiting a few years for me, would you, Cassie?"

She laughed, her cheeks warming. "I'd be honored to wait for you."

"Last guy who made a pass at my woman ended up with a bloody nose, boy," Jared warned mildly, pushing away his empty dinner plate. "Consider yourself warned."

"Is that right?" Shane asked, his tone sounding so much like his father's that Cassie couldn't help giggling. "Maybe I'd manage to do more than bruise your jaw if I took you on."

Jared fingered the bruise and eyed his son in challenge, looking rather intimidating to Cassie despite the smile in his eyes. "Think so?" His voice was all the more dangerous because it was so very quiet and polite.

"Or maybe not," Shane backed down hastily, holding both hands palm-up in surrender. "Just making conversation."

"Why don't you just finish your dinner," Jared suggested, turning his head to wink at Cassie.

"Yes, sir," Shane agreed, catching the wink and smiling. "Whatever you say, sir."

"Why couldn't he always be that agreeable?" Jared asked with a wistful sigh.

Her hand over her mouth to muffle her laughter, Cassie resisted the urge to circle the table and hug both of them until their faces turned purple. These two were so very special—and for tonight, at least, they were hers.

She intended to enjoy every minute with them.

* * *

They were less than half an hour away from Cassie's apartment when the trip came to an abrupt, terrifying end.

After so many hours on the road without incident, Cassie was relaxed and driving confidently, looking forward to getting home and preparing Shane's usual late-night snack before sending him to bed so she and Jared could be alone. She'd already decided not to even think about her job or Jared's family until the next morning, after another night of his lovemaking to give her the courage to face the future.

She wasn't looking in the rearview window when the accident occurred. She'd just driven beneath a green light, knowing Jared was following close behind. And then she heard the squeal of brakes, the blast of a car horn, followed by the sickening, unmistakable sound of two vehicles colliding behind her.

Slamming on her brakes, she looked back. Her stomach lurched when she realized that another pickup truck had run the red light, slamming at full speed into the passenger's side of Jared's truck. She hadn't even seen it coming, she realized frantically, jerking her car to the side of the road and leaping out the door almost before she brought it to a full stop.

There was no sign of movement from the horribly tangled vehicles in the intersection. The wreckage looked dark and ominous in the artificial glow of the streetlights.

"Call an ambulance!" she screamed to another motorist who'd stopped in response to the accident. Terrified of what she'd find, she ran toward Jared's truck. "*Jared! Shane! Oh, my God, no!*"

Chapter Nine

Cassie reached the driver's side of Jared's truck at the same time as a massively built black man who'd been in the car behind Jared. "Better stand back a minute, lady," he said, holding up an arm to keep her from coming any closer. "Let me look inside first. It might be—well, you know."

She pushed him frantically aside, terror giving her strength even against his muscle. "I know them," she said, her breath catching in a sob. She reached for the door handle. "Jared! Shane!"

Quickly grasping the situation, the man stopped trying to interfere and moved forward to help.

Jared was slumped in his seat, his hands still draped over the steering wheel, the shoulder strap of his seat belt holding him upright. Cassie's heart stopped when she saw the blood. The left side of his face was covered with it.

"Jared?" she whispered, reaching a trembling hand out to him. "Jared, can you hear me?"

She'd never heard a more beautiful sound than his groan. Her knees went weak. She clung helplessly to the doorjamb. "Jared?"

He muttered something and shook his head, as though to clear it. That movement tore another groan from him. His left hand lifted to his head. His eyes opened, bleary and dazed. "Cassie?"

And then his gaze sharpened as full awareness returned. "Shane!"

He twisted frantically in his seat, even as Cassie strained to see around him. "Oh, God. *Shane!*"

Cassie sobbed. She couldn't see the boy, but the agony in Jared's voice spoke volumes.

"Oh, no, please," she heard herself praying, her voice little more than a broken whisper. "Oh, Shane."

Even though it was late—just after 10:00 p.m.—a crowd was beginning to gather. The sound of sirens was already dimly audible. Broad hands fell on Cassie's shoulders, tugging gently. "I've had some experience with this sort of thing," the big man who'd stopped with her said. "Let me see if I can help."

Cassie had always taken such great pride in handling emergencies with clearheaded competence, having never given in to nerves or hysteria in her life. Yet now she found herself trembling uncontrollably, tears streaming down her face as she stared helplessly into the truck.

She'd never faced anything so personally devastating for her.

Oh, God, please let Shane be alive. Don't take him from Jared—or from me. Please.

The first police cruiser pulled close and two officers jumped out, immediately taking charge of the scene, moving back onlookers, clearing a path for the emergency crews on their way. A fire truck rounded a corner, lights and sirens activated.

Again, Cassie felt hands on her arms, drawing her away from the wreckage. She fought them off. "No! I have to know they're all right!"

"Ma'am, we can't help them if you don't give us room," an earnest young officer told her, holding her when she would have pulled away, his hands kind, but firm. "You can stand right here, close, but out of the way. Okay?"

"Please," Cassie whispered, looking up at him through a blinding film of tears. "I love them. Help them."

The young officer searched her face, then tightened his grip on her arms. "Sit down," he urged, tugging downward. "Let's get your head between your knees."

He didn't have to force her downward. Her knees buckled. Had it not been for the officer's support, she would have fallen. Two more hands reached out from her other side, and the familiar deep voice of the black man who'd stopped to help spoke over her head. "I'll stay with her if you need to get back to work."

"Thanks," the officer said gratefully.

People moved around them in the parking lot of the closed-for-the-night business in front of which the accident had happened. The spectators' voices were hushed but avid as they surveyed the scene with a mixture of revulsion and fascination. "That guy looks dead," someone said from nearby.

Cassie lifted her head sharply, gasping when the world spun in response. "I have to go to them," she whispered, placing a hand flat against the pavement to give herself support as she rose.

"Give yourself a minute," her companion urged. "You're still white as a ghost. You try to stand up now, you're just going to pitch back over."

But already the world around her was steadying, her eyes drying as characteristic determination kicked in. "I have to go to them," she repeated. "Please."

The man eyed her cautiously for another moment, then nodded. "Okay. I'll give you a hand up. Take it easy, now. And my name's Frank, by the way."

"Thank you." She clung to his strong, dark hand as she pushed herself to her feet with his help. "What's happening? Where's the ambulance?"

"On the way, ma'am. Steady now."

Cassie craned on tiptoe, trying to see around the officers standing in the open driver's door of Jared's truck. "Is he alive?" she asked, barely able to push the question past the lump in her throat. "Is Shane alive?"

"That the boy?"

She looked up at Frank hopefully, nodding. "Could you see him?"

"I saw him. He's hurt, but he was alive when the officers took over. Hey, you're not going to faint again, are you?"

"I haven't fainted yet," Cassie murmured, though she maintained a grip on his supportive arm.

Just hearing that Shane hadn't died in the accident had sent a wave of knee-weakening relief through her. If only his injuries weren't serious. . . .

Belatedly, she remembered that there had been another vehicle involved in the accident. Looking over the buckled hood of Jared's truck, she saw a group of police and firemen gathered at the second pickup. "Is the other driver hurt badly?"

Frank followed her gaze. "I think he's dead, ma'am."

"Oh, no." Cassie closed her eyes for a moment, then opened them quickly when the wail of a rapidly approaching ambulance caught her attention. It was closely followed by a second ambulance. "Thank God. They're finally here."

"It's only been five or six minutes since they were called."

It had seemed like a lifetime. Cassie watched anxiously as paramedics rushed to the scene, emergency equipment in hand.

Frank's gloomy diagnosis of the other driver's condition was confirmed. The officers gathered around the other vehicle and waved the paramedics toward Jared and Shane, shaking their heads as though to say there was nothing to be done for the other driver.

Cassie started forward when she saw Jared being assisted out of the truck, a bandage being pressed to his head by a woman who was beginning to look harried. Cassie saw at a glance that Jared wasn't being cooperative, particularly when he was urged toward one of the waiting ambulances. He shook off the hands that had reached out to help him.

"He's my son, dammit," Cassie heard him snarl as she took a step closer. "He's my son!"

Evading a police officer who stepped toward her, Cassie slipped closer to Jared, placing her hand on his arm. She searched his face. He was pale, blood-streaked, disheveled, his eyes wild, but at least he didn't look seriously injured. "Jared?"

He looked down at her. She couldn't feel hurt that he blinked as though it took him a moment to remember who she was. She understood that all his concentration, all his emotions were focused on his son.

"Cassie," he said after the briefest hesitation, raising his hand to touch her face. "Are you all right?"

She covered her hand with his. "Of course I'm all right," she assured him, trying to smile. Knowing how miserably she failed. "Are you?"

His eyes turned back to the truck around which so many people were working with what appeared to be feverish haste. "I don't know yet."

A slender young man in a white uniform approached them, his attention focused on the bleeding cut on Jared's left temple. "Here, let me look at that," he offered.

Jared waved him away impatiently. "I'm okay. My son's the one who's hurt."

"Yes, sir, I know, but he's being attended to. At least let me see if I can stop your bleeding. You won't be any help to your son if you pass out, will you?"

"Let him look at you, Jared," Cassie urged, both hands on his arm now. "I'll check on Shane."

Jared nodded reluctantly and allowed the paramedic to lead him toward an ambulance. "I'm not leaving until my son does," he warned the young man.

"No, sir. I don't blame you," the paramedic answered compassionately. "We'll do what we can to treat you here until your son is transported."

Confident that Jared was in good hands, Cassie turned to the truck. "Excuse me," she said to a police officer who was passing here.

"Need to stand back, lady. This ain't a free show," he growled, hurrying toward the intersection where curious motorists were causing a traffic hazard with their rubbernecking.

She sighed and tried again, tapping the shoulder of a man in a fireman's uniform. "Please, can you—?"

"Sorry, ma'am. I've got to fetch a piece of equipment. Talk to an officer," the fireman replied hastily, though not unkindly.

Again, it was Frank, the big man who'd stopped to help after the wreck, who came to Cassie's assistance. He took her elbow and helped her to the young officer who'd drawn her away from Jared the first time.

"I'm Lieutenant Franklin Thompson from the Houston Police Department," he introduced himself, his deep voice carrying just a trace of command, as though he were a man accustomed to being in charge. "The lady wants to know the condition of the boy in the truck. He's a friend of hers."

Responding instinctively to the voice of a fellow officer, the young policeman cooperated immediately, looking up from the clipboard on which he'd been filling out a report.

"He's trapped in the wreckage by the front quarter panel of the vehicle, ma'am," he explained carefully. "He's alive and stable, I understand, but the full extent of his injuries can't be determined until he's extricated. We're going to have to get the other truck out of the way, then pull him out with special equipment."

"The Jaws of Life?" Cassie asked, having heard the term on the television and read about it in the newspapers.

"That's right, if necessary. In the meantime, it would be best if you and the father stay back. I know you're concerned, but the boy's being assisted by experienced professionals. I don't suppose you can convince Mr. Walker to be taken on to the hospital for treatment of his own injuries, could you?"

Cassie looked back at him. "What would you do if it were your son trapped in that mess?" she asked quietly.

The officer didn't even hesitate. "I'd tear him out with my bare hands if they'd let me."

"Then you know exactly how Jared feels," Cassie replied. She felt very much the same way herself. "He won't leave until he knows Shane's out. Neither will I. But we will stay out of your way."

"I promise I'll keep you both informed about what's going on," the officer assured her.

"Thank you. We'd appreciate that." Cassie turned toward Frank. "And thank *you*, Lieutenant. You've been so much help."

He smiled. "A cop's a cop, even when he's on vacation." And then he led her back to Jared, who was sitting with visible reluctance in the back of an ambulance, one medic taking his blood pressure while the slender young man who'd led him away bandaged his head.

"Here's your friend," the latter said to Jared, looking up with a friendly smile when Cassie and Frank approached. "He's been getting a little impatient," he added for their benefit.

"What's going on out there, Cassie?" Jared demanded.

Cassie repeated what the officer had told her. "They're doing the best they can, Jared."

Jared glared at the paramedic standing over him. "Are you about finished?"

"You're going to need stitches for this cut, but the bleeding has stopped," the young man answered, apparently unconcerned by Jared's curtness. "Your blood pressure's fine, considering the stress you're under, and there's no sign of a concussion. You'll be okay until we can get you to a hospital to be checked out more carefully."

"Not without my son," Jared repeated, already pushing himself off the gurney on which he'd been seated.

"No, sir. Not without your son."

If it hadn't been for the terrible gravity of the situation, Cassie would have smiled at the paramedic's wryly resigned tone. As it was, she could only take Jared's hand when he stepped from the ambulance and reached for her.

She wrapped her fingers tightly around his, both of them turning to watch the painfully slow process of extricating Shane from the mangled cab of Jared's truck.

* * *

Jared rode in the ambulance with Shane when the boy was finally transported to the hospital some forty minutes later. Cassie followed in her car, still shaken by the one glimpse she'd had of Shane as he'd been loaded into the ambulance.

He'd been so pale, so still, so vulnerable-looking. What if there were internal injuries? What if he didn't even make it to the hospital?

How would Jared survive if he lost the son he loved so very deeply, after so many other losses in his life?

Her heart wept for both of them.

Shane, still unconscious, was wheeled straight into an emergency examining room upon arrival at the hospital. Though he protested, Jared, too, was led away by hospital staff determined to care for him whether he cooperated or not, followed by a clerk with a stack of admission forms.

Cassie was left to pace the waiting room, her hands wringing in front of her, her head aching from stress and exhaustion. She glanced at her watch. It was almost eleven.

Finding a bank of pay telephones at one end of the emergency lobby, she dialed Tony's home number. Her employer answered.

"Tony, I'm so glad it's you."

"Cassie? Where are you?"

"I'm in Dallas. Oh, Tony." Her voice broke.

"Cassie? Cassie, what is it? What's wrong?" Tony sounded increasingly anxious when it took her a moment to answer.

She drew a steadying breath. "There's been an accident," she said, trying to stay calm and coherent. "Jared and Shane were following me into town and they were broadsided by another vehicle."

"Oh, damn, Cassie, how bad is it? Are *you* okay?"

"I'm fine. My car wasn't involved. Jared seems okay, though he hit his head on the side window. But Shane—" She had to stop again to swallow hard against a rush of tears.

"Jared's son? Cassie, is he—?"

"He's alive," Cassie broke in quickly. "He was trapped in the truck for quite a while until they could pull him out. He's hurt, but I don't know how badly. They're examining him now."

She named the hospital. "Can you come, Tony? I could really use you right now," she added, desperately needing a friend's support.

"We'll be there in fifteen minutes," Tony answered, though they both knew it was a good twenty-five-minute drive from his home to the hospital. Cassie knew, as well, that Tony would be there in fifteen, if at all possible.

"Drive carefully" was all she said.

It was just under twenty minutes later when Tony and Michelle hurried into the waiting room. Cassie bolted from the hard plastic chair on which she'd been perched.

"I'm so glad you're here," she breathed, taking Tony's outstretched hand in both of hers. "Jared still hasn't come out, and no one's told me anything. I don't know what's going on, and I'm so worried about Shane."

Penetrating black eyes studied her face. "You look awful," Tony said with more concern than tact. "You sure you're okay, Cassie?"

She managed a nod, then almost immediately shook her head. "Not until I know how Shane is," she whispered. "Oh, Tony, he's such a sweet boy. I couldn't bear it if..."

Remembering Michelle, she swallowed the rest and turned to the woman standing quietly behind them. "Michelle. I'm sorry. I didn't mean to ignore you."

"I understand." Michelle D'Alessandro was one of the most beautiful, most elegant women Cassie had ever met. She had been more than a little intimidated the first time she'd met her employer's wealthy, classy wife. But that was before she'd realized that Michelle was kind-hearted, sweet-natured and more than a little shy beneath her polished sophistication. "Thank you for calling us. I wanted to come."

"It's getting so late." Cassie checked her watch again, fretting at the length of time that had passed since she'd seen Jared and Shane. "God, I wish I knew what was happening in there."

Tony turned toward the admissions desk. "I'll see what I can find out."

"Let's sit down," Michelle suggested to Cassie. "You look ready to drop."

"I've been on the road most of the day," Cassie agreed wearily. "And then this..."

"Can I get you some coffee? Vending-machine coffee is usually dreadful, but it might help."

Cassie shook her head. Her stomach was tied into so many knots she was afraid she wouldn't be able to keep anything down. "Thanks, anyway, Michelle."

Ignoring the other people around them in the sterile lobby, Michelle sat beside Cassie on a narrow vinyl bench. "Jared changed his mind about visiting us, I take it."

"Yes." Cassie cleared her throat. "I—I talked him into it. I thought it would be good for both him and Shane to meet their family."

"You can't blame yourself for this, Cassie. You were only doing what Tony and I asked you to do. The accident was just that—an accident."

"A drunk," Cassie corrected bitterly. "I've found out that the other guy was drunk, and that he had a history of drunken driving. He paid for it this time with his life."

She couldn't bear to think that the price might have been even higher.

Tony rejoined them, the frustration on his handsome face indicating that he'd learned little more than Cassie had been able to find out before he'd arrived. He stood beside the bench, his hand resting on his wife's shoulder. "All they'll tell me is that they're being examined and treated and that a doctor will be with us as soon as possible."

Cassie made a sound of disgust. "That's what they kept telling me," she complained. "And I've been here almost an hour. What could be taking so long?"

"Hospital procedures can be very lengthy sometimes," said Michelle, who had been a hospital volunteer for several years. "Surely it won't be much longer."

Cassie sighed and buried her face in her hands, feeling as though she'd aged decades in the past few hours. Everything had been going so well. How could it have gone this drastically wrong?

"Tell me about Jared and Shane, Cassie," Michelle said, obviously trying to distract her from her worry. "I'd like to know something about them before I meet them."

Cassie straightened, wondering how to explain Jared to this sister who didn't remember him.

"Jared is reserved and rather quiet," she said finally, so easily picturing his usually grave face. Remembering how he'd looked when passion had swept away his reserve.

"He has a great deal of pride," she went on quickly. "He's conservative and a little bossy, but he has a dry sense of humor that comes out when you least expect it. And he absolutely adores his son."

Tony lifted a dark eyebrow, studying Cassie's face. She felt herself flushing beneath the intensity of that regard. "Sounds like you've gotten to know him fairly well in such a short time."

Cassie avoided his eyes. "We have spent quite a bit of time together during the past few days," she concurred.

Michelle interceded, to Cassie's relief. "Is Shane like his father?"

"In some ways they're very much alike, though Shane is more outgoing. He's fourteen—bright, mature, funny. I'm..." She wiped her eyes. "I'm crazy about your nephew, Michelle."

"I'm sure I will be, as well," Michelle said, reaching over to squeeze Cassie's hand. "He's going to be okay, Cassie. If there's one thing Tony's taught me, it's to believe what my heart tells me. And my heart's telling me now that I'm going to have a chance to get to know my nephew."

Cassie had always been an optimist. She tried desperately to cling to that optimism now. "I'm sure you're right, Michelle," she murmured, the words almost a prayer. "I'm sure you're right."

Jared couldn't remember ever feeling more drained than he did when he left the examining room in which he'd finally been allowed to see his son.

Shane was sedated, sleeping deeply, so Jared didn't linger once his questions had been answered to his satisfaction. Having been assured he'd be located as soon as Shane was settled into a hospital room for the night, he headed for the waiting room, knowing Cassie must be frantic by now.

His head ached, though he'd refused the pain pills he'd been offered. He wore eight stitches at his left temple, but that cut and a few bruises were his only injuries from the accident. He fervently wished Shane had been as fortunate.

He wanted Cassie, needed to feel her hand in his, her arms around him. Though he'd spent most of his life on his own, learning not to depend on anyone but himself, just this once he needed the emotional support of someone who cared about him, without strings, without qualifications.

He needed Cassie.

With her copper hair gleaming in the bright fluorescent lighting, she wasn't hard to spot in the emergency waiting area. He had eyes for no one else when he started toward her, his booted stride eating up the distance that separated them.

As though she sensed his approach, she looked up, her eyes meeting his. And then she was on her feet, and a heartbeat later she was in his arms.

He buried his face in her hair and allowed himself the first long, deep breath he'd taken since he'd turned and seen his son's face after the accident. He felt the tremors running through Cassie's slender body and drew her closer, heedless of anyone who might be watching.

"God, Cassie," he muttered, drawing strength from her almost palpable concern for him. "Oh, God."

She drew back only far enough to search his face anxiously. "Jared? Is Shane—is he—?"

"He's going to be okay," he answered quietly, reassuringly, seeing the panic that had sprung into her eyes and chiding himself for causing it. "His right arm is broken and he has a concussion. He's also got a couple of cracked ribs and possible whiplash."

"What about his right leg?" Cassie asked, remembering that the leg had been caught beneath a jagged piece of metal that had come through the cab of the truck with the impact.

"Badly bruised," Jared answered, identifying strongly with her obvious relief that it hadn't been more serious. "Had the metal come through a few inches lower, he might have lost the leg."

"Oh, Jared." Cassie went limp against him, her fingers clutching his badly wrinkled, bloodstained shirt. "I've been so frightened."

"Yeah. Me, too. But he's going to be okay, Cassie. Shane's a tough kid."

"Like his father," she murmured, looking up at him with a trembling attempt at a smile.

"Yeah," he murmured, lost in her tear-filled green eyes. "Like his dad."

And then he kissed her, a long, tender kiss of shared relief, of aching emotion, of a deep, powerful hunger that went far beyond the physical.

He drew back at last to look down at her with a weak smile. "Know where we can get some coffee while Shane's being settled into a room? God knows I could use some."

"Yes, I— Oh!"

Jared was startled by Cassie's squeak, looking at her in question when she suddenly covered her face with one hand and went scarlet behind it. "Cassie? What's wrong?"

"I think she's finally remembered she hasn't been waiting alone," a man's voice answered unexpectedly.

Jared turned his head to find himself face to face with a tall, dark, Italian-looking guy with dark, searching eyes and a quizzical expression. Behind him stood a slender, brown-haired woman in her mid-twenties, her blue eyes locked on Jared's face. He stared back at her, finding so many familiar features that he had no doubt who she was, though he hadn't seen her in twenty-four years. It was like looking at a feminine version of himself, or Shane.

"Shelley?" he asked hesitantly, his hand freezing at Cassie's waist. "Are you Shelley?"

She nodded, her blue eyes filling with tears. "Hello, Jerry. It's so very good to see you."

Shaken to his boots, and still too emotionally drained to conceal it, Jared thrust his free hand through his hair and let out an unsteady breath. He wasn't ready for this, he thought grimly, taking a hard swallow as he tried to think of something to say. He hadn't had a chance to prepare for a family reunion.

But regardless of whether he was ready, he couldn't deny that the woman standing in front of him was his sister and that he had once loved her. Nor was he unaware that his first reaction had been to take her in his arms, even though she was little more than a stranger to him now.

"Damn," he muttered.

He really wasn't ready for this.

Chapter Ten

Realizing what his sister had called him, Jared looked at her in question. "You said Jerry. That's what you called me when you were little."

She nodded, her smile unsteady. "I know."

"You couldn't possibly remember. You weren't even three when we were split up."

"I don't remember very clearly," she replied. "But all my life I've had dreams of playing with a boy named Jerry and a girl named Layla. I didn't know until earlier this year that those dreams were really early memories."

"I answer to Jared these days," he murmured, all but shuddering at the thought of being tagged with "Jerry" again at this point in his life.

Her smile deepened. "And I'm Michelle."

"It must have been unnerving for you to find out you had so many brothers and sisters," Jared commented rather awkwardly, not quite sure what else to say. What were they expecting of him?

She nodded. "It was staggering, to say the least. But exciting, too. I grew up thinking I was an only child, and that I was all alone when my adoptive parents died. I was pleased to learn that I wasn't alone, after all."

"Now you've got more family than you ever imagined," the dark man with her commented with a smile.

Michelle returned his smile. "Jared, this is my husband, Tony D'Alessandro—who happens to come from a huge, extended family himself."

Jared studied the other man closely, deciding he liked what he saw. Looking to be in his early thirties, clean-cut, clear-eyed D'Alessandro was just the opposite of the old movie stereotype of an unshaven, disreputable, somewhat sleazy P.I. On first impression, Michelle seemed to have found herself a good husband. For her sake, Jared was glad.

He extended his hand. "So you're Cassie's boss—the guy who refused to bail me out of jail."

Tony grinned and gripped Jared's hand firmly. "No offense, of course. I'd have bailed you out eventually. Just thought I'd let the New Mexico cops help Cassie keep track of you for a couple of days until I had a chance to check you out for myself."

Jared dropped Tony's hand and draped his arm around Cassie's waist. "Cassie didn't need any help keeping track of me," he said smoothly. "She knows her job. And she's damned good at it. You're lucky to have her working for you."

"*Jared…*" Cassie murmured uncomfortably, shifting her weight.

Tony's left eyebrow rose, but he nodded. "I'm aware of that."

"Good." Jared glanced at Cassie's flushed face, knowing she wouldn't appreciate his talking her up with her boss. "About that coffee . . ."

"There's a canteen on the next floor," Michelle volunteered. "It's only a few tables and vending machines—the cafeteria's closed at this hour—but at least it's a place to sit down and have a cup of coffee."

"Sounds good." Jared inhaled deeply, releasing the breath in a long sigh. "I'm wiped out."

"I'll let them know where we'll be if you're needed," Tony offered, turning toward the desk.

Cassie was being unusually quiet, Jared realized. Still keeping her close with the arm he'd wrapped around her waist, he glanced down at her. "Cassie? You okay?"

She nodded, her mouth trembling a bit. "Just tired."

"If you'd like to go on home, Tony and I will stay with Jared until he's reassured that Shane is settled for the night," Michelle suggested, glancing curiously from Cassie to Jared, obviously wondering about their relationship.

Cassie shook her head before Jared could voice the protest that sprang immediately to his lips. He knew she was tired, but he couldn't bring himself to let her go. He needed her with him now.

It was the first time he'd really needed anyone since . . . well, in longer than he could remember. And he was too damned tired to even worry about that at the moment, he thought wearily.

"I want to stay," Cassie said. "I'd like to make sure for myself that Shane's okay." She managed a smile, though it was a pitiful attempt. "I'll be fine as soon as I get some coffee in me."

Conversation was rather stilted over eight cups of coffee in the all-night canteen. Cassie was still unnaturally subdued, Tony polite but watchful, as though taking his time to judge whether Jared represented any threat to either Michelle or Cassie.

Jared watched Tony with Cassie, a little suspicious at first of the obvious affection between them. He relaxed when he realized that Tony treated Cassie with much the same fond exasperation he might have shown a younger sister. And Cassie responded with affection, respect and just the right touch of impertinence, as though to tell him that he could give orders as her employer, but only to a point.

Jared approved. He didn't like the thought of anyone trying to break Cassie's reckless spirit, despite his own admonitions to her on occasion during the past . . . damn, had it only been four days since they'd met?

Shaken by the realization that he'd fallen faster and harder for this woman than he'd ever thought possible, Jared didn't hear Michelle speak his name the first time. He blinked when he heard her, realizing she must have spoken before. "I'm sorry, Michelle. What did you say?"

She'd asked a question about his years in the navy. He responded, giving her a brief rundown of the past twenty-four years, leaving out more than he told her, particularly when it came to his unsuccessful marriage. About that, he said only that he'd been married young, divorced a few years later, and had been granted full custody of his son after leaving the navy two years ago.

"Do you think you should call Shane's mother to tell her about the accident?" Michelle asked.

Aware that she couldn't have known better, Jared kept his answer mild, knowing that Cassie was listening intently beside him. "No. She gave up all rights to Shane two years ago. This doesn't concern her."

More than ready to change the subject, he turned the questioning to Michelle, who told him she'd been adopted by a childless couple, raised in a comfortable, secure home, and worked part-time now for her late father's company as administrator of charitable contributions.

Jared wondered why the pleasant, uneventful life she'd described didn't quite mesh with the shadows he occasionally glimpsed in her eyes. Michelle may have been raised in a comfortable, secure home, but she hadn't been completely happy, he decided. Maybe someday she'd tell him why.

Not that it was any of his business, of course, he reminded himself abruptly. It had been twenty-four years since he'd been responsible for this young woman.

"Mr. Walker?"

Jared turned his head in response to his name, finding Shane's doctor behind him. He stood, aware that Cassie did the same. "What is it?"

Dr. O'Reilly lifted a hand to indicate there was no reason to worry. "I just wanted to tell you your son's awake and asking for you. Thought you might want to speak to him a moment before we sedate him again."

"Is that necessary? The sedation, I mean," Jared asked with a frown.

"It will help him sleep more comfortably tonight. He needs the rest."

Jared nodded. "All right. And, thanks. I do want to see him."

Dr. O'Reilly smiled. "I was sure you would. I'll take you to his room."

Jared started after the doctor. Then stopped when he realized he was the only one doing so. He looked over his shoulder. "Cassie?"

She didn't move. "Yes?"

"Come on."

He saw her eyes light up, though she hesitated. "You want me to come with you?"

"Shane will want to see you." Which was only half the truth, of course. Still, Jared spoke confidently, knowing his son well enough to anticipate the request. Shane would know that Cassie would have been worried sick about him.

Cassie glanced at Michelle and Tony, then stepped quickly to Jared's side. "I'd love to see him."

Jared took her hand in his, aware of how right it felt to have her at his side.

He really was going to have to give these complicated feelings some thought. Later.

Her eyes on the boy in the hospital bed, Cassie held back when Jared stepped to Shane's side. Her throat was almost unbearably tight, her eyes burning with the tears she refused to shed in front of Shane. She needed just a moment to recover from the shock of seeing him lying there so still and small in his bandages and cast, his face looking so very young beneath the bruises and traces of blood which hadn't been completely washed away.

"Hi, Dad." Even Shane's voice seemed suddenly younger, higher, less confident than she'd heard it before. "You okay?"

"I'm fine, Shane," Jared answered gruffly, leaning over the bed.

"Your head?"

"Just a cut. A few stitches."

"Does it hurt?"

"Nah." Jared spoke the obvious lie without a blink. "You hurting much?"

"Not too bad," Shane answered, as easily as his father. Cassie couldn't help smiling a little. Neither of them would have admitted if they *had* been in terrible pain. Hopelessly macho, the both of them.

God, how she loved them!

"Where's Cassie?" Shane demanded, trying to look around his father. "Is she okay?"

Touched that the boy would ask about her so soon, Cassie stepped closer to the bed. "I'm right here. And I'm fine."

He looked relieved. "I can't really remember much about what happened," he admitted. "You weren't hit, were you?"

"No. I'd already passed through the intersection by the time the other driver came through and hit your truck."

"I never even saw him until he was right on us," Jared murmured, his expression bleak. "If I'd hit the brakes a little sooner, or had a chance to turn the wheel . . ."

"I didn't see him, either, Dad," Shane reassured him. "You couldn't have done anything differently. Besides, it turned out okay. Neither of us is hurt bad. A broken arm's no big deal."

Cassie had to blink back tears again at the earnest note in Shane's voice. He was trying so hard to help Jared fight the guilt that was as unfounded as it was inevitable.

A muscle twitched in Jared's hard jaw, but he nodded and managed a faint smile for his son's benefit. "The nurse is waiting outside to give you something to help you sleep tonight."

Shane made a face. "I don't want them to knock me out."

"It'll help you rest, son. Don't give them any trouble, you hear?"

Shane chuckled weakly, his eyelids heavy as he glanced expressively at his bandages and the IV tube running into his left arm. "Not much chance of that," he murmured.

"You could still take on half the staff and win, kid," Jared told him affectionately, gently ruffling the boy's hair.

"But maybe you'd better just take it easy tonight. I'll be back in the morning."

" 'Kay. You get some rest, too."

"I will."

"Cassie?"

Cassie moved to stand at the opposite side of the bed from Jared, looking down at the boy with a tremulous smile. "Yes, Shane?"

"I'm expecting to need that guest room tomorrow night, okay?"

"I'll have it ready, just in case," she promised. She leaned over to brush her lips across his cool cheek. "Good night, Shane. See you tomorrow."

He gave her a smile, though she could see the pain in his eyes. " 'Night, Cassie."

"We'll send the nurse in now," Jared said, taking Cassie's hand. She knew he was as aware of Shane's discomfort as she was, and that he was suffering with his son. He held her hand in a grip almost tight enough to make her wince, telling her just how hard it was for him to leave.

They rejoined Michelle and Tony in the canteen, finding them waiting patiently for word about Shane.

"He's doing fine," Jared announced, the relief visible in his eyes. "He's hurting, but coherent. Shane's tough. He'll be back on his feet in no time."

"Oh, I'm glad to hear that," Michelle said. "I can't wait to meet him."

"He's looking forward to that, as well," Jared replied. "He was really excited to hear that he has two aunts and some cousins wanting to meet him."

As interested as she was in watching Jared's reactions to his sister, Cassie couldn't quite stifle the yawn that escaped her. It was well past midnight now, and she'd had a very long day after very little sleep the night before.

Jared turned to her immediately. "You're out on your feet. Time for you to get some rest."

"Jared, you'll stay with us tonight, won't you?" Michelle asked politely. "There's no need for you to stay in a hotel when we have plenty of extra bedrooms."

Cassie bit her lower lip, wondering how Jared would respond. She wanted him with her, of course, but didn't quite have the nerve to repeat her invitation in front of her boss and Jared's sister.

What would they think if they knew she and Jared had become lovers so quickly? Would Tony be disappointed with her for losing all sight of professional behavior on this particular case?

Jared seemed to suffer no such qualms. He thanked Michelle for her offer, then added, "But I already have a place to stay tonight."

Both Michelle and Tony looked directly at Cassie, who responded with a fiery blush that must have confirmed all their suspicions.

She cleared her throat noisily. "We knew it would be late when we arrived tonight," she explained. "We'd planned to call tomorrow and make arrangements, then get everyone together."

Tony's eyes glinted, and Cassie tensed, remembering the times she'd teased him during his early involvement with Michelle, wondering if he would fire her now or have the courtesy to do that in private. But all he said was, "No need for you to come in to the office in the morning, Cassie. Get some rest and we'll talk tomorrow, all right?"

"Thanks, Tony."

Cassie glanced cautiously at Michelle, who looked from her to Jared, then back again. And then she smiled with what looked to Cassie like approval before laying a hand on

Jared's arm. "As much as I regret the accident, I'm still very glad you're here, Jared," she said softly.

Cassie watched as Jared's face softened fractionally. He covered his sister's hand with his own. "You've grown into a beautiful woman, Michelle. It's good to see you again."

Michelle was obviously touched, her eyes going damp. "I'll call Layla first thing in the morning. She's so anxious to see you. She's told me dozens of stories about the things you did together when you were younger."

Jared nodded. "I remember." And then he dropped his hand and turned to Cassie. "Let's go."

Knowing Jared had reached an emotional overload of sorts, Cassie nodded and led him briskly to her car. She kept their conversation light and impersonal during the ride to her apartment, giving him a chance to pull his defenses together.

As much as she resented those defenses at times, she knew he needed them tonight. And she wanted to give him enough space that he didn't start feeling cornered before he'd even spent an entire day in Dallas.

Preceding Jared into her functional, two-bedroom apartment in a midpriced complex located in a quiet Dallas neighborhood, Cassie was glad she'd spent a day at housework before leaving town to track Jared down. After a week of sitting empty, the apartment was a bit stuffy, but at least it wasn't cluttered with newspapers, magazines and odd pieces of clothing, as she'd been known to leave it occasionally.

"Can I get you anything?" she offered, leading Jared into the living room, off of which opened the kitchen, dining area and the short hallway leading to the two tiny bedrooms and guest bath.

He shook his head. "I need a shower and sleep more than anything else right now."

She understood. Her own body was so desperately in need of rest that she ached to her toenails. "There's a shower stall in my bath and a tub in the guest bath."

"Where's your bedroom?"

"First door on the right."

He nodded and carried his bag toward the hallway she'd indicated. "I won't be long."

"Take your time." She watched him disappear, wondering if she should prepare the daybed she kept in the spare bedroom, which usually served as her study. Considering how tired they both were, lovemaking seemed unlikely—but would Jared want to sleep with her or alone?

She knew which she'd choose. She couldn't think of any nicer way to rest than curled next to him. But maybe he'd prefer privacy for tonight.

She carried her bag to her bedroom, listening to the shower running in the attached bath as she dropped it at the foot of the bed. And then she moved into the guest room, deciding it was best to be prepared for either eventuality.

She'd just finished smoothing clean sheets onto the daybed when Jared spoke from the doorway behind her. "What are you doing?"

She turned self-consciously, tucking a curl behind her left ear. Her knees went weak at the sight of him, his hair wet, chest still damp, a towel draped around his hips. He wore nothing else.

"I wasn't sure where you wanted to sleep," she explained, dry-mouthed in reaction to him. He looked so very good, even with the bandage at his temple, the day-old bruise on his jaw and the newer bruises marking his ribs and stomach from the abrupt tightening of his seat belt during the accident. The seat belt that may well have saved his life, just as Shane's had probably saved his.

Jared glanced at the daybed and then over his shoulder toward the other bedroom. "Where were you planning to sleep?"

"Why, in my own bed, of course."

"Then that's where I want to sleep. Unless you'd rather I stay in here. If so, just tell me."

How typical of Jared to express his wishes so bluntly, Cassie thought with a weary ripple of amusement. "I would love to share my bed with you, Jared. Though I can't promise anything more energetic than a good-night kiss when we get there."

His grin was endearingly lopsided, his expression understanding. "I don't have the energy to ask for anything more," he assured her. "Come to bed, Cassie. Just let me hold you tonight."

She went to him without hesitation, knowing there was nowhere in the world she'd rather be.

As tired as she was, Cassie wouldn't have been surprised to have slept twenty-four hours without even stirring. But the bedroom was still dark when she woke, the bedside clock letting her know she'd gotten only three hours' sleep. And the bed beside her was empty.

Where was Jared? Had he decided to sleep in the other bedroom, after all? Was his head hurting?

Concerned, she slipped out of the bed, not bothering to don a robe over her thin white cotton nightgown. Her bare feet made no sound on the carpet as she crossed the hallway to look into the spare bedroom. She saw at a glance that the daybed hadn't been disturbed since she'd last seen it.

Knowing Jared had been as tired as she was, if not more so, she grew more anxious, though she tried to reassure herself that perhaps he'd only gone into the kitchen for a glass of water.

She stopped abruptly in the doorway to the living room. Wearing only a pair of jeans, Jared stood at the window overlooking the apartment compound, his back to her as he stared without moving. He obviously hadn't heard her, wasn't aware that she was watching him.

She thought of going back to bed, giving him that space she'd decided he needed. But something in the set of his shoulders drew her forward. She was close enough to touch him when she spoke in little more than a whisper. "Jared? Is something wrong? Is your head hurting?"

He started in response to her voice, his head jerking in her direction. The thin light streaming in from outside glittered in his shadowed eyes—and from a drop of moisture on his cheek. Her chest contracted sharply.

Tears? From Jared? "Oh, Jared, what is it?"

He was still for so long that she thought he wasn't going to answer. And then he released a gust of breath and dashed at his cheek with the heel of his hand—much as Shane would have, she couldn't help thinking.

"I almost lost him," he said, his voice a deep growl. "Dammit, Cassie, I almost lost him. If that truck had hit us one minute later, six inches farther back, Shane wouldn't have made it."

She couldn't bear to see him suffering. She wrapped both hands around his arm, resting her head against his bare shoulder. "Don't, Jared. You're torturing yourself need-lessly. Shane's going to be fine."

"I know that. But I can't stop thinking about how close it was."

"Think about how lucky you both were, instead."

"Yeah. I'm trying."

They stood quietly for several long moments, Cassie's head against his shoulder, Jared still staring out the window. Cassie's heart ached for him. She'd never felt closer to anyone else in her life. Though she'd never really been in love before, she'd always known that the true test of the emotion came in the difficult times, not the easy ones.

She and Jared had been through more in four days than some couples experienced in as many years. Perhaps that was why it was so easy for her to love him, Cassie mused. She'd watched him under pressure, at leisure, angry, laughing, distraught. She'd seen him as a father, as a lover, as a fighter. As a man. And she loved every side he'd revealed to her in those days, even knowing that there were aspects of him she still hadn't seen, may never get close enough to see.

But did Jared feel the same way? Did he still see Cassie as a temporary companion, a convenient buffer between himself and his sister while he was in town? Did he really need her as much as she believed he did?

She shivered at the thought that she may have been deluding herself about his feelings, that he could so easily walk away from her as soon as Shane was released from the hospital.

Jared's arm went around her immediately. "You're cold. Let's get you back in bed."

"You need your rest, too," she urged, looking up at him. "Come with me, Jared."

He nodded and walked with her to the bedroom, where he stripped off his jeans. Together they climbed back into the rumpled bed. "C'mere," Jared said, tugging Cassie into his arms.

She slipped a hand behind his neck, feeling the muscles bunched there. She tightened her fingers, kneading a stubborn knot at the juncture of his shoulder. He groaned softly. "That feels good."

"Turn on your side and I'll rub your neck."

"No. You're tired. Get some sleep."

"Jared—" She shoved at him. "Roll over. You're in my bed, so I get to be the bossy one this time."

He made a sound that was very close to a chuckle and finally rolled over as she'd requested, his back to her. Cassie went to work on the knotted muscles in his neck and shoulders, satisfied to feel them slowly easing beneath her ministrations.

If Jared would accept nothing else from her, at least she could pamper him tonight. She tried very hard to convince herself that was enough—for now, at least.

Chapter Eleven

Cassie was rather startled when Jared spoke after lying still beneath her hands for several minutes. She'd thought he was falling asleep, but his voice was fully awake. "I almost lost Shane once before, you know."

Her hands stilled, then resumed their massage. Jared needed to talk. She needed to listen. "When?"

"Two years ago, when he ran away. Kay married a jerk who wasn't openly abusive to Shane, but was totally indifferent to his welfare. He and Kay spent most evenings getting quietly drunk while Shane was left pretty much on his own. I had finally figured out what was going on—" his voice was gritty with self-censure "—and I'd been trying for well over a year to get custody of my son. Kay fought me, more as a way of getting in a few last digs at me than because she really wanted Shane."

"Couldn't the courts see that she wasn't a good mother to him?"

Jared shrugged the shoulder she was rubbing. "No one cared enough to really investigate. Kay did a good job of looking like the loving, concerned mother when she was in public. Hell, she'd kept me fooled for nearly ten years, until Shane finally got old enough to tell me just what was going on. I knew she drank too much, of course, but I thought she put Shane first. I was wrong. I guess I was too involved with my own problems to want to know the real truth."

There was that guilt again. She knew now that he'd never completely defeat it—that it wasn't entirely unfounded, though he'd devoted himself to making up for the mistakes he'd made during Shane's early years.

She didn't insult him by trying to assure him he hadn't made any mistakes. But she did want him to know that he wasn't making them now, not with Shane, anyway. "You're a good father, Jared. Shane's one of the most well-adjusted, levelheaded, brightest boys I've ever met. He didn't achieve those things alone."

Jared rolled to his back and threw an arm over his head, staring at the darkened ceiling. "I've done what I could the past couple of years. God knows there was a lot of damage to undo."

"Why did he run away from Kay and his stepfather? How did you find him?" Cassie asked, sensing he needed to finish his story.

"He'd warned his mother that if she continued to contest me for custody, he'd run away. She didn't believe him—and I thought I'd convinced him to give it up, that I wasn't going to stop fighting for him until I won. But the last time my petition was turned down, Shane lived up to his threats and took off looking for me. Kay didn't tell him I'd just been shipped out for a six-month tour. And she didn't notify me for almost a month that Shane was gone."

"A month!" Cassie gasped. "She let that boy live on the streets for a month before she contacted you?"

"She knew how furious I'd be, how bad it would look for her," Jared confirmed in disgust. "She notified the authorities after about a week, but they were getting nowhere looking for him. Soon as I found out, I arranged for emergency leave and went looking for him.

"It took me almost six weeks to find him after I got back in the States. He'd been living in alleyways and bus stations in Memphis, which was the last place I'd been stationed before shipping out. He would run whenever anyone tried to question him or whenever anyone looked dangerous to him. He spent a couple of dollars a day on food, then swept sidewalks and ran errands in exchange for food when the money he'd taken with him ran out. He's bragged that he never begged for money, never stole anything during that time."

"Oh, God, Jared. A twelve-year-old boy on the streets of Memphis! He could have been—"

She bit the words off abruptly, knowing they'd only make him feel worse. But the images that flashed through her mind were horrifying. She couldn't even imagine how Jared must have felt during those long, desperate weeks, how many sickening possibilities he must have envisioned during his search.

"Yeah." The one grim word spoke volumes. "I'd always loved my son, but it took that to make me realize exactly how much he meant to me. How blind and self-absorbed I'd been before. I was so glad to find him alive and in one piece that I couldn't let go of him for days. Took me two weeks to get around to yelling at him for running off. He sat there grinning while I chewed him out for a good three hours. When I finished, he just said, 'I knew you'd find me, Dad.' I didn't know whether to hug him or take a strap to him."

. "You hugged him." Cassie spoke with confidence.

"Yeah. I hugged him. And told him if he ever did anything like that again, I was damned well going to use the strap."

"Kay stopped fighting for custody after that?"

"I didn't give her a hell of a lot of choice. I was granted an honorable discharge from the service to take care of my son, and Kay signed over all claim to him."

Cassie curled her lip. "She's a fool. How anyone could choose a bottle over her own son—especially a wonderful boy like Shane—is beyond my comprehension."

"She's a sick woman, Cassie. She had a rough time of it growing up—an abusive father, a victimized mother. It doesn't excuse her, of course, but—"

"No, it doesn't excuse her," Cassie broke in flatly. "She's an adult now, responsible for her own actions. You didn't have an ideal childhood, either, but you turned out just fine."

Jared's rough laugh held little humor. "Yeah, well, there are plenty of people who'd disagree with you. I'm thirty-five years old, I've got no job and no permanent home. I'm just out of jail and my son's in the hospital—not exactly a fine, upstanding citizen, am I?"

"If you're waiting for me to agree with you, you're wasting your time."

Jared turned his head toward her, his expression tightening at whatever he saw in the faint light. "Don't look at me like that, Cassie."

"Like what?" she whispered, though she thought she knew.

"Like you're seeing something in me that's not there."

She shook her head. "I don't think I'm doing that."

"Dammit, Cassie. I don't want to hurt you."

"Then, don't." She touched a tender fingertip to the corner of his tautly drawn mouth, wanting to ease his mind so he could sleep. She thought she knew just how to do that.

"I don't know if I can help it," he argued. "You expect too much from me."

"I'm not expecting anything more than you're willing or able to give, Jared." She leaned over him, brushing a strand of hair away from the bandage at his temple. "Does your head hurt?"

He frowned. "Not much. Cassie—"

She lowered her head to press a kiss against the bruised skin just below the bandage. Her breasts brushed his chest, the thin cotton of her nightgown the only thing separating them. "Is there anything I can get for you?"

He gripped her forearms, holding her a little away from him. "If you don't stop that you're going to start something you're too tired to want right now," he warned roughly.

She bent her leg upward, over his thighs, her knee coming into gentle contact with his groin. She hid a smile as she dropped another kiss on his bruised jaw. Jared was tired, as she was. But, like her, he wasn't *too* tired.

She rubbed her smooth leg very slowly against his rougher one.

Jared groaned, his fingers tightening on her arms. "Cassie. Go to sleep."

"I will," she murmured, her lips moving against his throat. "Soon." And then she slid a hand down his chest and beneath the sheet that covered them from the waist down.

Jared released her arm to bury his right hand in her hair, cupping the back of her head when she lowered her mouth to one flat brown nipple. She touched her tongue to the hard point, her nose tickled by his chest hairs. She curled her fingers around him, loving the hot, pulsing strength of him.

Jared bit off what sounded suspiciously like a curse, and then moved with stunning speed to flip her onto her back beneath him, his hands going to the hem of her nightgown. "Just don't say I didn't give you a choice," he muttered, sweeping the fabric out of their way.

She smiled and curled her arms around his neck, lifting to welcome him into her body. Jared had shared so much with her tonight. This was something she could share with him, something he needed as badly as she did.

By the time they fell asleep, still wrapped in each other's arms, their bodies heavy with satisfaction, damp and warm from their lovemaking, the problems and questions that awaited them seemed very far away.

Cassie woke several hours later when Jared climbed out of bed. She stretched, aware that full sunlight was streaming through the windows this time. "Good morning."

Jared's smile didn't quite touch his eyes. "Morning. Mind if I take the first shower?"

"Go ahead. I'll make some coffee. I'm sure you'd like to get back to the hospital soon."

"Yeah." He went into the bathroom and closed the door behind him.

Cassie groaned in wry exasperation. She really was going to have to talk to Jared about his morning manners. Did the man never smile before noon?

Or was he only like this on mornings after he'd revealed too much of himself during the night?

Wrapping herself in her robe, she muttered beneath her breath as she headed for the kitchen to put the coffee on. That done, she came to a sudden decision. If she was ever going to teach Jared to love her, she was going to have to start with a course in morning etiquette. And now was as good a time to start as any.

Build all the walls you want, Jared Walker. I'm not going to stop trying to get in until you convince me without doubt that you're happier in there all alone.

Jared looked startled when Cassie stepped nude into the shower with him. "What are you doing?"

"I thought we'd save some time and shower together," she replied, taking a bar of soap from the soap dish. "Want me to do your back?"

His eyes narrowed. "Cassie—"

"I was just wondering," she continued blithely, rubbing the soap between her hands. "Do you *ever* smile in the morning?"

"Never before my coffee." Though the words sounded gravely teasing, he continued to watch her warily, as though he wasn't quite sure what to expect from her next.

She slid her soapy hands very slowly from his chest to the tops of his thighs, missing very little along the way. "Then I guess I'll just have to give you a better reason to smile than caffeine, won't I?"

He drew her toward him, a familiar spark lighting his dark blue eyes. "You're a dangerous woman, Cassie Browning."

She smiled and went up on tiptoe. "So I've been told," she murmured against his mouth.

A moment later she found her back pressed against the tiles, her thighs draped over Jared's as he crowded closer. And, as her eyelids grew deliciously heavy, she noted in smug satisfaction that Jared was smiling just before his mouth covered hers.

Shane was awake when Cassie and Jared entered his hospital room an hour and a half after their rather extended shower. He looked up with a smile when they came in. "Hi. They took the IV out."

"You must be feeling better," Jared remarked, noting that his son's eyes were brighter and that he had significantly more color in his face than he had had the night before. Relief coursed through him as he realized that Shane really was going to be all right.

"Yeah. I'm ready to get out of here. You wouldn't believe what they expected me to eat for breakfast."

Cassie laughed and kissed Shane's cheek with an easy affection that Jared watched intently. She really was fond of his son, he thought, warmed by the knowledge even as he worried that both Shane and Cassie would end up hurt.

"I'll bet you ate every bite of whatever they brought you," Cassie accused.

Shane grinned. "Yeah. I did. But it tasted like—"

"Watch the language," Jared interrupted when Shane gave him a teasing look.

"Just get me out of here, okay, Dad? I want to see Cassie's place."

"It's not much to look at," Jared replied, sitting on the edge of the bed and avoiding Cassie's eyes. "Real dump. Broken-down furniture, bullet holes in the walls. Things that move around in the night."

Shane laughed. "Yeah, right. You going to take that without a fight, Cassie?"

"I was just going to tell your father that I hope he finds a warm place to sleep tonight. You and I will get along just fine in my 'dump.'"

"That's assuming the doctor says it's okay for Shane to leave the hospital today," Jared warned, ignoring Cassie's threat. "I haven't talked to anyone yet."

"They'll let me," Shane said confidently. "I've just got a bump on the head and a broken arm. Skinny Mahoney didn't spend the night in the hospital when he got both legs busted by that bull, remember, Dad?''

"Skinny Mahoney got tossed out on his ear for making an obnoxious pass at the nurse who was trying to take his blood pressure,'' Jared reminded him with the beginnings of a smile.

"Yeah. He's an obnoxious kind of guy. But he didn't have to stay in the hospital just to let his bones heal up,'' Shane persisted.

"We'll see,'' Jared said, not wanting to raise false hopes, though he privately agreed that Shane would recuperate just as quickly at Cassie's place. He wasn't all that sure he should continue to impose on her that way, nor let either her or Shane get too accustomed to being together that much. Or would having Shane and Jared as full-time houseguests for a while make Cassie see that she had been better off before she met them?

And why was he feeling just a little resentful that Shane seemed every bit as pleased to see Cassie this morning as he had his father?

"You going to sign my cast, Cassie?'' Shane demanded, looking with some pride at the pristine white plaster. "I'll let you be first, then there's a couple of nurses I'm going to ask.''

"You mean you've already been flirting with the nurses?'' Cassie demanded in mock surprise. "You haven't even been here twelve hours yet!''

"They said I'm obviously a fast healer,'' Shane bragged. "I didn't even need a pain pill this morning. I mean, I'm kinda sore all over, but it's not all that bad.''

"Just don't get cocky and overdo it, son,'' Jared warned. "You were pretty banged up in that wreck. There's no reason to rush your recovery, you hear?''

"Yeah, I know." But Shane looked anything but patient. "What about the insurance, Dad? Have you contacted anyone yet?"

"I made some calls from Cassie's place before we left," Jared replied, amused that his son had already thought of the practicalities. "Fortunately, the guy who hit us was well insured, so we'll be covered for everything."

"What *about* the guy who hit us?" Shane asked suddenly. "What happened? How's he doing?"

Jared cleared his throat, aware that Cassie was watching him to see how he'd handle this question. "The guy was drunk, Shane," he said evenly, deciding to handle this as he did all Shane's questions—with total honesty. "He's dead, son."

Shane paled a bit, but didn't look surprised. "I thought he must be. No one would say for sure..I'm really sorry for the guy, you know, Dad?"

Jared nodded, his throat tight. This, too, was typical of his son. Shane held no grudge against the driver who'd come so close to taking his life with his drunken irresponsibility.

It humbled Jared to realize that his boy was a better man than he was.

There was a light tap on the door and Michelle looked in, smiling when her eyes met Jared's. "Hi. Are visitors allowed?"

He stood. "Come on in."

Shane stared at the woman who approached his bed, then looked wide-eyed at his father. "Wow, Dad. She looks just like us! Only prettier."

Jared almost flinched at the observation, feeling the ties of family drawing more tightly around him. "Shane, this is your aunt, Michelle D'Alessandro."

"Hello, Shane. And thank you for the compliment." Michelle smiled sweetly, and just a touch shyly, at her nephew. "It's very nice to meet you."

"It's nice to meet you, too," Shane answered politely, still studying her carefully. "Are you the one with the three kids?"

She laughed and shook her head. "That's your other aunt, Layla. I've only been married a few months."

"So you're the one who's married to Cassie's boss."

Michelle gave Cassie a quick smile. "Yes, that's right."

Shane looked suddenly serious. "I think he should give her a promotion or something for everything she's done for me and my dad. She deserves it."

"Shane..." Cassie murmured, cheeks flaming.

"Shane..." Jared growled in admonition, not wanting Shane to embarrass Cassie further, though Jared had said much the same thing to Tony only the night before. Shane had been on his best behavior for the past few days, but had been known to let his mouth get ahead of his brain at times.

"Well, she does!" Shane insisted.

Michelle didn't seem to be offended. "My husband and I are both very grateful to Cassie for everything she's done," she said.

"She didn't just do it 'cause it was her job," Shane added. "She really likes us, don't you, Cassie? In fact, she and Dad are—"

"Why don't you tell us about Layla's kids, Michelle," Jared broke in ruthlessly, giving his son a frown of warning. "Shane's been curious about his cousins."

Though Michelle's eyes danced with laughter as she looked from her brother to Cassie, she nodded and described Layla's lively children, Dawne, Keith and Brittany, who ranged in age from eight to two.

"Maybe when you find them, some of your other brothers and sisters will have kids my age," Shane suggested rather hopefully.

"Maybe they will," Michelle replied, looking as though she fully understood Shane's desire for the companionship of others his age. "But, in the meantime, my husband has dozens of young cousins your age, and they're a very close family. Maybe someday you can join us at one of their big gatherings for barbecue and a softball game."

"That sounds great," Shane approved. "I like playing softball."

"Then you should fit right in. They're fanatics about the game."

Jared wasn't sure how he felt about Michelle making plans for Shane to be included in her husband's family gatherings. He and Shane had been on their own for so long. Surely he wasn't feeling threatened by this new family who might become important to the boy?

He wasn't proud that so far this morning he'd been jealous of Cassie and now Michelle. It wasn't like him at all.

How the hell had he gotten himself into this situation, anyway?

Cassie was pleased with the remarkable progress Shane was making, though he was already beginning to wilt a bit. She could tell he needed to rest.

Sensing that Jared would want to stay with his son most of the day, she came to a decision. "I think I'll go to the office for an hour or so, if you don't need me for anything," she said. "I really should catch up with Tony about what's been going on while I was out of town."

Jared nodded. "Don't let us keep you from your work."

"I'll see you later this afternoon." She turned to Shane, laying a hand on his shoulder. "I'll sign your cast when I get back. In the meantime, you keep your other hand off the nurses, you hear?''

Shane chuckled, shifting his head restlessly on the pillow in a way that made Cassie suspect sympathetically that his injuries were hurting more than he was willing to admit. ''I'm not making any promises,'' he murmured. ''There's one redhead with these incredibly big—''

Cassie giggled and covered his mouth with her hand. ''You're terrible, Shane Walker!''

''I was only going to say she has incredibly big syringes,'' Shane said with exaggerated innocence. ''Why, Cassie, what did you think I was going to say?''

''Somebody beat this kid while I'm gone, will you?'' Cassie asked no one in particular. And then she leaned over to give him a quick, careful hug. ''See you in a little while, Shane.''

''Don't be long,'' he replied wistfully, suddenly looking young and uncomfortable again.

''I won't.'' Cassie glanced at Jared, all too conscious of the eyes on them. ''Call the office if you need me, okay?''

He nodded. ''We'll be fine,'' he assured her, his expression carefully shuttered.

Had Michelle not been in the room, Cassie would have planted a kiss on his mouth just to shake that cool composure of his. Instead, she merely nodded and left, knowing she left an important part of herself behind in that small hospital room.

Cassie walked into the tastefully decorated reception area of D'Alessandro Investigations, smiling at the attractive black woman behind the desk. ''Hi, Bonnie. Is Tony in?''

Bonnie returned the smile. ''Cassie! Good to have you back. I hear you had all kinds of excitement while you were gone.''

"Too much excitement," Cassie agreed, wrinkling her nose.

"For a P.I.? There's no such thing. Tony's in his office. Go on in."

"Thanks." Uncharacteristically nervous, Cassie cleared her throat, took a deep breath, and smoothed her hands down the black pleated slacks she wore with a teal-and-black printed shirt.

Bonnie watched her in open curiosity. "Something wrong, Cassie?"

"No. Why?"

"Well, you look—I don't know, like you're going in to have a meeting with the boss or something."

"I *am* going in to see the boss," Cassie reminded her.

"True. But you've never really treated him like a boss before. You're not in trouble or anything, are you?"

Cassie managed a shaky smile. "I'll let you know."

She tapped twice on Tony's office door, waiting until she heard him give permission to enter before turning the knob.

"Come on in, Cassie," he said when he saw her in the doorway. "Close the door behind you," he added.

She swallowed and did so. "I saw Michelle this morning," she said, just to make innocuous conversation. "She was at the hospital, visiting Shane.

Tony waved her to the chair across his desk and leaned back in his seat. "How's the boy this morning?"

"He's doing amazingly well. He was talking and smiling and determined to be released from the hospital today."

"Think he will be?"

"I don't know. Jared hadn't talked to the doctor yet when I left."

Tony looked at the pencil he twisted between his fingers. "Where do you suppose they'll stay tonight?"

Cassie cleared her throat again. "I suppose they'll stay with me."

Tony's left eyebrow rose. "Is that right?"

Her nervousness vanished in a surge of impatience. "All right, let's get it out in the open," she said, leaning forward and planting her hands on her knees as she met her employer's dark eyes. "I got personally involved with this one. I went with a hunch that Jared hadn't done anything wrong and did everything I could to get him out of jail. I was even going to bail him out with my own money if he hadn't been released when he was.

"I adored Shane from the moment I met him, and bought him dinner and got him a room rather than calling the juvenile authorities to report that he was on his own. I followed them to Arizona and kept after Jared until he agreed to change his decision about coming back with me to Dallas—and I wasn't just trying to get him to visit his sister," she finished defiantly.

Though he wasn't smiling, Tony's eyes glinted with amusement by the time she finished. "Is there any rule you didn't break, Cassie?"

"I didn't break any laws, that I know of," she replied carefully, beginning to relax just a bit.

"There's no law against falling in love," Tony commented, setting down the pencil. "And I'd be a real jerk to yell at you for it when I did exactly the same thing, wouldn't I?"

Cassie shifted in her chair. "I never said I was in love with Jared."

"You didn't have to. I recognize the symptoms."

Cassie pushed her hair back with both hands. "Have I been incredibly stupid, Tony?"

He shrugged sympathetically. "There were times when I wondered if I'd ever get past Michelle's lifelong reserve and teach her to trust me. Particularly when her attorney produced evidence to make it look like I was only after her money. We worked our problems out successfully, but Jared's older and harder and he's been kicked around a lot. His defenses have to be firmly in place."

"Except when it comes to Shane, they are," Cassie agreed. "There are times when he almost lets me in—and then he slams a door in my face. It's so frustrating."

"You haven't known him very long. Give it time."

"I just hope I have the time. For all I know, he could take off tomorrow, or next week. I think being faced with family again is making him uncomfortable."

"That's just something he'll have to work out. He *does* have a family, and they care about him, whether he wants them to or not. It's up to him whether he's going to become a part of them or risk losing them again. We knew there were no guarantees when we set out looking for him."

"No guarantees," Cassie repeated. "I knew that. I just didn't know at the time how very much it would come to matter."

"Cassie, if you need to talk, I'm here. I just want you to know that I hope you and Jared work this thing out. I won't get in your way—as your boss or his brother-in-law. Fair enough?"

"More than fair." She smiled shakily at him. "Thanks, Tony. You're a good friend as well as a terrific boss."

"Just call me a sucker for love. Now, I know you'll want to get back to the hospital in a while, but how about giving me a hand with some paperwork for an hour or so? I could really use some help around here."

"Of course. And I promise I'll be back full-time tomorrow. By the way, how are Chuck's teeth?"

Tony grimaced. "Firmly back in place. I had a long talk with him about protecting his face when he takes a punch.

He could use some lessons from you on hand-to-hand combat."

Cassie laughed. "Remind me to tell you sometime about the brawl Jared and I got into at a little bar in New Mexico."

Tony groaned and shook his head. "I don't think I want to hear about it."

"Don't worry, boss," she quipped impudently. "I was on my own time. Now, where's that paperwork?"

Cassie had been working for an hour when she finally gave in to an ever-growing urge to place a telephone call. Maybe the need had developed when she'd witnessed Jared's sweet, but rather awkward reunion with his sister, watched as they'd struggled to establish a bond despite the years that had separated them. Knowing Tony wouldn't mind if she took a short break, she punched a series of digits on the telephone dial, charging the long-distance call to her personal calling card.

It was only a moment later when a familiar deep voice answered the low buzz on the other end of the line, so very far away. "Browning Air Freight. What can I do for you?"

"Cliff? Hi, it's Cassie. I'm glad you're in."

"Cassie?" Her brother seemed surprised to hear from her. "Hey, kid, what's wrong? Has something happened at home?"

Cassie bit her lip in a rush of guilt. Had she called her brother so infrequently that he automatically assumed something must be wrong for her to be calling now?

"No, Cliff, nothing's wrong," she assured him hastily. "I just wanted to talk to you for a minute. Are you busy?"

"Of course not. So how have you been, Cass? How's the P.I. racket?"

"Interesting," she answered with a smile, twirling the telephone cord around her finger. "My latest case involves reuniting a family of siblings who've been separated twenty-four years. I guess that's why I suddenly needed to talk to you. I don't want us to end up like that, Cliff."

There was a thoughtful pause from the other end. "I don't want that, either, sis," Cliff said at length, his voice uncharacteristically serious. "Guess we haven't stayed in touch lately, have we?"

"No. But I'd like to try to change that. It's true that we don't get to see each other very often because we live so far apart, but that doesn't mean I don't love you, Cliff."

"I love you, too, Cass. And I'm really glad you called."

She smiled. "Me, too. So, how are you? Is the business going well?"

"Yeah, great. Some months I even come out in the black."

"Good for you. How's your love life?"

Cliff laughed. "I'm in the wilds of Alaska, remember? Most interesting female I've seen lately was a long-legged moose."

"I hate to tell you this, Cliffie, but you're starting to sound a little kinky. Maybe you'd better spend a few weeks in civilization soon."

"You may be right. What about you? Any interesting prospects on the dating scene? You ready to make Grandma a happy woman yet and change your single status?"

Cassie thought immediately of Jared, of course. But she didn't have the time—or money—to go into a lengthy explanation during this call. "I'll let you know if it happens."

"Does that mean it's a possibility?" Cliff asked, sounding intrigued.

"You know me. Always on the lookout for possibilities," she teased, skillfully evading specifics.

They talked another few minutes, catching up on family gossip, making plans for a Christmas reunion, and then Cassie said she had to get back to work. "It was really good to talk to you, Cliff."

"Yeah. It was. I've got your number. I promise I'll start using it more often."

"You do that. Take care."

"You, too. 'Bye, Cassie."

Her smile was misty when she hung up, but her mood was much lighter. If she'd learned one thing during the past few days, it was the incomparable value of family. She wouldn't take hers for granted again.

Tonight, she'd call her parents. She was definitely overdue for a long, cozy chat with them.

Jared was watching television with Shane that afternoon when Michelle dropped in for a second visit. This time she wasn't alone. The woman who followed her into the room looked very much like her, with only a smattering of gray in her brown hair. Jared came to his feet.

"Layla?"

"Jared." The word was little more than a whisper. Layla stared at him a moment, then threw herself in his arms. "Oh, Jared."

He caught her to him, dozens of memories flashing through his mind, prominent among them the last time they'd seen each other. They'd held each other then, too. And, as she did now, Layla had cried.

He remembered exactly what he'd told her then. "Didn't I promise we'd see each other again, Sissy?"

She gave a watery chuckle and wiped her eyes with her hand. "I thought I'd never hear you call me that again."

"Looks like you were wrong." He held her away from him. "You haven't changed."

Her cheeks pinkened. "I'm thirty-four years old. Not a little girl anymore."

"No. But still as pretty as you were then."

She touched his cheek. "You used to tell me how pretty I was when you wanted me to do your chores so you could go play with your friends. What is it you're after now, Jared Mitchell?"

He chuckled, trying not to show her how touched he was to see her again. Seeing Michelle had affected him, but he and Layla had shared so much in the brief years they were together. More than any of the others, really. "I hear you're a mother now. Still taking care of the little ones, eh?"

"A habit I couldn't break, I guess. I missed my baby brothers and sisters when they took them away."

"Yeah." His smile faded. "Me, too."

"You never looked for us, Jared?" She sounded wistful.

He swallowed and shook his head. "I meant to. But by the time I was old enough to be out on my own, I decided you were probably all better off without me."

"Looks like you were wrong," she answered quietly, her imitation of him deliberate.

He looked away. "I wasn't sure at first that this was a good idea, Layla. It's been such a damned long time."

"Too long," she agreed. "But you're still my big brother, Jared. And I still love you."

She kissed his cheek, then looked toward the bed before Jared had to come up with a reply. "I want to meet my nephew."

Shane was watching them in fascination, Michelle's hand on his shoulder. He gave Layla a sweet smile. "Hi, Aunt Layla. I'm Shane."

"Oh." Layla approached him slowly, her dark blue eyes—so like the others in the room—devouring his face. "You look just like your father did when I knew him, though of course he was a few years younger. Oh, Shane, it's so nice to meet you."

"Aunt Michelle's been telling me about Dawne and Keith and Brittany. She says Keith's a pistol."

Layla laughed and nodded. "Yes, he is. He'll enjoy meeting his male cousin. My husband only has a couple of nieces."

It occurred to Jared that a lot of plans were being made in this hospital room today. He knew, of course, that Shane would need a few days to recover before they hit the road again. But everyone seemed to be taking for granted that Jared and Shane would be staying in Dallas indefinitely.

The imaginary ropes grew tighter around his chest.

What the hell had he gotten himself into?

Chapter Twelve

After shamelessly begging the doctor to let him go, Shane was released from the hospital late that afternoon. Cassie picked him and Jared up and took them straight to her place, where she pampered Shane so thoroughly that Jared wryly predicted the boy would never want to leave.

Cassie and Shane only smiled at each other. Cassie, for one, would have been quite content for Jared's prediction to come true.

"Would you like some more ice cream, Shane?" she offered. The three of them were sitting in her living room, watching television, and it had been nearly half an hour since his last snack.

"No more snacks," Jared interceded firmly before Shane could answer. "Cassie, he's had enough."

"A glass of milk, then? Or water. Are you thirsty, Shane?"

"I'm fine, Cassie. Really," Shane assured her, then yawned. "Sorry. Guess I'm getting a little tired."

"You should be in bed," Jared said.

Shane frowned. "But, Dad, it's not even ten o'clock yet."

"I know, but you still haven't got all your strength back. Come on, son. I'll give you a hand."

Shane sighed, but conceded, pushing himself out of his chair with his left hand, his right resting in the sling that supported his cast. He limped to the couch where Cassie sat, bent unselfconsciously down to her and gave her a smacking kiss on the cheek. "G'night, Cassie. See you in the morning."

"Good night, Shane. Let me know if you need anything, okay?"

Jared was back in fifteen minutes. He sat beside Cassie on the couch and reached for the lukewarm soft drink he'd been drinking earlier.

"You think he'll be comfortable enough during the night?" Cassie fretted, looking toward the hallway to the guest room. The door was closed, no light coming from beneath it. "He's still so pale and weak-looking."

"He's fine, Cassie. Just needs a few days to take it easy."

"I guess I'm being silly," she conceded with a sheepish smile. "These maternal feelings are all new to me."

Jared stretched one leg out in front of him, studying his boot with apparent concentration as he asked, "You ever think about having kids of your own?"

"Sometimes," she admitted shyly. "I always thought I'd like to have a child before I turn thirty."

The thought of having Jared's child turned her knees to water, though she knew full well he wasn't proposing anything of the sort. He was just curious, most likely.

He gave her a quick glance, his expression still unreadable. "Why haven't you?"

She blinked. "I thought maybe I'd get married first."

"Most women your age are already married."

She couldn't help giggling. "Now you sound like my grandmother. She all but went into mourning on my twenty-fifth birthday. I tried to convince her that lots of women are waiting until after that for marriage and children these days, but she acted like I was already too long on the shelf to ever hope for anything more."

Jared smiled briefly. "How does she feel about what you do for a living?"

"We've told her I'm in computer research. It's close enough to the truth, but it's something she can handle. If she found out I work for a P.I., she'd be convinced I was like those guys on TV—dodging bullets, breaking into secured buildings, sleeping with...er..." Her voice trailed off as she realized what she'd almost said.

"Sleeping with the clients?" Jared finished for her.

"Well—you're not a client, are you? Besides, I was just describing what my grandmother probably thinks a P.I.'s life is like."

Jared grunted something unintelligible and stared for a few minutes at the television, where a moussed-and-powdered news anchor was trying to look earnest and intelligent as he read the day's top headlines.

When Jared spoke again, he'd made an abrupt change of subject. "Michelle wants us to have dinner at her house later this week, when Shane's feeling more like getting out. Layla and her family will be there, too."

Cassie tried to look pleased that Jared and Shane would be spending an evening with their family. "You're welcome to borrow my car to get there. Or have you made arrangements with the insurance company for a rental?"

Jared lifted an eyebrow in her direction. "Why would I want to borrow your car? You'll be going with us, won't you?"

"Oh, I—" She twisted her hands in her lap. "Are you sure I'm invited? This sounds to me like a family thing."

"You go, or I don't." Jared spoke with blunt finality.

"But, Jared, you came to Dallas to see your sisters."

"No." He set his glass on a coaster and turned purposefully to face her. "We talked about this before. I came to Dallas because you're here. Dammit, I'm not staying here because of the free lodging, Cassie. You're the woman I'm involved with right now, not my landlady. You have every right to be with me when we join the others."

You're the woman I'm involved with right now. As a declaration of deep feeling, the words left something to be desired. But, from Jared, they were almost a commitment—temporarily, at least, she reminded herself before she could begin to hope for more.

"I'd love to go with you if you want me to, Jared."

He nodded in curt satisfaction. "I want you there."

"Then I'll go."

He nodded again, then changed the subject once more. "Shane and I are both out of clean clothes. Is there a Laundromat around here somewhere?"

"There's one here in the apartment complex," she said. "The small building to the left of the tennis courts."

"Then I'll do some washing in the morning while you're at work. You need me to throw in a couple of loads for you while I'm at it?"

She stared at him in astonishment. "You're offering to do laundry for me?"

He chuckled at the look on her face. "You don't have to look so stunned."

She shook her head and smiled. "For some reason, I find it hard to picture you measuring washing powder and fabric softener."

"You think I buy new clothes once a week? Who do you think's been doing our laundry for the past two years?"

"I hadn't really thought about it. Do you cook, too?" she asked, teasingly.

"I make one hell of a spaghetti sauce. And chili that will curl your eyelashes. Shane's specialty is chicken casserole. He found the recipe in a cookbook."

"Shane cooks, too?"

"We both get tired of eating out sometimes."

Cassie smothered her smile and leaned forward with a mock-grave expression, laying her hand on Jared's knee. "Feel free to stay here as long as you like."

He grinned and pulled her into his arms. "I don't do windows."

"That's okay," she assured him, winding her arms around his neck. "I'm sure you have other talents."

"Several. Want me to demonstrate a few tonight?"

"I would love that." She brought her mouth to his before she could give in to the temptation to tell him that she loved him more with each day she spent with him.

The next three days were among the happiest—and the most insecure—of Cassie's life.

She left each morning for work after having breakfast with Jared and Shane and returned each evening to find the housework done and dinner on the table. They spent the evenings playing board games, watching television, laughing and teasing. And then Shane went to bed, and Cassie and Jared were alone, to talk quietly for a while and then to turn to each other with a hunger that seemed to grow deeper each time they made love.

Shane was rapidly recovering his strength, making Cassie and Jared marvel at the amazing resiliency of youth. He seemed happy with the way things were going, settling comfortably into Cassie's guest room, already scattering enough of his belongings around him to make the room his. When she learned that Shane enjoyed reading, Cassie bought him a stack of Western and adventure books, as well as a couple of excellent novels based on true events in American history. She was beginning to fret about him being out of school for so long.

Shane had even made some friends. While helping his father with the laundry, he'd met the fifteen-year-old twin brother and sister who lived with their mother in the apartment directly across the compound from Cassie's. The three had hit it off immediately, Heather and Scott—the twins—apparently impressed by Shane's slightly battered appearance and experience-based maturity.

Shane spent a couple of hours with them each afternoon when they returned from school, and already he was regaining his color and energy just from the time spent outdoors in the warm autumn weather, to Cassie's delight.

Despite the advice of an attorney Tony recommended, Jared refused to sue the estate of the driver who'd caused the accident, not wanting to cause more grief to the man's widow and three children. He said the settlement offered by the other driver's insurance company—enough to cover all medical expenses and provide him with a new pickup to replace the totalled one—was perfectly adequate, that neither he nor Shane would seek a large profit from the tragedy. Cassie told Tony that the decision served as a perfect illustration of Jared's pride and self-sufficiency.

"So is the guy going to stay in Dallas, or what?" Tony asked as Cassie was preparing to leave the office Friday afternoon.

She sighed. "I wish I knew. He hasn't said a word about his plans. Every time Shane hints that he likes it here and wouldn't mind enrolling in a Dallas school, Jared changes the subject."

She didn't add that Jared's expression always turned shuttered when that particular subject came up, so that she couldn't even begin to guess at his feelings. If he was feeling restless or trapped or even content to be staying with Cassie while Shane recovered, he was doing an excellent job of hiding those emotions.

He was a pleasant, cooperative, considerate houseguest. At night, he was the most giving, passionate lover Cassie had ever even fantasized, but he'd given her no reason to believe he was thinking of making their arrangement permanent.

As careful as she'd been not to push him, not to allow herself to hope for more than he might be willing to give, the uncertainty was driving her crazy. It was so hard not to make plans, not to say things that might sound like she was arranging a future for them. It wasn't in her nature to keep her own wishes hidden for long. Yet she was terrified of doing or saying something that would scare him off.

"I just don't know what he wants," she said with a sigh.

Tony frowned. "It's really not fair of the guy to keep you in limbo like this."

She couldn't help coming to Jared's defense. "He's never made any promises, Tony. Nor have I asked for any. I simply offered him a place to stay while Shane recuperated, and he accepted."

"Something tells me you're giving him a hell of a lot more than a place to stay."

Cassie flushed. "Really, Tony."

"Yeah, I know. None of my business. I just don't want to see you get hurt, Cassie."

"Neither do I," she admitted, pushing a strand of hair out of her face. "But I still can't help hoping..."

It wasn't necessary for her to finish the sentence.

Tony's scowl deepened, but he kept his opinions to himself. "Michelle's looking forward to having everyone for dinner tonight."

"Shane's been talking about it all week. I promised to hurry home so we won't be late."

"Maybe Jared will tell us his plans sometime during the evening."

"Just don't push him, okay, Tony?" Cassie asked carefully. "I don't want to make him feel cornered."

Tony muttered something beneath his breath, then sighed and promised Cassie he'd try not to say anything that would embarrass her in front of Jared. "It's just that I can't help feeling a bit big-brotherly with you," he added.

She smiled and reached up to kiss his cheek, the first time she'd dared such a familiarity with her boss. "Thanks for caring, Tony. See you tonight."

Cassie took great pains with her appearance for the evening, selecting a deep emerald dress that had always been one of her favorites and taming her curls into a more sophisticated style than the casual brushing she usually gave them. She even wore a touch of eyeliner, something she rarely bothered with when she applied her usual light makeup.

Shane whistled when Cassie joined him and Jared in the living room. "Wow, Cassie. You really do have legs, don't you?"

Cassie realized it was the first time he'd seen her in a dress. She tended to wear jeans and sweaters at home, slacks and blazers for work. She ruffled Shane's hair. "Of course I have legs."

"Very nice ones, at that," Jared added, giving Cassie a smile that made her breath catch in her throat.

"Thank you," she managed to reply.

Shane grinned.

Both Jared and Shane wore slacks and oxford-cloth shirts. They'd been to the doctor that day, and Jared's stitches had been removed, leaving only a thin red scar at his temple. Cassie assured them they looked very handsome, though she knew she was understating. Even with their scars and fading bruises, Jared and Shane were a strikingly attractive pair. Any woman would be proud to be seen with them, she thought with a wistful longing.

"Now that we've all admired each other, I guess we'd better go," Jared announced, his smile fading.

Cassie looked up at him in question. "You don't sound like you're looking forward to the evening."

He shrugged. "Family dinners aren't really my thing."

"How would you know, Dad?" Shane asked logically. "We've never really been to any."

Jared didn't acknowledge that the boy had made a point.

Both Jared and Shane were startled when Cassie drove her car through the gates of what could only be called a Tudor mansion half an hour later.

"What's this place?" Shane asked from the back seat, craning his neck to stare at the massive stone fence surrounding them.

"This is where Michelle and Tony live," Cassie explained, bringing the car to a stop in the circular driveway. A flight of stairs led from the driveway to massive double doors at the entryway of the house, which looked to Jared to be at least fifteen thousand square feet.

He hadn't been prepared for the elegance of his sister's home.

Jared climbed out of the car and glanced around the beautifully lighted and landscaped grounds. "You didn't tell me your boss came from this kind of money," he muttered when Cassie stood beside him.

"He doesn't. This is the home where Michelle grew up. The Trent family home. It's been hers since her parents died."

Jared looked down at her with narrowed eyes. "Michelle's adoptive parents were wealthy?"

"I told you they were quite comfortable," Cassie reminded him.

"You didn't say they were filthy rich," he answered bluntly.

"Not filthy, maybe, but definitely rich," Cassie confirmed. "Trent Enterprises is one of the largest corporations in the area. They're into everything."

"Damn." Jared shoved his hand through his hair, wishing he were anywhere but here. He'd have avoided a hell of a lot of trouble if he'd just gone on to Flagstaff last week instead of following Cassie to Dallas, he thought grimly. He supposed he was paying the price for thinking with his gonads instead of his brains again.

He hadn't seen his sisters since Shane was released from the hospital on Monday, though they'd both called Cassie's place every day to check on the boy. He had begun to feel comfortable with them, but now he was tense again, a touch defensive. What the hell were they expecting from him?

He sensed something was wrong the moment Michelle's housekeeper led them into the enormous wood-panelled den where his family awaited them. Both Michelle and Layla welcomed Jared with strained smiles and troubled eyes.

What had upset them? he wondered, frowning as he studied the other occupants of the room. He recognized Tony, of course. A rounded, pleasant-faced man of his own age was introduced as Layla's husband, Kevin Samples. Jared shook the man's hand, liking the guy right off. He'd already been told Kevin was an accountant. He could tell now that the man was quiet, unassuming, and absolutely adored his wife and three kids.

Layla's children were brought forward next to be introduced. Jared couldn't help smiling when he saw them— eight-year-old Dawne, five-year-old Keith and two-year-old Brittany. They reminded him so much of himself and his own brothers and sisters at the same age.

He gave Layla a smile of approval, noting in amusement that Shane seemed particularly fascinated with the children, who looked at their wounded older cousin with wide-eyed awe.

And then Michelle turned toward an older man standing to one side of the room, and Jared knew that he'd found the source of the tension humming beneath the polite pleasantries.

"Jared, Shane, Cassie, I'd like you to meet my uncle, Richard Trent, who lives in California. Uncle Richard popped in unexpectedly to visit me this afternoon, and I asked him to join us for dinner so he could meet everyone," Michelle explained.

Richard Trent, a tall, distinguished-looking man in his late fifties to early sixties, nodded at Cassie and Shane, then turned to Jared. The suspicion in the older man's eyes had Jared going on the defensive before Trent even spoke. "I understand you've had a run of bad luck since you came to town."

Jared nodded. "A car accident. As you can see, my son was injured, but we were lucky, on the whole."

"Where do you and your son live, Walker?"

Jared crossed his arms, trying to look relaxed. "We spent the past year in Oklahoma, but we're in the process of relocating."

"Oh? To where?"

"We haven't decided," Jared answered smoothly.

Trent lifted an eyebrow. "Just what is it you do?"

Though he would have thoroughly enjoyed telling the man it was none of his business, Jared forced himself to be polite, for his sister's sake. "Ranch work, mostly."

As though sensing the antagonism between Jared and the older man, Shane spoke up quickly. "Dad and me are going to own a ranch someday. Quarter horses and polled Herefords. We're saving up for a down payment."

Jared gave his son a repressive frown. He'd taught the boy not to discuss their business with strangers. This was a hell of a time for Shane to forget that.

"I didn't know you were interested in owning a ranch, Jared," Layla said, her voice just a bit too bright. "But it doesn't surprise me. Even when you were a little boy, you loved horses and cowboy movies."

"I like cowboy movies, too," little Keith piped in, tugging at Shane's leg as he spoke. "Like *Fievel Goes West*. You ever see that one, Shane?"

The adults laughed—all of them except Jared and Richard Trent.

"So, just how were you planning to finance your ranch, Walker?" Trent murmured, glancing meaningfully at the luxury surrounding them. "Bank loan? Or did you have some other scheme in mind?"

Michelle gasped. "Uncle Richard! That's really none of our business."

Trent feigned surprise that she'd be annoyed with him. "I'm a businessman, Michelle. I'm sure your brother understands that businessmen are always interested in hearing the plans of aspiring entrepreneurs."

"Oh, I understand," Jared replied, his narrowed eyes locked with Trent's speculative ones. "I understand completely."

Layla slipped to Jared's side, placing a hand on his arm as though to offer support—or perhaps to hold him back.

"So that's how you've built up these muscles," she said, still a bit too cheerily. "All that hard ranch work. I see you're still living up to your line of the poem, Jared."

He looked at her in question. "What poem?"

"Surely you haven't forgotten," Layla chided. Michelle smiled, obviously understanding the reference. "Don't you remember that all seven of us were born on different days of the week? You were Saturday's child. And Saturday's child has to work for a living."

Jared remembered now. Their mother had been particularly taken with that little poem, quoting it to them often. A wave of sadness went through him as he pictured her, thin and tired, rocking the baby and reciting the verses. He suppressed it immediately, deciding he'd blocked the memory because it had been easier to do that than to live with the old pain.

"What about you, Aunt Layla?" Shane urged, visibly intrigued by this glimpse into his father's childhood. "What day were you born?"

"Monday's child," Jared murmured, still lost in the past. He gave Layla a slight smile. " 'Monday's child is fair of face.' "

Layla flushed in pleasure. "You *do* remember."

"Yeah." His smile faded. "I remember."

Shane frowned suddenly. "I thought two of the brothers were twins."

Layla tore her understanding gaze from Jared's. "Strangely enough, Joey was born just before midnight on Thursday, and Bobby just after midnight Friday morning. They have different birthdays."

"Cool!" Shane responded and laughed.

Richard Trent glanced at his watch, quite obviously bored by the reminiscences of a family in which he had no part. "Do you suppose your housekeeper is ready to serve dinner, Michelle?"

Michelle's smile faded. "I'm sure she is. Shall we go into the dining room now?"

As the others left the den, Tony detained Jared with a hand on his arm.

"Try not to let Trent get to you," he muttered. "He thought I was after Michelle for her money, too. He's definitely the suspicious type, but he and his wife and son are the only members left of Michelle's adopted family. It's hard for her to sever all ties to them."

"Yeah," Jared growled. "For her sake, I'll try to ignore him. But what I'd really like to do is knock that smug smile right off his face."

Tony chuckled. "Believe me, I know the feeling. If he weren't Michelle's uncle, I probably would have already tried a time or two."

Feeling rather friendly toward his brother-in-law at the moment, Jared nodded and walked with him into the dining room, his scowl returning when he saw the crystal chandeliers and elegant table settings. He noted that Michelle seemed perfectly comfortable that Layla's three children scrambled into chairs at the long table, apparently as welcome there as the adults, despite the quelling looks Richard Trent gave them.

Thanks to the children, conversation was quite lively while Betty served the meal. Sitting between Shane and

Jared, Cassie joined in easily, obviously doing her part to keep the evening pleasant.

Jared found himself unable to participate, except to answer direct questions. His full attention was centered on Richard Trent, who continued to watch Jared with a mixture of suspicion and disapproval. If this was the way Michelle had been treated as she'd grown up, he thought at one point, it was no wonder that there were old shadows behind the present contentment in her eyes.

"I like your house, Aunt Michelle." Shane said, obviously happy with the evening thus far. "It must have been cool growing up here."

"Thank you, Shane. It was a happy home," Michelle replied. Then she added softly, "Though I would have loved to have had my brothers and sisters with me. It was rather lonely at times, being an only child."

"My brother and his wife did their best to give you everything you wanted while you were growing up, Michelle," Richard chided her.

"Yes, of course, they did," Michelle answered evenly. "But, like most children, I longed for playmates."

"I'm sure you had your friends," Richard argued. "Your parents hardly kept you a prisoner here. Though they were, of course, careful to screen the people you associated with. When one has attained a certain level of wealth and power, it is always prudent to watch out for those who would take advantage of you. After the unfortunate incident in your childhood, I would think you'd understand why Harrison and Alicia were rather overprotective afterward."

Jared noted that Michelle paled in reference to the "unfortunate incident." He ran his eyes quickly around the table, judging for himself who else understood the reference. Tony looked grim, Cassie annoyed, Layla stricken, Kevin sympathetic. Apparently, Jared was the only adult who *didn't* know.

"What unfortunate incident?" he asked bluntly, sensing that whatever it was would explain a great deal about Michelle's occasional haunted looks.

Silence greeted the question, except for little Brittany's babbling from the booster chair next to her mother. Knowing who'd be most likely to give him a direct answer, Jared looked to Tony. "Well?"

Tony glanced at the children, and Layla distracted them by turning their attention to their dinners. "Michelle was kidnapped when she was eight years old," he said quietly. "Her father hired my dad, who was also a P.I. at the time, to find her. He did, and the kidnapper was arrested without incidence."

Kidnapped. Jared set his fork on his plate, losing interest in his food. He looked at Michelle, thinking she suddenly looked very young and vulnerable. "You weren't harmed?"

"No," she answered. "Only horribly frightened. The incident left me wary of trusting people, but Tony helped me get past that." She gave her husband a loving smile, her uncle a quick frown of reproval, and then smoothly changed the subject, asking Shane about his arm.

Shane, whose mouth had fallen open in shock at the story, reassured her that he wasn't in terrible discomfort, then made everyone laugh with his self-directed humor about the difficulties of eating with his left hand. Jared was proud of the boy for sensing that laughter was desperately needed at the moment.

Laughter was the farthest thing from Jared's mind just then. The thought of his younger sister in the hands of a kidnapper made him want to tear someone apart with his bare hands.

Realizing that his feelings were both protective and possessive, he almost sighed. Despite his attempts to maintain his distance from his sisters, he'd already started to care for them again.

A bond had been formed—or maybe it had always been there, only to be rediscovered with their reunion. No matter how far Jared would travel from them now, he'd always know that his family was here—and he'd want to see them occasionally, to know how they were. Just as he found himself wanting to know what had happened to the twins and the baby.

He picked up his fork again and let the conversation flow around him, too deeply lost in his own thoughts to care any longer about whether Michelle's uncle suspected him of being an opportunist who was only after his wealthy sister's money. Jared had more important things to worry about now.

Like what the hell he was going to do with the rest of his life, now that Cassie and his sisters had come into it. And whether those imaginary bonds were suddenly growing so tight that he would never be able to escape them, even if he wanted to do so.

Chapter Thirteen

Cassie excused herself after dinner, visiting the elegantly appointed guest bathroom to touch up her lipstick and give herself a moment to relax in private. Jared's tension had conveyed itself to her, and she'd already been nervous about spending the evening with his family.

She hadn't socialized much with her employer and his wife before. And then, there was the additional pressure of knowing everyone there was aware that she and Jared had become lovers within days of meeting each other. She'd caught more than one speculative glance during the evening and knew the others were wondering where her relationship with Jared was headed.

She only wished she could have given them an answer.

She didn't mean to eavesdrop on Michelle's parting with Richard Trent. Cassie had just approached the foyer through which she'd have to pass to reach the den when she heard their voices. She paused, uncertain whether she should intrude.

"Are you sure you want to make this choice, Michelle?" she heard Richard Trent asking, his tone so stuffy and censorious that Cassie's lip curled involuntarily.

Michelle's voice was sad when she answered. "You're the one who's making the choice, Uncle Richard, by putting it that way. You're the one who can't accept that I needed to find my brothers and sisters, that the Trent money doesn't mean as much to me as having my family with me."

"You know your aunt and I wanted you to come stay with us in California after your mother passed away," Trent reminded her coolly. "You had a family."

"Please, let's be truthful with each other just this once. You never really accepted me as a Trent, Uncle Richard. To you, I was always the mongrel child your brother adopted. You made the offer for me to come live with you only because of some misguided sense of responsibility to my father, not because you love me."

"So, you've chosen this group of strangers over the only family you've known since you were two years old."

"To be honest, Uncle Richard, you're much more of a stranger to me now than anyone else here tonight. I'm sorry, but that's the way I feel."

"Then I wish you joy with them," he replied icily. "And if you really trust that drifter of a brother of yours, then you have less sense than I'd credited you with."

"Please excuse me, Uncle Richard," Michelle said in a voice that shook with anger. "I have to get back to my family now."

"Goodbye, Michelle."

"Goodbye, Uncle Richard. Please give my best to Aunt Lydia and Steven."

Cassie heard the door close with a final-sounding snap. Richard Trent had obviously said all he'd intended to say. Biting her lip anxiously, she stepped into the foyer, concerned about Michelle, furious about Trent's implications regarding Jared.

Michelle looked up when Cassie approached. Her blue eyes, so like Jared's, were dark with pain and regret.

"I'm sorry," Cassie said quickly. "I didn't mean to eavesdrop, but I couldn't help overhearing part of that. Are you all right?"

Michelle sighed faintly and nodded. "I'm fine. I was never close to him, but . . . well, he was my adoptive father's brother. And I loved my father very much."

"I'm sorry," Cassie repeated.

Michelle tossed her head and forced a smile. "Don't be. I have Layla and her family now and, thanks to you, my brother and my nephew. As well as a husband who loves me almost as much as I adore him. I couldn't possibly ask for more."

Cassie fought down an unbecoming ripple of envy at the obvious love and security Michelle had found with Tony. Would Cassie ever know that contentment with Jared? She knew he'd thoroughly spoiled her for any other man.

Cassie had always suspected that there would be only one great love in her life, and Jared was the one. But did he— *could* he—ever feel the same way about her?

She tried to keep her worry hidden as she accompanied Michelle into the den to rejoin the others.

Cassie could tell that the others were as relieved as she that Richard Trent had departed, taking his suspicions and his disapproval with him. Shane took one long look at Michelle and began to entertain her with a series of silly jokes that soon had his younger cousins squealing with laughter while the adults looked on with indulgent amusement.

Cassie watched Shane with a deep, warm pride, knowing he was exerting himself to make Michelle smile because he'd sensed his aunt's distress over Richard Trent's behavior. Shane was such a loving, caring, perceptive boy, she mused. It would break her heart for him to leave her life almost as much as it would if Jared chose to do so.

She watched Jared closely during the remainder of the evening, noting that he was pleasant and polite, talking easily enough to Tony and Kevin, reminiscing a bit with Layla. Yet in some way Jared held himself apart from the others, almost like an observer rather than a participant in the activities. He'd relaxed some since Trent's departure, but his eyes were guarded, his smile not quite natural.

Cassie knew him well enough to be aware that something was bothering him. Boredom? Restlessness? Defensiveness?

Unfortunately, she didn't know how to interpret his mood—he'd never allowed her to get quite that close to the darker, deepest part of him.

Close—but not close enough. Would she always feel that way with him? Would he ever learn to open up to her—or even want to try?

She knew she couldn't go on much longer in limbo. Soon she would have to ask Jared about his plans, put an end to her agonizing over the possibilities.

She'd never considered herself a coward, but she was terrified at the thought of initiating a confrontation that could send Jared away from her.

Seemingly oblivious for once to Cassie's tension and Jared's remoteness, Shane chattered contentedly from the back seat on the way back to Cassie's place, pronouncing himself pleased with the evening, on the whole.

"Michelle's uncle is a jerk, isn't he? No wonder she was so happy to find her real family, if that's all she had before. Everyone else was great—Aunt Layla and Kevin and the kids, I mean. Aren't they?"

"They're very nice," Cassie agreed when Jared didn't say anything. "I met them for the first time at Michelle and Tony's wedding."

"Did you meet Tony's family, too? The Italian ones?"

"Dozens of them," Cassie answered with a slight smile. "I don't remember all the names, but they're a close, boisterous, very friendly clan. Tony's crazy about them."

"Michelle was telling me how much fun they have at family gatherings," Shane explained. "She said they're having a barbecue next weekend and I can go with her and Tony, if I want, to meet some of the cousins my age. I'll still be in this stupid cast, of course, so I can't play softball with them, but it would be fun to meet them. She said some of them even go to the same school that Heather and Scott go to—I'm going to ask if they know any kids named D'Alessandro. It's okay with you if I go to the barbecue, isn't it, Dad?"

Cassie almost held her breath at the question, staring fiercely ahead as she drove, though most of her attention was on Jared.

"I don't think you'd better be making plans for next weekend, son," Jared answered quietly. "The doctor said today that you're up to traveling again if we take it easy. I made a couple of calls this afternoon. The job in Arizona's still open, but it won't be much longer. If I'm going to take it, we need to head that way in a couple of days. We should be able to pick up our new truck Monday afternoon, so we can leave anytime after that.''

Cassie's fingers tightened on the steering wheel until her knuckles shone white. She clenched her jaw to keep from begging Jared not to go. She sensed him watching her and made a massive effort to keep her face expressionless.

Shane was quiet for a long, taut moment. And then he spoke, sounding for the first time since Cassie had known him like a rebellious teenager. "I don't want to go to Arizona.''

"Maybe we'd better talk about this later," Jared said, realizing that Cassie's car was hardly the place to conduct such an important discussion.

"Fine," Shane replied flatly. "But I don't want to go to Arizona. I like it here. You've always talked to me before you made decisions like this.''

"Dammit, Shane, I have to work!" Jared snapped, making both Cassie and Shane jump at the sudden vehemence of his voice. Almost as though the frustration that had been seething inside him for the past week had suddenly boiled over. "We can't go on sponging off Cassie forever.''

"You're not sponging off me," Cassie pointed out carefully. "You've bought groceries and supplies, and helped out a lot around the house. I've enjoyed having you both stay with me.''

"We've invaded your home and your privacy," Jared returned. "I'm sure you're ready to get your life back to the way it was before you met us.''

"No," she whispered, seeing the road ahead through a thin film of tears. "I'm not ready for that at all.''

An uncomfortable silence reigned in the small car during the next ten minutes, until Cassie parked in her assigned space and turned off the engine. Shane opened his door first, flooding the interior with light. Without looking at Jared, Cassie peeled her uncooperative fingers off the steering wheel and reached for her purse.

Jared got out of the car slowly, then stood on the sidewalk staring toward Cassie's apartment without moving.

"Jared?" Cassie asked. "Aren't you coming in?"

He didn't quite meet her eyes. "I think I'll take a walk," he murmured. "I'm not ready to go in just yet."

"I'll walk with you," she offered, moving toward him.

He stopped her with a shake of his head. "If you don't mind, I'd really like some time to myself."

Cassie bit her lip and nodded. "Be careful," she couldn't help saying as she stepped back.

"I won't end up in jail this time," Jared replied, turning away. "Don't wait up."

Cassie and Shane stood side by side on the walkway as Jared strode briskly away, disappearing into the darkness beyond the security lights.

For the boy's sake, Cassie shook herself out of the threatening depression. "We'd better go in. It's getting late."

Shane nodded glumly and turned with her toward the apartment. He'd almost stopped limping during the past day or so; now Cassie noticed that the limp was back. As though he were suddenly too dispirited to master it.

She felt obligated to try to cheer Shane up. Closing the apartment door behind them, she tossed her purse on a chair. "Would you like a soft drink or anything?"

He shook his head, his good hand buried in the pocket of his jeans, his expression as closed as Jared's had been earlier. "No, thanks. I think I'll turn in. I'm kind of tired."

Her heart twisted at his obvious unhappiness. She put a hand on his arm, feeling the tension radiating from his slender body. "Shane, your father didn't mean to hurt you. He's just feeling . . . pressured, I think. So much has happened to him this past week. Surely you understand that."

Shane nodded reluctantly. "I know. But, jeez, Cassie, why's he still planning on leaving? I mean, I know why he left my mom—they were miserable together and she didn't want him to stay. But his sisters want him here. We don't know anyone in Arizona, don't have anyone who gives a darn about us there. Why would we want to leave here to go there?"

Cassie weighed her words carefully, trying to defend Jared when what she really wanted to do was agree wholeheartedly with Shane. "Your father is a very proud man, Shane. You know that."

"Yeah. What's that got to do with anything?"

"It bothers him that he doesn't have a job now, that he feels . . . well . . . dependent on me. And he's worried about getting you back into school."

"There are jobs here," Shane argued. "And schools. Heather and Scott really like their school. I could go there."

"And maybe you will," Cassie reassured him, though she didn't want to raise false hopes. In either of them. "Your father just needs a little time to sort out his feelings. Maybe you'd better not push him right now, Shane."

"I'll try," Shane conceded with a sigh. "But I'm not just moving to Arizona without telling him the way I feel about it."

"I'm sure he doesn't expect you to."

Shane studied Cassie's face with an intensity that made her rather self-conscious.

"Cassie? Do you want us to go?" he asked hesitantly, as though he worried about her answer, but had to know.

"Oh, Shane." Her eyes filled with tears again, despite her effort to hold them back. She put her hands on his shoulders and held his gaze with her own. "Of course I don't want you to go. I love having you here, both of you."

His eyes sparked with hope. "You do?"

"Yes. I've been very happy these past few days. I would miss you terribly if you leave."

"We've been like a family, you know?" he asked wistfully. "I was kind of hoping to make it permanent."

She almost moaned at hearing her own thoughts put into words. But she had to make him understand that she and Jared had to work out their relationship in their own way, and that in this area at least, Shane didn't really have a vote.

"Shane, I don't know what's going to happen, what your father will choose to do. But you have to know that he loves you more than anything else in the world and that he doesn't want to hurt you. Whatever he decides, it will be because he thinks it's best for both of you. You've always trusted him before, haven't you?"

Shane nodded, chewing his lower lip.

"Then trust him now. He needs to know you're on his side, Shane."

Shane exhaled gustily. "I'll think about what you said."

It wasn't a surrender, and they both knew it. But Cassie told herself she'd done all she could do for now. The rest was between Jared and his son.

She and Jared had their own problems to face.

It took Jared two attempts to fit his key into Cassie's door. Scowling, he let himself in, moving with exaggerated stealth. It was late—after 1:00 a.m.—and he was sure Shane and Cassie were both sleeping. He didn't want to wake them.

He was tempted to stretch out on the living room couch and allow himself the escape of sleep. He was tired of thinking tonight, tired of old memories and frustrating indecisiveness. Tired of remembering the way Cassie and Shane had looked when he'd walked away from them earlier.

Without consciously deciding to do so, he found himself standing outside Shane's room. He opened the door quietly and looked inside. As he'd expected, Shane was sleeping, sprawled bonelessly in the tangled sheets of the daybed, his cast gleaming white in the shadows. Had he gone to sleep still angry with his father?

Jared sighed soundlessly and closed the door. He glanced across the hallway. Even as he told himself not to risk waking Cassie, he found himself walking that way, needing to look at her as he'd needed to see his son.

He hadn't expected to find Cassie's bed empty. He whipped his head around to find her sitting in the big wooden rocker she kept in one corner of the room, her knees pulled up beneath the cotton nightgown that was all she wore as she looked at him from the shadows.

"I thought you'd be asleep," he said awkwardly.

"No."

Jared cleared his throat and shoved a hand through his hair. "It's late. You shouldn't have waited up for me."

"I couldn't sleep."

He wished she wouldn't sit so still, looking so small and vulnerable in the big chair. He was more comfortable with the Cassie who'd jumped fearlessly into a fight with three drunks than with this one, who could so easily be hurt by his clumsiness.

He wasn't sure he'd ever be able to forgive himself if he hurt Cassie.

She represented everything he'd spent the past decade avoiding: commitment, trust, marriage, maybe more children—a lifetime of responsibilities. Making himself vulnerable to someone again, risking the devastating pain of loss through death or disillusionment.

Almost losing Shane in the car accident had all but brought Jared to his knees. Wasn't it enough that there was already one person who meant so damned much to him?

Unable to think of anything to say, Jared took a step forward, cursing beneath his breath when he stumbled over a shoe.

"You've been drinking." Cassie sounded more as though she were making an idle observation than passing judgment.

Jared shrugged. "Yeah. I had a few beers at that yuppie bar a few blocks away from here."

"Did it help?"

"No," he admitted, thinking of his ex-wife's endless quest for peace of mind through alcohol. "It never does."

"Would you like to talk about it?"

"About what?" he asked, knowing as he spoke that he was stalling.

"About whatever is bothering you so badly," she answered patiently.

He dropped to the edge of the bed, his hands clasped loosely between his knees. "I don't know what to say."

"You could start by telling me what you're feeling right now," she suggested, her voice little more than a whisper from the shadows.

Jared stared at his hands. He'd spent so many years repressing his feelings that he wasn't sure he even knew how to identify them now. "I'm not very good at that sort of thing."

"At having feelings, or discussing them?" Cassie asked with just a touch of sympathetic humor.

His mouth twitched in what might almost have been a smile. "Take your pick."

Cassie hesitated a moment, then left the rocker to walk slowly toward him. "Why don't I help you out a little. I'll name some emotions, and you tell me if they apply."

He watched her warily. "I don't think that's—"

"Angry," she said, ignoring his objection.

He shook his head. "I'm not angry."

She came to a stop less than two feet away from him, her bare feet curled into the carpet, her hands clasped loosely in front of her, her glorious hair hanging loose around her shoulders. "Bored."

"No," he murmured, staring at her, at the way the thin light coming through the window made her skin seem as translucent as fine china. "Not bored."

"Depressed."

His body stirred, reacting forcefully to the hint of nipples and the triangle of dark hair just visible through the thin white cotton of her nightgown. "No."

"Frightened?"

He wanted her so badly it scared him to his toes. "Maybe."

She reached out to stroke his hair, her touch so light he hardly felt it. "Trapped."

His throat tightened. "Yeah."

Her hands were cool, soft when she cupped his face between them and leaned toward him. "You know your problem, Jared Walker?"

He knew his problem, all right. He was a hair's breadth away from attacking her, having her on her back beneath him before she could blink twice.

He tried to concentrate on what she was saying. "What do you think my problem is, Cassie?"

"It's been so easy for you to walk away before now," she answered quietly, holding his eyes with her own. "You were taken from your real family when you were eleven, and your one attempt at making a new family seemed to fail when your marriage ended. After that, you made it a habit to leave when things got sticky, to avoid entanglements of any kind. Shane did the same when he ran away from home two years ago.

"Since then, the two of you have had each other, but you've been on the move, never staying anyplace long enough to put down roots. You're feeling trapped now because you know it won't be so easy to leave this time. Shane wants to stay. Your sisters want you to stay. I want you to stay. Now you have to decide what *you* want. And that scares you, because it means making a commitment of some sort. One way or another."

"I'd stick to P.I. work if I were you," Jared said stiffly, his stomach clenching in reaction to her accusations. "You'd never make it as a shrink."

She didn't seem to take offense, at his words or the curt tone in which he'd spoken. "Are you saying I'm wrong?"

"I'm saying you don't know what the hell I'm feeling," he answered roughly.

"So tell me," she dared him. "What are you feeling, Jared?"

Without giving her warning, he tumbled her to the bed, then stretched out on top of her, his hips flexing to make her fully aware of the erection straining against his zipper.

"Now see if you can guess what I'm feeling," he muttered, his hands tangling in her hair.

If he'd thought to intimidate her, he realized immediately that it hadn't worked. Cassie simply twined her arms around his neck, bringing her mouth close to his.

"You want me," she whispered, her breasts brushing his chest, her soft legs shifting to better accommodate him.

"Yes," he growled, lowering his head to hers. "Yes, dammit."

He crushed her mouth beneath his with a hunger that felt too soul-deep to ever be thoroughly satisfied, no matter how many times he might have her. Cassie opened to him with such eager participation that he felt himself tremble in reaction. How could she keep giving so much of herself when both of them knew how easily he could hurt her, how very likely it was that he would?

He counseled himself to go slowly, to keep his touch gentle, his desires reined. But the fires inside him only burned hotter when he tried to bank them, leaving his self-control in ashes. His hands and his mouth raced over her, greedy, desperate, demanding. Cassie made no effort to resist him, responding instead with a sweet passion of her own. He moved, she shifted with him. He took, she gave and then took for herself.

Jared shoved her nightgown out of his way and fastened his mouth hungrily to her right breast, drawing the distended tip deep into his mouth. Cassie gasped and arched into him, her fingers clenching at his shoulders.

"Jared," she murmured, her voice little more than a broken sigh. "Oh, Jared."

He slid his fingers into the dark red curls between her thighs, finding the soft, swollen, love-damp flesh they protected. Cassie squirmed beneath his stroking, her breath catching, then shuddering out of her. His mouth at her throat, Jared slid two fingers deep inside her, his thumb making a slow, firm rotation.

"That's it, baby," he murmured when she bowed upward in reaction. "Let it happen."

Mindful of Shane sleeping across the hall, Jared covered Cassie's mouth with his own when she would have cried out with the first climax. He briefly regretted the need for quiet, wanting to hear the sounds he drew from her.

He hardly gave her time to catch her breath before he began again, tossing her nightgown aside, tearing at his own clothes until there was nothing left between them. Starting at her earlobe, he nibbled and tasted his way downward, leaving her breasts damp and swollen, her stomach quivering, her knees trembling.

Her toes clenched when he nipped at her ankles, then spread when he tasted the delicate arch of her foot. And then he shifted his attentions higher, making her dig her heels into the sheets and arch helplessly into his mouth as he gave her the most intimate kiss of all.

Cassie was trembling, her soft, supple skin covered in a film of perspiration. She whispered his name, pleaded with him to stop, then in the same breath begged him to go on. Her hands clenched in his hair, alternately tugging him away and then holding him closer. The second climax made her whimper.

Jared surged upward, thrusting inside her before the tiny convulsions ended, groaning when her inner muscles tightened around him. For the first time in over twenty-four years, he felt as though he'd found a place where he belonged. A home.

Cassie gathered him close, welcoming him to that warm, private place with a loving generosity that brought a hard lump to his throat. The last thread of sanity snapped, and he pounded into her again and again with a furious need that left him unable to slow down, unable to hold back anything from her.

Cassie wrapped herself around him and cradled him until the storm was spent, crooning endearments and encouragements, soothing him with her words, her tone, her body. Jared had never felt so deeply loved, so desperately needed. And even as he surrendered himself to a shattering orgasm that all but rendered him unconscious, he knew that he'd never been so humbled, nor so bone-deep scared of his feelings.

It was a very long time before he could make himself move. Even then, the most he could manage was to shift his weight off her, his arms tightening around her as he rolled to hold her against his heaving chest.

He felt the wetness on her cheeks and knew she was crying. He couldn't bring himself to ask her why, though he suspected she'd been as affected as he by the unprecedented intensity of their lovemaking. He was too damned close to tears himself to speak coherently. And, except for a moment of weakness the night Shane was hurt, Jared Walker hadn't cried in twenty-four years.

He knew when Cassie slipped into sleep, her cheek still damp against his shoulder. He cradled her closer, guarding her rest against anything that would hurt her. Himself included.

Nothing had ever been like that for him. The sensations had never been so intense, the need so great. No other woman's pleasure had ever mattered so much to him.

He stared blindly at the ceiling, wondering if he should sleep on the couch, after all. Knowing even as the thought crossed his mind that he wouldn't be able to force himself to leave the woman who lay in his arms.

You're feeling trapped because you know it won't be so easy to leave this time, she'd said. And though he hadn't told her, he'd known her words were the truth.

Walking away this time would probably be the hardest thing he'd ever done. But finding the courage to stay could prove to be the toughest challenge he'd ever faced.

Chapter Fourteen

Cassie had promised Tony she'd work Saturday. She slipped away early, leaving Jared and Shane sleeping. Jared looked as though he'd gotten very little rest during the night. Usually a light sleeper, he didn't even stir when Cassie left.

As she guided her car out of the parking lot, Cassie wondered if she'd be able to accomplish anything at the office when her mind was so occupied with her worries about Jared. She was no closer now to knowing his plans, or believing he would be willing to stay with her. She'd waited up for him last night with a vague idea of confronting him, demanding that he make a decision and end the suspense.

But then he'd tiptoed into her room, looking so sad and lonely and tormented that all she'd wanted to do was hold him, love him, offer him a temporary refuge from the pain. And Jared had responded to her ministrations with such desperate intensity that she still felt dazed in the aftermath, her body pleasantly sore from his relentless lovemaking.

He loved her. Something deep inside her had to believe that he loved her, even as she reminded herself that he might never be able to tell her so. Maybe he'd never even be able to admit it to himself. But his actions had spoken so clearly what he couldn't say in words.

But even believing Jared loved her, Cassie didn't try to convince herself that he would stay with her. He'd spent too many years guarding his emotions, too many years protecting himself from vulnerability to change those habits overnight—or even in the traumatic, eventful nine days since she'd met him.

He needed time to come to terms with his past and his emotions, time to be convinced that his relationships weren't all doomed to failure. Time for Cassie to prove to him how deeply she loved him, that she would love him no matter what they faced in the future. And time was one of the things he didn't seem willing to give.

It wouldn't be easy for him to walk away, not now. But he could do it. Cassie suffered no delusions about the depth of Jared's fortitude. If he decided it would be better for himself and Shane to leave, he'd go with barely a backward glance at the people who loved him here. And he'd leave a hole in Cassie's life that she would never be able to fill, no matter how hard she worked, no matter how many men she might meet in future.

She braked for a red light, automatically taking care with her driving. And then she slammed her fist against the steering wheel.

"Damn you, Jared Walker! Why do you have to be so stubbornly self-sufficient? Why can't you understand how incredibly selfish you're being?"

But Jared wasn't there to hear, of course. Cassie wasn't sure he'd listen even if he were.

Jared was awakened by the sound of a low, hoarse groan. It took him a moment to realize the sound had come from his own dry throat.

Blinking against the full sunlight streaming through the bedroom window, he rolled onto his back, wincing as his body protested the movement. He hurt all over, not just his head, but all his muscles—as though he'd spent the night fighting packs of demons. Which, he supposed, he had.

He looked around the room for Cassie, then, slowly coming out of his disorientation, he remembered that she had to work today. Had she left for the office yet? A glance at the clock brought him fully awake. Hell, it was nearly noon! He hadn't slept that late since...he couldn't even remember the last time.

Scrubbing his hands over his bristled face, he sat nude on the edge of the bed, elbows on his knees.

Great, Walker. You're unshaven, you're hung over, you've lain in bed until noon like some sort of useless bum. Fine example for your son.

He stumbled into the bathroom and turned the shower on full pressure, as hot as he could stand it. He felt himself slowly coming back to life beneath the steaming force of it. He didn't leave the shower until the water ran cold.

The sight of his own face in the steam-fogged mirror over the sink nearly tore another groan from him. He looked like hell. Red-eyed, bearded, haggard. A good ten years older than thirty-five. If this was what a life of leisure did to him, then he'd damned well better get back to work soon. As soon as humanly possible.

He hid the lower half of his face beneath a coating of shaving lather and reached for his razor. He intended to make significant improvements in his appearance before facing his son. Thank God Cassie hadn't been there to see him wake up in the shape he'd been in. He wasn't sure his pride could have taken that.

Cassie. He cursed when just the thought of her made his hand jerk, drawing a scarlet drop of blood from his jaw.

What the hell was he going to do about Cassie? How could he ever forget her sweet generosity during the night? The loving, tender, uncritical way she'd welcomed him back into her bed even after he'd treated her so curtly when he'd left her standing on the sidewalk as he'd walked away.

And how could he ever make himself leave her, even though he had so damned little to offer her if he stayed?

Ignoring the fierce scowl of the reflection in the mirror, Jared finished his shaving, brushed his teeth and stamped into the bedroom to pull on clean clothes. It crossed his mind that the easiest thing to do would be to leave before she came home, be out of her life once and for all with no lingering farewells to torment either of them. But he knew he couldn't do that, either to Cassie or to Shane.

This time, Jared had to think of someone other than himself.

He'd expected to find Shane watching television or reading. Instead, he found a note on the kitchen table, telling him that Shane was having lunch with his friends Scott and Heather and would be staying at their place to watch movies afterward. Jared was alone with his grim thoughts for the next few hours, with no place to go and no way to get there if there had been.

His mood more savage than before, he opened a cabinet and reached for the coffee—the real kind, not the decaf

Cassie usually made for herself. Today, he desperately needed the kick of caffeine.

Cassie looked away from her computer screen when a man's hand waved slowly in front of her eyes. "Tony? What are you doing?"

Her boss set a paper bag on her desk. "It's almost one. I've brought us some lunch."

"Oh. Thank you, but I'm not very hungry. I think I'll keep working on this—"

"Cassie," Tony interrupted firmly. "Did you have breakfast this morning?"

"Well, no," she admitted, "but—"

"Then eat. And that's an order from your employer. You're not going to be a lot of help to me this afternoon if you faint into your keyboard. And we've got a long day ahead of us yet."

She sighed and turned her chair away from the computer. "All right, I'll eat," she grumbled. "But I'm not at all sure this is in my job description."

"Sure it is," Tony answered cheerfully, pulling a chair close to the other side of her desk for himself. "It's right under the clause about catering to your boss's every whim. Fine print, of course."

"*Very* fine print, apparently."

"Right. Here, I brought you a diet cola to go with that."

She accepted the cold can with a nod of grudging gratitude, then unwrapped her sandwich with a marked lack of enthusiasm.

Tony took a big bite of his own sandwich and chewed slowly, his dark eyes never leaving her face. "You look like hell," he pronounced after swallowing.

She glared at him. "Thanks a lot."

"Did you and Jared have a fight?"

"No."

"A quarrel?"

"No."

"Do you want to talk about this?"

"No."

He frowned, looking as though there was something else he wanted to say. But then he relented. "All right. I won't push you. Much. I just want to remind you that I'm here if you need me."

"And I appreciate it," Cassie answered firmly, but with a faint smile. "This time, Tony, I have to handle my problems alone. This is between myself and Jared, and there's nothing you—or anyone else—can do to help. Okay?"

He nodded. "I should point out that you deserve this for breaking the rules and getting personally involved in a case. But since I'm such a good friend, I won't do that."

"Thanks," she answered wryly.

"You're sure you don't want me to go break the guy's arm or anything?"

Cassie was sorely tempted to let him do just that. She'd spent the morning fluctuating between aching sympathy for Jared and resentful anger with him for putting her through this. But, as she'd just told Tony, this was between herself and Jared. Not Tony or Shane or Michelle or Layla or any of the others who cared about them.

And, besides that... "He'd bash your head in," Cassie couldn't resist commenting. "Trust me."

Tony's left eyebrow shot upward. "You don't think I could take him?"

A reluctant smile tilted the corners of her mouth. "I think you'd put up a good effort," she said diplomatically. "But Jared would win. He's learned to fight dirty."

He'd had to, she thought wistfully. For so many years, there'd been no one else to fight for him. No one else who cared enough. And now it might be too late for him to trust that he didn't have to be alone anymore. That all he had to do was find the courage to reach out.

Jared had just finished his first cup of coffee and was pouring a second when the doorbell rang. Cassie wouldn't ring the bell, of course, but maybe Shane had forgotten the key she'd given him. Jared set his cup on the table and went to open the door.

He really hadn't expected to find his sister Michelle standing on the other side.

"Hello, Jared," she said when he only looked at her in surprise.

Annoyed with himself for his uncharacteristically slow reactions today, Jared forced a smile. "Hi. This is a surprise. Come on in."

"Thank you." She walked past him, glancing around the room with a discreet curiosity that let Jared know she'd never been there before.

"Have a seat," he offered, waving toward the couch. "Can I get you some coffee? I was just pouring myself a cup."

"Yes, that would be nice. Thank you."

"You take anything in it?"

"No. Just black, please."

He nodded and turned toward the kitchen, polite pleasantries out of the way. He couldn't help wondering why Michelle had come. Something about her expression had told him she wasn't just making a social call.

"I'm the only one here right now," he explained when he returned with their coffee. "Cassie's working and Shane's hanging out with some kids who live a couple of doors down."

"I knew Cassie was working today," Michelle admitted as Jared took a chair close to where she sat. "I was hoping for a chance to speak to you alone."

He saw the hint of nerves in her eyes and in the fine tremor in her hand when she held her coffee cup. "Relax, Shelley," he murmured, using the old name from half-forgotten habit. "I'm not going to bite."

She smiled, rather sheepishly, and set her cup and saucer on the coffee table. "I know. But I'm not sure how you're going to react to what I want to say."

Jared drained his coffee and set the cup aside. Was Michelle here to ask him to stay in Dallas? Or maybe to find out for herself if her adopted uncle's warnings had been necessary? "Might as well find out," he said bluntly. "What is it, Michelle?"

She took a deep breath. "First, I want to apologize for my uncle's behavior last night."

He shook his head. "That's not necessary."

"But it is. I thought if he met you for himself he'd understand that there was no need to worry about me. That you're too proud and honorable to pose the kind of threat Uncle Richard worried about."

"He couldn't know that," Jared felt compelled to point out. And then he added reluctantly, "You can't really be so sure of that, yourself, Michelle. You don't even know me."

"I know you," she answered evenly, her eyes meeting his without hesitation. "You're my brother, Jared. It's true that I don't remember much, if any, about the short time we had together as children. But I only had to spend a few hours with you to see that you're a good man, that you love your

son very much, and that you have maybe too much pride for
your own good."

His mouth quirked, but he nodded gravely. "Yeah.
Maybe."

"Which is exactly why I'm nervous about the offer I'm
about to make," she added quietly.

His eyes narrowed. "What offer?"

She wiped her hands on the legs of her pleated slacks, the
gesture very telling. Jared had spent enough time with her
already to know that Michelle was usually utterly calm and
composed, her elegant poise developed through years of
practice.

"I want to offer you a loan, Jared," she blurted, then bit
her lower lip in consternation, as if she regretted speaking
so frankly.

"Thanks, but that's not necessary," he answered roughly,
making a massive effort not to snap at her. He reminded
himself that she was only trying to help, that she couldn't
know how precarious his mood was today. "The insurance
company is taking care of Shane's medical expenses, we're
picking up a new truck on Monday, and I've got a job waiting for me in Arizona. I really don't need a loan."

Michelle made a sound of frustration and pushed a strand
of fine brown hair away from her face. "I'm not handling
this very well," she admitted. "I didn't mean I think you're
in any sort of financial trouble. I know you're not."

She'd probably had her P.I. husband find out to the last
penny every detail of his financial standing, Jared thought
with a touch of resentment. Even after having over a week
to get used to the idea, he still didn't like knowing that Tony
and Cassie had methodically tracked him down through his
records since childhood. "Right."

"Oh, Jared, please don't get defensive with me," Michelle said, reaching out to lay a hand on his knee. "I guess I'm not very good at this because I've never really had a family. I've been on my own for so long that I'm having to learn how to communicate with other people."

He could certainly identify with that. Had Michelle really been as lonely in her palatial home as he'd been in his far less glamorous surroundings?

He couldn't help softening, remembering the shock he'd felt at hearing about the trauma of her kidnapping. "I know your childhood wasn't an easy one, Michelle."

She shook her head impatiently. "No, that's not what I'm trying to say. I'm no poor little rich girl. Other than a few incidences, my childhood was quite pleasant. It was just that damned money—like a wall between me and my friends, between myself and anyone who could pose a threat to me. Potential boyfriends, employees, strangers. When I learned that I'd been raised in such luxury while my brothers and sisters had been given so little, I felt horribly guilty."

"You shouldn't have," Jared said, trying to keep his tone gentle. "Honey, it wasn't your choice. You were just a baby when we were split up."

"I know that, too. But I'd have traded all the money without hesitation for the chance to grow up with you and Layla and Miles and the twins and the baby."

The mention of Miles made Jared wince. He still hadn't quite accepted that his happy-go-lucky little brother would never be reunited with the rest of them. Would any of the others? "We can't go back and change the past, Michelle."

"No. But we can build a future. We don't have to repeat the mistakes of the past and let those old scars keep us apart now."

"I'm not doing anything to keep us apart," Jared said carefully. "Now that we've found each other again, I'll do my best to keep in touch. For my sake, and for Shane's. But I have to find my own way, Michelle. I have to work, find a place to live, get Shane back in school. The rest of you have lives. You've got to let me have mine."

"Which is why I'm here," Michelle hastened to assure him. "Shane said you and he have plans to own a ranch together."

He nodded warily. "Yeah. We've talked about it. I've been saving, but I don't have enough to make a start yet."

"And when you have enough, you plan to arrange for financing, right?"

"Yeah," he agreed. "But with a bank."

"Fine. Think of me as a bank. I can make you that loan, Jared. With interest and regular payments and legal papers drawn up by an attorney. Or we can arrange a partnership or a cosigning, or whatever you'd find most comfortable. This isn't charity, it's an investment on my part. Tony and I happen to think it's a shrewd one."

His head came up sharply. "You've discussed this with your husband?"

"Of course. Tony and I talk about everything together. When Shane mentioned your desire to own a ranch, Tony thought of one of his father's longtime friends. The man— Mr. McLaughlin—owns a small spread about thirty miles south of here. Mr. McLaughlin hasn't gotten wealthy from his operation, but he has made a good living, and the potential is there to expand and increase the profits.

"The problem is that he's getting older, and would like to retire with his wife to Florida, where their daughter lives. Tony had a cousin who thought about buying the ranch, but then changed his mind when he realized how much hard manual labor would be involved.''

Jared was interested despite his reservations. Deeply interested. "I've never minded hard work," he muttered, thinking of how excited Shane would be at the very possibility of having their dream come true. A ranch. A home. No more life on the road.

The very thought of that sort of permanence made Jared break out in a cold sweat. Was that really what he wanted?

"I don't know, Michelle. I don't like the thought of being in debt to you."

She shrugged, a deliberate imitation of his habit. "You'd have to be in debt to someone to own a place like that," she pointed out. "At least in the beginning. I'm not asking for a decision now, Jared. I'd expect you to think about this, of course. Look the place over. Study your options. I just want you to know that this is a legitimate business offer, with no strings, no obligations."

"I don't want you to think I'm not grateful that you made the offer," he replied, covering her hand with his own. "It took a lot of trust for you and Tony to come to this decision. That means a lot to me."

"Does that mean you'll consider it?" she asked eagerly. "You won't turn us down without giving it any thought?"

"I'll think about it. But no promises."

"No," she agreed with a smile. "No promises. And thank you."

He quirked an eyebrow. "For what?"

"For not letting that stiff-necked pride of yours keep you from at least listening to me. I know you were tempted to tell me to butt out of your life."

He couldn't help smiling. "Maybe you are getting to know me fairly well."

"I'd like to get to know you better," she said softly.

"Yeah. Me, too." He squeezed her hand before releasing it. "Cassie told me Tony's making some more headway with the search for Lindsay, that he thinks there's real hope he should be able to contact her within the next few weeks. You think she'll be interested in meeting us, even though she couldn't possibly remember any of us?"

"Oh, I hope so," Michelle said sincerely. "I can't remember her, either, but she's still my little sister. I'd like very much to get to know her."

Relieved at the change of subject, Jared leaned back in his chair and listened with a faint smile as Michelle told him about her emotional reunion with Layla a few months earlier. As interested as he was in hearing the story, part of his mind was still occupied with Michelle's unexpected offer of a loan.

He had to admit that his first instinct had been to turn her down flat, thanking her politely, but firmly refusing to even consider the offer. And then he'd realized he'd been reacting more from pride than logic.

Would he have been so quick to turn her down if she had been nothing more than a banker making the same legitimate offer, rather than the little sister he hadn't seen in so many years? And had her offer really been based on a business decision, or did she think he needed this assistance to support himself and her nephew?

He had a great deal to think about now, some very important decisions to make. But he needed time alone to do so. He just wasn't sure how much time it would take, and whether he had any time to waste. The job in Arizona wouldn't be there indefinitely, and the ranch could be sold at any time if this McLaughlin was serious about retiring and moving away. His head began to ache all over again at this additional bit of pressure.

He was rather relieved that Michelle didn't linger long. Claiming that she had errands to run, she left with one last plea for him to think seriously about her offer before making any final decisions about leaving Dallas. Jared promised again that he would.

He surprised himself almost as much as Michelle when he impulsively kissed her cheek as he saw her out the door. Her eyes were misty when she left, the gesture obviously having touched her.

You're in too deep, Walker, Jared found himself thinking as he stood alone in the room after she left. *With Cassie, with Michelle. With all of them.*

So what the hell was he going to do about it?

Chapter Fifteen

Cassie was exhausted when she arrived home that evening, her weariness resulting from a combination of stress and the hours of hard work she and Tony had put in on a security report to be presented to a client on Monday.

She wasn't sure what to expect from Jared when they saw each other for the first time after the emotional night they'd shared. She certainly hadn't expected him to greet her with a distracted smile and the news that he and Shane were expecting a pizza delivery at any moment.

"Dad's acting a little weird today," Shane murmured, catching Cassie alone in the kitchen for a moment. "Like his mind's a million miles away. He's been that way ever since I got home from Heather and Scott's a few hours ago."

Did that mean Jared was planning to leave? Cassie couldn't help wondering, her stomach clenching in dread. Was he pulling back to prepare her for his departure?

Perhaps she was being paranoid—but she thought she had plenty of reason to be.

Cassie put an arm around Shane's shoulders and gave him a hug—as much for her own comfort as his. "He has a lot on his mind, Shane."

"Yeah," Shane muttered. "Don't we all?"

Cassie sighed. *How very true.*

The pizza arrived, a large-with-everything that they ate in near silence in front of the television, though none of them looked particularly interested in the fluffy sitcom they were watching. Cassie noted that neither Jared nor Shane cracked a smile at the inane jokes—nor, for that matter, did she.

The pizza, usually her favorite fast food, sat like lead in her stomach when she finished. The tension in the room had grown so thick she could almost touch it.

Shane helped Cassie clear away the debris with his one good hand, then shifted restlessly on his feet for a few moments before saying, "I think I'll go to my room and listen to some music."

"No." Jared spoke for the first time in quite a while, glancing up from the chair where he'd sat in brooding silence. "Turn off the television, son. We need to talk."

Cassie shifted in her own chair, glancing toward her bedroom. Did Jared want her to leave them in privacy?

As though reading her thoughts, he looked at her, his expression inscrutable. "This concerns you, too, Cassie."

Oh, God. His tone was so serious, his eyes so shuttered. He was going to tell her he was leaving, she just knew he was.

Oh, Jared, no. Don't leave me. Please.

Struggling to hide her panic, she clenched her hands in her lap and nodded with feigned composure. "All right."

Jared looked from Cassie to Shane, noting the tension that seemed to grip both of them. They sat in almost identical poses, shoulders braced, feet planted, eyes focused unwaveringly on his face. Both of them trying so desperately to look brave, when both were so obviously afraid of what he was going to say.

He swallowed hard, aware of the massive responsibility involved in having two people care so deeply about him.

He drew in a breath. "As Shane pointed out last night, I've gotten into the habit of discussing things with him before making decisions that affect our lives. We need to have one of those discussions now. There are several options open to us, and we need to choose."

"I know what *I* want," Shane muttered.

Jared held up a hand to silence him. "Wait, son. Let me have my say first."

Shane nodded with obvious reluctance.

Satisfied that Shane was listening, Jared continued. "Option number one—the job near Flagstaff is still open, still waiting for me if I choose to take it. It's a big ranch with living quarters, meals and insurance provided. The pay's good and there's a decent school close by."

"It sounds like a good opportunity," Cassie seemed compelled to comment.

Jared looked at her approvingly, pleased that she was trying to be objective. "It *is* a good opportunity," he agreed. "My friend Bob Cutter set it up for me or the ranch owner would never have been this patient about my answer."

"What's option number two?" Shane asked impatiently, the knuckles of his left hand white against the denim covering his thigh.

Jared cleared his throat. "Michelle came by to see me today. Her husband knows a man who owns a small ranch thirty miles south of here, and the guy wants to sell."

Shane's eyes lit up. "A ranch. Really?"

Again, Jared silenced him with an upraised hand. "Wait. I'm not through. I haven't seen the place, don't know anything about it except that Michelle told me it's turning a small profit. Nothing spectacular, apparently, though she thinks it has potential if it's managed right."

"We could make it work, Dad. Couldn't we?"

Jared couldn't quite meet Shane's hopeful eyes. "It's not that easy, son. For one thing, there'd be the investment of getting set up with the place. It would take everything we've got and then some just to get started. Could be several years before we saw any extra money out of the operation."

Cassie's voice was strained when she asked, "Do you— would you be able to make an offer on the place?"

The next part still bothered him, but he knew he had to tell them. "Michelle offered to make a loan for the down payment," he said quietly. "It would be legal and binding, with current interest rates and regular monthly payments, all the papers drawn up by an attorney. She and D'Alessandro are willing to be mortgage holders or partners, whichever we choose."

Both Shane and Cassie were quiet for a moment, as if stunned that Jared would even consider the offer. Cassie finally spoke, tentatively. "Michelle wouldn't have made the offer if she didn't think it was a worthwhile investment, Jared."

He nodded. "I know. At first I thought she was offering a handout, but she set me straight on that pretty quick. It's a legitimate offer."

"Does that mean you're going to take it?" Shane asked, hardly daring to speak out loud.

"There are still a lot of ifs involved," Jared warned. "The ranch may not be what we have in mind, the deal could fall through, the guy could change his mind about selling. And even if we did get the place, we could have a couple of bad years that could wipe us out entirely. We're talking about a big risk here. A lot of hard work. A lot of responsibility. If I sign papers and agree to the conditions of the loan, I can't just walk away from it if either of us gets tired of the work or the routines. You understand that, Shane?"

"I understand," Shane answered quietly, holding his chin at a steady angle that made him look so much older than his years. "We're talking about a total commitment."

"Yeah," Jared agreed. "Total. You'd have to concentrate as hard as ever on your schoolwork, of course, and God knows I'd still want you to have a normal social life, but there'd be chores to do and occasional emergencies to deal with, whatever plans you might have made. I'd still want you to go to college, but maybe by that time we'd be doing well enough to hire extra help to take up the slack while you were gone. I know this is what we've talked about, Shane, but this is reality, not some vague dream for the future. It won't always be fun and it will rarely be easy."

"Yeah, well, neither of us has ever expected life to be easy, have we, Dad?" Shane asked, meeting Jared's eyes as he spoke, fourteen years of difficult memories mirrored in his expression. "I'm willing to give it all I've got. If you are, of course."

Which brought Jared to the one question he had to know the answer to. Aware of Cassie listening so intently from her chair, he leaned forward and faced his son. "Shane, I know this is what you want. But what if it's not what *I* want?

What if I tell you that I want to take the job near Flagstaff and that I plan to leave first thing Monday morning?''

Shane didn't even hesitate. ''Then I'll start packing to go with you. We're a team, Dad. Where you go, I go.''

Jared's breath left him in a soft whoosh as he realized that the bond between himself and his son hadn't been shaken by anything that had happened to them in the past few eventful days. Jared had needed to know that Shane's first loyalty still lay with him.

''What about you, Cassie?'' he asked, swiveling his gaze to her. ''What are you going to do if I head for Arizona in a couple of days?''

She was pale, but outwardly composed. She met his eyes without flinching. ''I'll help you pack,'' she said. ''And I'll kiss you goodbye. And then I'll probably end up following you again . . . unless, of course, you manage to convince me you don't want to see me anymore.''

So this was love. Jared wondered why he'd ever thought it such a painful, frightening emotion.

He spoke past the lump in his throat. ''You're taking an awfully big chance, you know.''

Her eyes were damp, but steady. ''Yes.''

Had there ever been any other woman like this one? Jared shook his head in bemusement.

''I've never met anyone like you, never had anyone more willing to take risks for me. From trying to clear me of false charges to being ready to fight a group of drunken rednecks. You nagged me to be reunited with my family, and now you're apparently willing to walk away from your home and your job to be with me. Even with no promises, no guarantees.''

Her smile was faint, but genuine. ''Yes,'' she repeated.

"Maybe it's time I start taking a few chances myself," Jared said roughly, getting to his feet. "Come here."

Cassie was in his arms almost before he'd finished saying the words. He held her close, his head bent protectively over hers, his arms locked around her slender waist.

"You won't have to follow me anywhere," he muttered. "Like it or not, you're stuck with me now—with both of us. So you'd damned well better not change your mind about wanting us."

"No," she whispered through her tears, wrapping her arms around his neck. "Oh, Jared, I'll never change my mind. I love you. Both of you."

He grabbed a handful of hair and tugged, tilting her face to his. "Turn around, Shane," he ordered just before crushing Cassie's mouth beneath his own.

"Yes, Dad," Shane replied, cooperating with a huge grin. Still turned away from them, he asked, "Does this mean we're buying the ranch?"

Jared tore his mouth from Cassie's long enough to answer. "We're a long way from buying the ranch," he warned, lost in the happy glitter of Cassie's brilliant green eyes. "But we're damned well going to take a look at it."

He tilted his head to kiss her from a new angle, unable to get enough of her taste—or the love he felt flowing from her.

"All right!" Shane rocked contentedly on his heels, then asked, still without looking around, "Think maybe we'll have some more kids? I'd kinda like a kid brother."

Jared choked against Cassie's sudden smile. Lifting his head again, he glared at Shane's back. "Don't push it, boy."

Shane's laugh blended with Cassie's. "Whatever you say, Dad," he replied agreeably.

"Go to your room."

"Yes, sir." Shane was whistling when he left. Though the tune was somewhat flat, it was easily recognizable. "The Wedding March."

Jared glared after the boy, then looked back down at Cassie in exasperation. "I do my own proposing," he growled.

She nodded, watching him expectantly.

He sighed. "Oh, hell. I don't have a damned thing to offer you, Cassie, but I'm asking you, anyway. Will you marry me?"

She touched his face with trembling fingers. "Don't you have anything to offer me, Jared?" she asked in an unsteady murmur.

"Only my heart," he answered gruffly, his cheeks warming as he struggled to verbalize his feelings for the first time in so very long. "I love you, Cassie. I have from the first time you visited me in that damned jail. And if you're willing to take one more chance on me, I swear I'll never give you cause to regret it."

"Oh, Jared." The tears that had brimmed in her eyes spilled onto her cheeks. "You've just given me everything I could ever ask of you."

"Does that mean you'll marry me?"

"Yes," she whispered, going up on tiptoe to press her mouth to his. "Yes, yes, ye—"

He smothered the rest with a heartfelt kiss that expressed all the emotion he couldn't put into words.

Epilogue

The third Saturday in October was warm and clear, to the delight of everyone who attended the party Michelle threw that afternoon on the beautifully landscaped lawn of the home she shared with her husband. It was an informal affair, the guests in jeans and sweaters, folding tables set up to hold sandwiches and snacks, canned soft drinks on ice in big barrels. Squealing children dashed around the legs of the adults, who carried on numerous noisy conversations sprinkled with laughter.

It was an interesting group, Cassie noted, standing to one side for a moment to watch the festivities. Most of the guests bore a distinctly Italian look, being members of Tony's huge family, but Layla and Kevin and their children were there, as well as Michelle's closest friend, Taylor Simmons, and of course, Jared and Shane. Yet, despite the disparities of background and interest, the guests mingled freely and easily, thanks in part to Michelle's excellent skills as a hostess.

Cassie smiled when Taylor Simmons approached her. They'd met a time or two before and she'd liked Michelle's dark-haired, smoke-eyed friend from the beginning, admiring Taylor's success as a fashion photographer and appreciating her dry humor.

"Taking a breather?" Taylor asked, leaning against the low brick wall behind Cassie.

Cassie nodded. "This group could wear you out in a hurry."

Taylor laughed and agreed. "Especially Tony's clan. Talk about energy!"

Cassie spotted Shane running across the lawn with two boys and a girl of approximately his age, Layla's smaller children following close behind. Shane had a week to go in his cast yet, but the broken arm wasn't slowing him down much. He'd fallen right in with Tony's young cousins, even seemed to be developing a crush on the pretty girl giggling with him now.

"They certainly know how to have a good time," Cassie remarked, still talking about the D'Alessandro family.

Taylor agreed again, her smile fading to a fond look as she glanced across the lawn to where Michelle chatted with Layla, and Tony's mother, Carla. "I'm so glad Michelle found Tony," Taylor mused. "I've never seen her this happy and outgoing, you know? She was so lonely before. And now that she's finding her own family, she's positively radiant."

Cassie smiled, thinking of the similar changes the past month had wrought in Jared. "Yes. They're all pleased to have found each other again after so many years."

"And speaking of which—that new husband of yours is one fine-looking man, Cassie. You were smart to snap him up so quickly, before the rest of us had a chance at him."

Cassie giggled, proudly twisting the week-old gold band on her left hand. She and Jared were guests of honor at this party, having just returned from a brief, but truly spectacular honeymoon. They'd had a small wedding, attended only by Jared's sisters and their families and Cassie's stunned, but delighted parents and grandmother. She'd only been disappointed that her brother hadn't been able to join them, though he had called and sent an extravagant gift, promising he'd see them at Christmas.

Cassie's family had been delighted with Jared, charmed by Shane, expressing their great relief that Cassie had finally found someone to marry. After meeting them, Shane had teased her mercilessly about her narrow escape from being a poor, lonely "old maid" until Jared had firmly put a stop to the jokes with a reminder that Shane should show respect for his new stepmother.

Shane had spent the past week with Michelle and Tony and, though he'd assured them he'd had fun, he was obviously looking forward to setting up housekeeping with his father and stepmother. He hadn't even complained about the tutor Jared had hired to catch him up on his studies, though he seemed eager to start classes at the school Jared had found for him close to the ranch they were still in the process of buying. The McLaughlin ranch had proven to be exactly what they'd hoped it would be, and all three of them were impatient for the legalities to be out of the way so they could set up housekeeping there.

"Don't expect me to apologize for snapping him up," Cassie teased Taylor, more content than she'd ever been in her life. "I'd have been a fool to let Jared and Shane get away once I found them."

Taylor heaved a deep, exaggerated sigh. "If you and Tony would hurry and find the twin brothers, maybe one of them will turn out to be my prince."

Cassie laughed and assured Taylor she'd do her best, though she felt a bit sorry for the other woman. Michelle had once mentioned that the true love of Taylor's life had died in a car accident just over a year ago. So blissfully in love herself, Cassie could imagine what a devastating experience that must have been for Taylor.

Jared joined his wife only moments after Taylor drifted away to chat with Michelle and Layla. Perceptive as always to Cassie's feelings, he tilted her chin with one finger and looked deeply into her eyes. "You look sad. What's wrong?"

Touched by his concern, Cassie wrapped her arms around his waist and hugged him. "I'm just sorry for anyone who doesn't have what we have. I love you, Jared."

Though he still hadn't quite grown accustomed to Cassie's open, generous affection, Jared willingly returned the hug before settling her within the curve of his arm, where they could watch the party together.

"I love you, too, you know," he commented after a moment, his gaze focused on Shane at play.

Cassie smiled smugly. "I know."

She rested her head on his shoulder. "How does it feel to be surrounded by so much family?" she asked curiously, thinking of what a short time had passed since it had been just Jared and Shane. Now Jared had a wife, in-laws, two sisters and their husbands, two nieces and a nephew, not to mention the missing family members still to be located.

Jared chuckled, obviously following her thoughts. "Different," he replied. And then, after a moment, "Nice."

"I'm glad."

Jared's arm tightened around her. "Cassie?"

"Hmm?"

"I want you to find my brothers. The twins, Joey and Bobby. I want to know what happened to them."

She lifted her head to look at him in surprise. "You know we've been looking for them all along."

"Yeah," he agreed, his expression grave, "but I'm only now coming to realize how much I want to see them again. Lindsay, too, once we find her. Family's important. They all need to know we're here if they want us or need us."

"Does this mean you're not interested in going back to that carefree bachelor life you led before?" Cassie asked, only half-teasingly.

"Not for anything in the world," Jared assured her deeply. "I'm home now, and I plan to stay."

Looking up at him, Cassie realized that for the first time since she'd met him in that New Mexico jail, his eyes were no longer haunted, the old memories and old loneliness having been replaced by a new contentment and purpose. Love glowed where pain had once burned, and she couldn't have been happier for him—or for herself.

She was very, very glad she'd taken a chance on Jared Walker.

*   *   *   *   *

Silhouette

SPECIAL EDITION®

™

It takes a very special man to win

That

SPECIAL

Woman!

She's friend, wife, mother—she's you! And beside each Special Woman stands a wonderfully *special* man. It's a celebration of our heroines— and the men who become part of their lives.

Look for these exciting titles from Silhouette Special Edition:

April   FALLING FOR RACHEL by Nora Roberts
Heroine: Rachel Stanislaski—a woman dedicated to her career discovers romance adds spice to life.

May   THE FOREVER NIGHT by Myrna Temte
Heroine: Ginny Bradford—a woman who thought she'd never love again finds the man of her dreams.

June   A WINTER'S ROSE by Erica Spindler
Heroine: Bently Cunningham—a woman with a blue-blooded background falls for one red-hot man.

July   KATE'S VOW by Sherryl Woods
Heroine: Kate Newton—a woman who viewed love as a mere fairy tale meets her own Prince Charming.

Don't miss THAT SPECIAL WOMAN! each month—from some of your special authors! Only from Silhouette Special Edition! And for the most special woman of all—you, our loyal reader—we have a wonderful gift: a beautiful journal to record all of your special moments. Look for details in this month's THAT SPECIAL WOMAN! title, available at your favorite retail outlet.

TSW2

Silhouette Books
is proud to present
our best authors,
their best books...
and the best in
your reading pleasure!

Throughout 1993, look for exciting books
by these top names in contemporary
romance:

CATHERINE COULTER—
Aftershocks in February

FERN MICHAELS—
Nightstar in March

DIANA PALMER—
Heather's Song in March

ELIZABETH LOWELL
Love Song for a Raven in April

SANDRA BROWN
(previously published under
the pseudonym Erin St. Claire)—
Led Astray in April

LINDA HOWARD—
All That Glitters in May

When it comes to passion,
we wrote the book.

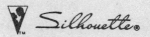

BOBT1RR

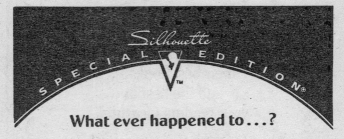

What ever happened to...?

Have you been wondering when a much-loved character will finally get their own story? Well, have we got a lineup for you! Silhouette Special Edition is proud to present a *Spin-off Spectacular!* Be sure to catch these exciting titles from some of your favorite authors.

TRUE BLUE HEARTS (SE #805 April) *Curtiss Ann Matlock* will have you falling in love with another Breen man. Watch out for Rory!

FALLING FOR RACHEL (SE #810 April) *Those Wild Ukrainians* are back as *Nora Roberts* continues the story of the Stanislaski siblings.

LIVE, LAUGH, LOVE (SE #808 April) *Ada Steward* brings you the lovely story of Jessica, Rebecca's twin from *Hot Wind in Eden* (SE #759).

GRADY'S WEDDING (SE #813 May) In this spin-off to her *Wedding Duet, Patricia McLinn* has bachelor Grady Roberts waiting at the altar.

THE FOREVER NIGHT (SE #816 May) *Myrna Temte*'s popular *Cowboy Country* series is back, and Sheriff Andy Johnson has his own romance!

WHEN SOMEBODY WANTS YOU (SE #822 June) *Trisha Alexander* returns to Louisiana with another tale of love set in the bayou.

KATE'S VOW (SE #823 July) Kate Newton finds her own man to love, honor and cherish in this spin-off of *Sherryl Woods*'s Vows series.

WORTH WAITING FOR (SE #825 July) *Bay Matthews* is back and so are some wonderful characters from *Laughter on the Wind* (SE #613).

Don't miss these wonderful titles, only for our readers—only from Silhouette Special Edition!

 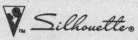

Silhouette

SPECIAL EDITION ™®

Once there were seven...

Seven beautiful brothers and sisters who played together, and weathered adversity too cruel for their tender ages. Eventually orphaned, they were then separated. Now they're trying to find each other.

Don't miss Gina Ferris's heartwarming

FAMILY FOUND

Saturday's child not only works hard for a living, he's also a sexy single father! This is one long-lost brother that doesn't want to be found. Don't miss Jared Walker's story in HARDWORKING MAN, available in April from Silhouette Special Edition!

Be sure to catch the other members of the Walker clan in FULL OF GRACE (SE #793) and FAIR AND WISE (SE #819).
